SHADOW WARRIORS

Second Son did not know how many were after them. She thought there were four, but there might be many more. Whenever she paused to look back, they were still there, never gaining ground, never losing any. It perplexed her.

Presently a deadfall barred their path. Fallen trees choked the earth for as far as Second Son could see in both directions. She bore to the right to go around, her son close behind.

Suddenly two more figures appeared up ahead. Second Son immediately stopped and raised her bow. As if they were unearthly specters, the pair vanished. To their rear the rest stayed just out of arrow range.

"What in the world are they up to?" Billy-Wolf wondered.

"I wish I knew," Second Son answered.

Billy-Wolf saw warriors converging from several directions at once. It was obvious that they would overtake him before he covered more than ten feet. Automatically, he whipped the Hawken to his shoulder, worked the hammer, and fired at the foremost man, who dropped.

Something else happened. Something amazing. At the booming blast of the rifle, every last warrior disappeared; one moment they were there, the next moment they weren't.

MOUNTAIN MAJESTY

Mountain Majesty

BOOK EIGHT

THE SAVAGE LAND

JOHN KILLDEER

BANTAM BOOKS
NEW YORK • TORONTO • LONDON • SYDNEY • AUCKLAND

THE SAVAGE LAND

A Bantam Domain Book / October 1995

*Bantam Books are published by Bantam Books, a division of Bantam
Doubleday Dell Publishing Group, Inc. Its trademark, consisting of the
words "Bantam Books" and the portrayal of a rooster, is Registered in
U.S. Patent and Trademark Office and in other countries. Marca Reg-
istrada. Bantam Books, 1540 Broadway, New York, New York 10036.*

PRINTED IN THE UNITED STATES OF AMERICA

RAD   0 9 8 7 6 5 4 3 2 1

chapter

— 1 —

The forest lay dark and dank under the mantle of spreading twilight. Shadows lengthened rapidly as a pair of warriors wound down from the high country toward a verdant valley, their heavy burden slung between them on a long pole.

The pair were Chipewyans. Both were dressed in finely crafted shirts, pants, and moccasins made from the tanned hides of caribou. Both were armed with knives and bows. Since they needed their hands free to carry the big black-tailed buck they had slain less than an hour ago, their bows had been unslung and slipped into their quivers.

In the lead tramped the older of the pair. Streaks of

gray flecked his otherwise raven hair. His back was to his companion, or the younger warrior would have noticed the darting glances he gave the surrounding forest from time to time.

It was deathly still on that mountain slope. No breeze blew. No animals cried out. Silent ranks of spruce trees and pines hemmed them in on both sides.

Neither of them had spoken for some time when the younger warrior commented, "Mattonabee will be pleased. He was not very happy yesterday when we came back empty-handed."

"It is not easy finding game in a new land. A hunter must learn where the animals like to drink, where they lay up during the day." The gray-haired warrior sighed. "I would take Mattonabee more seriously if he were to do more hunting himself. He spends too much time warming his backside by the fire to suit me."

The younger warrior regarded the other's broad back. "You must be careful not to repeat those thoughts in the hearing of others, Father. If word should get back to him, he would be very angry."

"I am not afraid of Mattonabee, son."

"You should be. His medicine is very powerful."

The father glanced over a shoulder. "If he is as mighty as you claim, why was he not able to stop the Cree from driving us from our land?"

The son had no answer. He shifted the pole to relieve a cramp and thought of the delicious meal he would savor that night. Since his arrow had finished off the buck, it was his right to pick the part of the animal he wanted when it was butchered, and he would pick the stomach. His wife would cook it, contents and all, adding shredded fat and the heart and lungs chopped into small pieces for flavoring. His mouth watered at the prospect and his stomach rumbled, reminding him of his gnawing hunger. Neither he nor his father had eaten since dawn.

A game trail offered a means of going faster. The father noted the tracks of deer and elk and bear. This country, he reflected, was ripe with wildlife. He did not see why they had to move on soon. In his opinion they had fled far enough.

The sudden squawk of a jay drew the father up short. He stared in the direction the sound had come from, deep into the murky woods, his weathered brow knit.

"What is the matter?" the son asked. "It was just a bird."

"Something startled it."

"A lynx or a bobcat, perhaps."

"Perhaps."

But the father doubted it very much. He went on, faster than before. The uneasy feeling that had overtaken him some time ago grew stronger with every stride. A less experienced woodsman might have blamed the feeling on raw nerves, or on fatigue or hunger, or any number of things. But the father knew better.

There had been telltale clues, such as the faint snap of a twig heard not once but twice. There had been the soft rustle of a thicket at the limits of his vision. Now there had been the cry of the jay. Taken singly, they meant little. Taken together, they meant trouble.

Of even more importance than all of those signs was the certainty the father had that they were being watched. He could not say how he knew. He could not point to a definite cause, and say this or that was to blame. He just knew.

The son had been paying close attention to his father since they stopped. For the first time he realized that something was amiss. His father's posture, his father's gait, they all pointed to it. He surveyed the forest but saw no reason for alarm.

Gradually the sky grew ever darker. The shadows blended into a solid black background broken by vague shapes. Far below, the lush valley beckoned. Near its center flickered pinpoints of light, the campfires of their people.

The father wished they were there already. It was his own fault for having insisted that they push on after the buck when he had known they could not possibly kill it and reach the village before nightfall. At the time, though, it had seemed the right thing to do. The band badly needed food. Too many of them had been going to bed with empty bellies.

Presently the two hunters emerged from the dense trees onto a wide shelf covered with high grass. Halfway across, the father raised a hand to signal a halt. "We will rest," he announced, grunting as he slowly lowered his end of the buck.

They had not stopped since the sun was straight overhead, so the son did not object. But he did wonder why his father had picked this particular moment to do so if they were in danger.

In fact, the older warrior had a very good reason. No foe, man or beast, could now approach them without being seen. They also had a clear view of the timberline and the forest on the slope below. If anything moved, they would spot it right away.

The father rested his right hand on the antler hilt of his copper knife. He cocked his head and strained his ears but heard nothing out of the ordinary.

The son did the same. He tried not to show his worry, but he had an idea why his father was disturbed. Much earlier that day they had come on fresh grizzly sign, and to his way of thinking that meant they were probably being stalked by one of the massive monsters. Next to polar bears, grizzlies were the most formidable creatures alive. He sincerely hoped he was wrong.

As time went by and no menace showed itself, the father began to doubt his instincts. He was human, after all. He could make mistakes. If there were something out there, he mused, it should have given its presence away.

The father was bending to grab the pole when a low, ominous growl rumbled from the brush bordering the shelf. Instantly both warriors pulled their birch bows and strung them with their babiche strings. Each man notched an arrow tipped with a sharp stone point.

"Do you think it is a grizzly?" the son whispered anxiously.

The father had no idea. It might be a bear. It might be a mountain lion. Whichever, they were at a distinct disadvantage. In the dark they could not see as well as it could. They would have to wait until the beast was almost on top of them before they resorted to their bows. So their first arrows must not miss. Should they fail to strike a vital organ, the animal would be on them before they could fire again.

The growl was repeated. This time the father pinpointed the exact spot, about sixty feet away under towering firs. He peered intently into the night without result.

"It must be after the buck," the son guessed. "The scent of blood drew it to us."

"True," the father agreed, "but we will not leave the deer behind if we can help it." He refused to abandon their kill when so many were depending on that meat to get them through another day.

"What are we to do, then?" asked the son. "We cannot carry the buck and shoot our bows at the same time."

The father had no ready answer. Fire would scare the beast off, but they dared not lower their guard to gather kindling. Nor would it be wise for them to try to sneak up on the creature. The senses of animals were twice as sharp as any human's.

The father saw his son lift his bow and start to pull back the string. "What do you think you are doing?"

"It might run off if we fire a few arrows into the brush."

"And what if one of your shafts should wound it? Do you remember that time your cousin was out hunting caribou and put an arrow into a great brown bear by mistake?"

The son promptly lowered his weapon. Yes, he most certainly did remember. The enraged bear had shot out of a thicket and attacked their hunting party before any of them quite knew what had happened. His cousin had lost an arm, later bleeding to death. Another man had his skull caved in by a single swipe of an immense paw. The son would not like to see that happen again.

"We will wait," the father proposed. He figured that eventually the creature would tire of lingering and wander elsewhere in search of easier prey, or else its hunger would drive it into the open, where they would have a shot at it.

It was hard, though, to stand there in the open, exposed and vulnerable, while a fierce snarling beast prowled so close at hand. The father could understand why his son kept glancing at the trail that led down into the valley.

There was a loud crack, as of a branch being broken. The animal moved to the south, making no attempt to employ stealth. Brush crackled, grass was trampled underfoot.

The son moved nearer to the father. "What is it doing?" he whispered. "Getting ready to charge?"

"I do not know," the older warrior confessed. This animal was not acting like any he had ever encountered. Mountain lions were usually much more secretive; a man never knew one was nearby until it pounced. Grizzlies would bluff on occasion to scare humans from their territory, but their bluff consisted of pretending to charge and then turning away at the very last instant. They did not shadow men for half a day. They did not lurk in undergrowth and growl on and on.

Moments later the forest fell silent again. The father held his breath and listened but did not hear so much as a leaf stir. When enough time had gone by, he allowed himself to relax and said, "We will go quickly. Once we reach the open valley, we will be safe."

They replaced the arrows in their quivers but slung the bows over their shoulders. Each of them hoisted an end of the pole, and without delay they hurried down the game trail.

Towering trees hemmed them in, trees so tall that the stars were blotted out. It was as if they were hastening through a narrow tunnel, their moccasins making little noise on the thick carpet of pine needles underfoot.

The father glanced back often. He would rather bring up the rear since that was where the beast would in all likelihood appear, if it showed itself at all, but he did not ask his son to switch places. It would do no good. His son would refuse. Like him, his son was a proud man who would resent any notion that he could not hold his own.

A sharp bend loomed before them. The father slowed to go around it and nearly clipped a pine with the pole. Firming his grip, he jogged on at a steady pace. The surrounding woods were eerily quiet. No owls or other night birds punctuated the darkness with their cries. No wolves howled. No coyotes yipped. It was as if all the wild creatures had gone elsewhere or were in hiding.

A long, straight stretch opened in front of them. The father went faster, his son's heavy breathing assuring him that all was well. They traveled hundreds of feet and were almost to another turn when the father glimpsed movement in the vegetation bordering the turn. Immediately he halted.

The son, taken unawares, tripped over his own feet and nearly fell. He had to hold fast to the pole to keep his balance. "Why did you do that?" he demanded.

"Something is up there," the father said, pointing. He let his end of the pole drop with a thud so he could notch another arrow to his bow. "I will go see what it is. You stay here."

"No," the son said, and would have argued the point except at that exact moment a wavering howl erupted from the gloomy pines near the turn.

It was a howl unlike any either man had ever heard. It was a howl unlike any ever uttered by wolf or coyote. It rose as high as the keening wind on a stormy night, then sank as low as the death groan of a dying man. It never held the same note for more than a few seconds, undulating up and down the scale of sound. At times the howl was almost musical, at times it was the raspy growl of an enraged beast. It went on and on, finally ending as abruptly as it had begun.

Father and son faced one another. In unison they blurted the name that terrified every member of their tribe like no other could: *"Windigo!"*

Stark fear came over both warriors. They moved shoulder to shoulder. The younger man quaked, making no attempt to hide his panic. It took every ounce of his will to keep his teeth from chattering as he asked plaintively, "What do we do?"

"We run," said the father. "Go around that bend and do not stop for anything. If the creature comes after you, shoot it." So saying, he gave his son a shove and the startled youth bounded off in great leaps like a frightened deer. The father followed on his son's heels, his gaze glued to the forest.

A piercing shriek rent the air. It was akin to the caterwauling of a cougar and the feral challenge of a wolverine combined in a single horrifying cry. It made the skin of both men break out in goose bumps.

The son came to within a dozen feet of the bend. He thought that he saw a hint of motion. Without waiting to be sure, he let his shaft fly. Whether he hit the Evil One or not, he could not say. The next moment he was around the turn and fleeing for his life, running as he had never run before. He did not think to look back. He did not think to check on his father. Legs pumping, arms flailing, he raced on and on. His lungs ached terribly. His legs were lanced by pain. Still, he sped into the night, unwilling to stop for fear the devourer of men would get him. Only when at long length the son burst from the forest onto the valley floor did he come to a lurching halt and turn.

His father was nowhere to be seen.

The son gaped. He started back into the woods, then froze as a high-pitched scream wavered down from above, a scream of sheer terror, a scream that he knew issued from his father's throat and would be the last sound he ever heard his father utter. It tapered to a gurgling whine, then stopped.

In its place the wind picked up, whispering through the treetops, sighing sadly as if at the loss of a valued life.

Shocked to his core, the son waited in vain for some sign that his father was all right. He knew it was hopeless.

He knew what had happened. But he stood and stared dumbly into the darkness until the sliver of moon was high in the sky. At which point he turned and shuffled like one dead toward the village, saying over and over again that one word.

"*Windigo. Windigo. Windigo . . .*"

chapter
2

Second Son crept to the top of a rise and flattened. She raised her head slowly so as not to draw attention to herself. Below the ridge on which she lay glistened a winding stream, and beside it in a clearing on the other side grazed her quarry.

For the past two hours the warrior woman of the Burning Heart Band of the Tsistsistas had been doing her utmost to get within arrow range of a small herd of animals unique to her experience.

From the banks of the mighty Mississippi to the limitless expanse of the Great Water her husband called the Pacific Ocean, Second Son had hunted practically every animal alive at one time or another for their supper pot. But never in her wide-flung travels had she tried to bring down the kind she was now after.

Cleve liked to refer to them as "billy goats with jackrabbit legs." Trappers out of Fort Hall simply called them mountain goats. In the language of the Tsistsistas there was no word for them, so Second Son had taken to thinking of them as Little Horns. Although White Ghosts would fit just as well.

They were incredible animals. Their favorite haunts were the lofty spires and rocky peaks no other creatures visited except for high-soaring eagles and hawks. Shaggy hair as white as driven snow covered their bodies and made them easy to spot from a distance. But spotting them and getting close enough to shoot one were two different things.

Only when mountain goats descended from the airy heights did a hunter have a chance. Second Son had been keeping her eyes on this herd for many weeks. Off and on she had visited the area, noting their habits, memorizing their daily routine. As with any hunter worthy of the name, she knew that she must know her prey as well as she knew herself to have any hope of success.

Today was the day Second Son had looked forward to. She had arrived before first light. After tethering her mare, Shadow, she had concealed herself on the far side of the ridge, near the crest. It was the ideal place to wait since it overlooked the pool where the Little Horns regularly drank.

Now, her ash bow in hand, Second Son watched the seven males closely. There were no females in this herd. The sexes stayed apart except during rutting season, which began during the Long Night Moon. She had seen the herd of females only once, high up. It appeared that they had more sense than the males and always stayed well out of reach.

Three of the bigger Little Horns were at the water's edge. One had stepped into the pool and stood there with its muzzle dipped low. Yet another had crossed two thirds of the way to the far side. Once it climbed out, it would be directly below the low ridge and well within bow range.

Second Son could imagine her husband's surprise when she placed her prize at his feet. The blond giant had mentioned again just a few days ago that he thought she was wasting her time.

"I'm sorry, darling," Cleve had said. "But every trapper hereabouts tells me that it's impossible to kill one of those critters. Many have tried and all have failed. You'd be better off going after deer or buffalo."

Her husband had laughed in that playful way he had and given her a hug, which turned into a wrestling match when he tried to tickle her. She did not like being tickled and he knew it. But husbands had a knack, as Cleve had once put it when talking about a relative of his, of letting words go in one ear and right out the other.

Why that should be, Second Son did not know. But no matter how many times she told him not to tickle her, every now and then he would do it. It was enough to make her want to hit him over the head with a war club. Fortunately for Cleve she loved him, so she couldn't. But there were times when she was strongly tempted.

The large male gained the near bank, bringing the warrior woman's reverie to an end. She tightened her fingers on the arrow and eased up onto her knees. By design she had positioned herself between a bush and a scrub pine so her silhouette would not stand out against the sky.

The Little Horn began to munch the sweet grass. Second Son elevated the bow and carefully pulled the sinew string back toward her right cheek. She went to sight on the mountain goat's chest, then stiffened when she detected movement out of the corner of her left eye.

The Cheyenne woman was not the only hunter abroad that day. Slinking toward the pool, belly low to the ground, tawny form rippling with sleek sinew, was a male painter, as Cleve called them. The big cat had not spied her. Its whole attention was fixed on the very mountain goat the warrior woman was on the verge of slaying.

Second Son was not about to let the Little Horn be taken right out from under her nose. She had put too much time and effort into this hunt. She would not be denied.

Quickly sighting down the shaft, Second Son steadied her arms, held her breath, and just as the mountain goat raised its head to stare suspiciously toward the high weeds that screened the painter, she let the arrow go.

The shaft flew straight and true, its barbed point glittering in the sunlight. It caught the goat between the ribs and sheared through hide and muscle to penetrate a lung and its heart. In sheer reflex the male managed to whirl and take several swift steps before death crumpled it in midstride. In a flurry of whirling legs and pointed black hooves, it tumbled end over end, coming to rest at the water's edge.

Instantly the rest of the herd fled. They were across the clearing and to the base of the mountain in the blink of an eye. Up the slope they streaked, weaving as they ran.

All this Second Son barely noticed. She was more concerned with the painter, which had stood when the herd spooked and was studying the animal she had shot, its long tail twitching excitedly. Taking the two steps needed to bring her to the top, she nocked another shaft, her fingers a blur.

The painter was on the move again, closing on the body, its head tucked low to its shoulders, that tail now as straight as one of the warrior woman's arrows.

Second Son whipped the bow up. It was short and thick

through the middle and much more powerful than it appeared. Cleve had been surprised the first time he had tested its strength, commenting that he'd had no idea she was as strong as Samson, whatever that meant. Swiftly she took aim on her competition but could not see it clearly for the grass.

Seconds later the painter padded into full view. It glanced once at the fleeing herd, then at the dead goat.

"Ho! Stupid cat!" Second Son called out in the tongue of the Tsistsistas. "That one is mine! Go find yourself another meal!"

The painter whirled at the sound of her voice and cut loose with a rumbling snarl, its thin lips pulled back to reveal its tapered fangs.

"You heard me, cat!" Second Son challenged. "Leave this place or die! The Little Horn is mine."

She did not really expect the painter to dispute her. These *couguars*, as the Frenchmen she had met were fond of calling them, were timid at heart, and would rather run from a person than fight. Many times she had encountered them. Never once had one come after her.

Which made Second Son all the more amazed when this specimen did just that. Venting another snarl, it flashed up the slope in a blur, covering fifteen feet at a leap. She angled the bow to compensate.

Since the cat was charging straight at her, it did not present much of a target. Second Son had a choice between its head and its chest, which was really not much of a choice at all because its skull was thick enough to deflect an arrow. She aimed squarely at the center of its chest. When the cat had covered half the distance, she sent the shaft flying.

A cougar's reflexes are second to none. This one tried to avoid the arrow by swerving to the side, but the shaft was going too fast and embedded itself in the big cat's flank.

The predator whipped around as if kicked by a mule. It paused for the briefest of moments to glare at the feathers jutting from its hindquarters. Then, with a piercing cry, the painter sprang higher. Its features were distorted in bestial rage the likes of which few human eyes had ever witnessed.

Second Son was ready. She had drawn a second shaft from her quiver and notched it. There was less time to aim, but she did not need much. Years of practice enabled her to rely on instinct as much as skill. She simply trained the arrow on the cougar and released the string.

At the very instant that the warrior woman fired, the painter leaped at her, its front legs outstretched, its wicked claws unsheathed and curled to rip and tear. The leap saved its life, for the shaft struck it low in the chest instead of in the center. The point dug a furrow the length of its stomach but did not strike any vital organs.

Suddenly the cat was on her. Second Son spun, swinging her bow as if it were a club. She hit the painter on the side of its head with enough force to send it tumbling. But it recovered in the blink of an eye and whirled to confront her, its teeth bared, its ears flattened, its tail lashing the air like a whip.

Second Son knew she was in a desperate situation. The cat was as long as she was tall and outweighed her by many pounds. It had teeth and claws as sharp as any knife ever made, backed by muscles of virtual steel. All she had was the bow with no arrow nocked to the string and her long butcher knife in a beaded sheath at her side.

Pain drove the painter to try to finish her off quickly. It closed in, its front paws flashing, seeking to slice into her legs. The warrior woman backpedaled and brought the bow down on top of its head with all her might. It had the desired effect of causing the cat to retreat, but as it did, the cougar swung a paw and clipped the bowstring. Just like that, the string was nearly severed, rendering the bow next to useless.

Second Son glanced down the ridge at her horse. If she could reach Shadow, she had a chance of outrunning the cat. Yet once the painter realized the mare was there, it just might go after Shadow instead.

Now the beast circled slowly, its body held so close to the ground that blood from its belly wound smeared the earth. It favored its left hind leg, where the other arrow was half-buried. Apparently it had learned the hard way not to take her lightly and was not going to rush in again until it saw an opening.

The Cheyenne woman backed away just as slowly. She contrived to circle lower so she would be that much nearer the mare. As yet the cat had not noticed the horse, but it was just a matter of time before it would. She wished that she had a lance. Or, better yet, she wished that she had listened to Cleve and let him buy her a brace of pistols and a rifle to have for her very own. She had declined because she had always used the traditional weapons of the Tsistsistas and they had always served her well. Now she wondered if perhaps she had been too hasty in her decision.

The cat took an abrupt swipe at her thigh. Second Son blocked it with the bow. But as she swung, her left foot stepped onto a loose flat rock, which slid out from under her. Before she could stop herself she fell backward, landing hard on her shoulders, and went sliding down the slope. Dust spewed out from under her. Frantically she tried to stop, but she kept gaining momentum. She careened off a boulder, racking her shoulder with torment. A rending snap told her the bow had broken.

Still sliding, Second Son was only vaguely aware of the cougar following her down. It did not like the dust that flew up into its face, and kept tossing its head and hissing.

Then Second Son came to a jolting stop against a log. She pushed onto her knees to find the painter in front of her and a boulder to her right. Off to the left a dozen yards stood Shadow, watching with head raised and ears pricked. She hardly was able to set herself before the cat screeched and launched itself at her chest.

A piece of ash as long as Second Son's arm was all that remained of the bow. Where it had broken, the hard wood bore a jagged point. It was not much of a weapon, but it was all she had, so she drove it up and in even as she ducked under the beast's raking paws. The point cut into its chest but did not stop the cougar from coming down on top of her. A paw hit her a glancing blow on the shoulder, enough to flatten her, slicing through the buckskin and into her flesh.

Second Son did not scream in terror. She did not cringe or succumb to numbing fear or do any of those things that many would have done. She was a warrior in the Burning Heart Band of the Tsistsistas and warriors did not show fear to their enemies. Warriors fought on until they prevailed or life left them. That was the warrior way.

So as the cat came down on her, Second Son's right hand swooped to her sheath and the butcher knife leaped clear. She thrust the blade into its chest at the very moment a second swing of a huge paw opened up her side. Then the heavy painter slammed down and there was not enough room for her to move her arm to stab. She was effectively pinned, at the animal's nonexistent mercy.

Her fate seemed sealed. Yet as the cougar went to take a rending bite out of her throat and its hot breath fanned her face, it unexpectedly let out a yowl of pain and jumped up off her.

Second Son lost no time in pushing to her feet. She saw the cougar spinning and leaping and pawing at its own chest in a frenzied attempt to dislodge the piece of ash, which had driven deep into its body when it pounced on her.

The beast was distracted. Second Son took immediate advantage, pivoted, and sped to Shadow. The mare knew what was in store and was poised for flight. It took but a moment for Second Son to unwrap the reins from the bush to which they were tied and swing up. With a jab of her heels she goaded the faithful horse into a gallop. They flew like the wind down the slope.

A glance back showed that the painter had dislodged the ash and was in pursuit. Second Son knew that the big cats were fast over short distances but lacked stamina. If she could keep ahead of it long enough, she would escape.

The cougar began to gain. Shadow was galloping all out and could not go any faster. Second Son held the bloody butcher knife ready to use should the painter overtake them. She did not take her eyes off the beast as it hurtled toward them at unbelievable speed.

Tense moments went by. Shadow held her own. The cat put on one last burst of speed and came within reach of the mare's legs. It lashed out and missed. By purest chance one of Shadow's pounding hooves slammed into its temple and sent it rolling across the grass.

Second Son whooped. The painter rose, dazed and wobbly. It made no effort to resume the chase but simply stared after her as she raced toward the end of the meadow. With a toss of its head, as if in disdain, the beast turned and limped off toward the ridge, back toward the stream—and the dead Little Horn.

No! Second Son thought. She hauled on the reins, bringing Shadow to a sliding stop close to the pines. Second Son glared at the cat in spite as intense as its own. Unless she did something, it would deprive her of her prize. It would drag the mountain goat off into the brush and she would never find it. The cat would win.

Second Son was not about to let that happen. Before her lay a number of downed saplings, victims of the high winds so common in the mountains. She slid down and ran to them, examining each, lifting those she liked to test their weight and heft. Finding a suitable one, she worked rapidly, trimming the slender branches. The top had to be broken off, leaving a sturdy but slender six-foot pole.

A check showed that the painter was almost to the ridge. The warrior woman began trimming the slim end of the pole. Chips sailed every which way as she whittled the wood down to a sharp point. The sapling had not been downed long, so it was easy to cut and shape.

The cougar had stopped to lick its wounds. It bent around to nip at the shaft in its flank as if striving to pull the arrow out.

Second Son kept one eye on her nemesis as she finished fashioning her makeshift lance. When it was done she hefted it a few times to test its balance. Then, sliding the butcher knife into her sheath, she vaulted onto Shadow, wheeled the horse, and headed back across the meadow at a walk.

The painter was so intent on tearing the shaft from its body that it did not notice her until she rose and emitted her war whoop. It stopped and straightened, regarding her with what could only be described as a puzzled look.

Holding the lance in her right hand, Second Son brought the mare to a trot. The cat took a few steps toward her, then halted, as if uncertain. A grim smile touched Second Son's full lips. She urged Shadow into a gallop and leaned forward so her body was better balanced. Her pine lance was slightly heavier than those she had learned to use when barely old enough to ride, but it would suffice. She would *make* it suffice.

The big cat stared at her, its tail flicking as always, its eyes narrowed. Perhaps the novelty of having prey turn on it gave it pause. Whatever the reason, it did not move until the warrior woman was fewer than fifty yards away. Then it snarled and came at her like a living bolt of lightning.

Second Son arched her back and raised the lance overhead. She bent to the side to give herself a clearer view of the onrushing beast. There was no turning back now. Either she emerged the victor or she would perish, and most likely the mare would die along with her.

The painter never slowed, never faltered. It raced to meet them, as graceful as it was deadly.

Tensing her right arm and bunching her shoulder muscles, Second Son waited for just the right moment. The distance between them narrowed to thirty yards, then twenty, then ten. In another heartbeat the cougar was almost upon her, and it leaped to bring her down. It was then that she hurled the lance with all the power in her supple frame.

The cat and the lance met in midair. The tip tore into its chest, sinking in deep. In the middle of its spring the painter seemed to deflate like a punctured water skin.

Second Son galloped past unscathed, and turned to see the cougar hit the ground with a loud thud, feebly paw at empty air, and go limp. It would never rise again.

Slowing and turning her horse, the warrior woman rode back and sat staring down at the vanquished creature. She took no pleasure in the killing, as some whites she had met were inclined to do. It simply had to be done.

In the less than thirty winters Second Son had lived, there had been many similar incidents involving various savage animals and even more savage men. They were a normal occurrence, as much a part of her life as breathing and eating. She had learned to take them in stride, as Cleve would say.

Now, dismounting, Second Son placed a foot against the cat's chest, gripped the lance with both hands, and tugged and wrenched, working it out. Next she squatted and slipped her hands under the warm body. It took some doing for her to drape the cat over her shoulder and stand, and then to transfer the animal to the mare. Shadow shied skittishly, quieting only after Second Son stroked her neck and spoke softly.

Taking the lance, she climbed on and rode over the ridge to the stream. Beside the Little Horn she reined up and gave the cat a push so that it plopped down next to the goat. She had her work cut out for her, but first she had to tend her wounds.

The cuts on Second Son's shoulder were the worst. She bathed them and the claw marks in her side and cut a strip from the bottom of her shirt to make bandages. There was very little blood and she would not be crippled. Heamma-wihio had watched over her.

By this time the sun hung low in the western sky. Second Son would be hard-pressed to finish the work she needed to do before nightfall.

Taking her knife, she bent to the Little Horn. Before skinning it, she inspected the animal closely, the first she had ever seen so near. Of main interest to her were the horns, which were black daggerlike affairs that curved backward. The beard she found amusing. As she lifted a leg, she noticed the hooves were different from any other animal's. They had sharp outer rims for gripping smooth rock and soft soles that provided traction on steep surfaces.

Pressing the tip of the butcher knife to the hide, she slit the hind legs open down the back of each. Then she cut in a straight line right down the middle of the belly, from the hind end to the chin. After slicing down the inside of the front legs, she was ready for the messy part of the job.

Second Son peeled the hide off the goat just like her husband might peel off a sock at night. As she peeled, she cut the ligaments and muscles holding the hide to the carcass. She was careful to slant the edge of her knife toward the body so she would not accidentally nick the hide and ruin it.

Once the mountain goat was skinned and the meat rolled up in the pelt, Second Son gave the painter the same treatment. Except, since she wanted to save the tail for her son, she slit down it lengthwise for several inches, then pulled the tailbone out.

All this took nearly two hours. The sun had partially dropped below the western horizon, blazing the sky in brilliant hues of red and orange and yellow, when she straightened and stretched. As she did, the mare nickered softly. Instantly Second Son was alert. She turned, and happened to glimpse a two-legged figure sneaking down the ridge toward her.

chapter

— 3 —

Cleve Bennett was bigger than most men. His size was not so apparent when he was by himself since he was not bulky as were most his size. Rather, every part of the man from Missouri was so ideally proportioned that the parts gave no true hint of the whole. Not unless he was near another person did it become readily apparent, such as now.

Cleve spat into both palms, gripped the ax handle firmly, and said in passable Tsistsista, "Stand back. I would not want to chop off your head by mistake." With that, he swung the ax into the white pine in front of him. The blade dug deep, testimony to the power contained in his broad muscles.

A few feet away Second Son's nephew, Rakes the Sky

with Lightning, smiled one of his rare smiles and stepped back out of harm's way. Folding his arms across his bronzed chest, he admired the skill his white relative displayed. Lightning himself was awkward with the long-handled tool. But then, he could count the number of times he had needed to chop down a tree on one hand.

The young Cheyenne warrior was a product of the prairie that had spawned him. He had spent the greater portion of his short life living amid the sea of waving grass that stretched from the Muddy River to the Shining Mountains. Many a day had gone by when he had not set eyes on a single tree.

That is, until that awful morning the Burning Hearts were attacked by a vengeful band of wicked whites who had slain practically every last man, woman, and child. Lightning had been burned so severely that he had almost died. It was thanks to the valiant efforts of his cousin Billy-Wolf Bennett that he was still alive.

Alive, and scarred. Thinking of their narrow escape caused Lightning to lift a hand to the left half of his face. Involuntarily, he shuddered. His wrinkled skin was a constant reminder of their horrible ordeal, and of the loving wife he had lost.

Not a day went by that Lightning did not think of Twisted Leg and the baby she would have borne had the vile whites not butchered her. Knowing that the killers had paid with their own lives was no consolation. His loss was too great, the hurt too deep. Thinking of it brought an anguished look to his twisted features.

Cleve Bennett did not notice. The free trapper was intent on felling the white pine. They needed to down a few more trees to finish the cabin they were building, and Cleve was eager to complete the task.

The big man yearned to give his family a home again. For close to two years they had been without a roof over their heads. All because he had gotten the notion to join the Beeville Expedition and travel to California.

At the time it had seemed like the right thing to do. But that was the way with notions. How was anyone to know that a decision he believed to be as right as rain would later turn out to be as wrong as the day was long?

Two years! Just reflecting on the hardships he and Second Son had undergone was enough to spur him to tear into the pine with a vengeance.

There had been the grizzly bear attack that had nearly ended his life.

There had been the priest in Monterey who had branded his wife "an abomination to God and man alike" simply because she went around dressed like a man and acting like a man, which, after all, was only in keeping with her status as a warrior.

There had been their capture by the ferocious Karok Indians, who had turned around and sold them to another tribe. Not to mention the brutal winter they spent as virtual slaves.

So much had happened, so much of it bad, and all due to his wanderlust! Cleve frowned and swung the ax for the umpteenth time. The tool thudded heavily into the bole, wedging deeper than ever. It would not be long.

Planting both feet flat, Cleve studied the angle of the cut he had made to be sure the tree would fall as he wished. Then he buried the ax one more time.

A grinding crunch filled the air. The white pine swayed, tilted, and swept toward the earth. It snapped off limbs from a nearby forest giant, scraped the trunk of the other tree, and crashed down with a resounding thud.

Beaming, Cleve wiped his sweaty brow with the back of his shirtsleeve. "One down, two to go," he said to his nephew, and only then observed the haunted look in the younger man's eyes. He did not need to ask why. Lightning had not been the same man since Twisted Leg's death.

Cleve stepped in close to the tree and commenced trimming the branches. For most, a single swipe of the ax was more than enough. When he was done, he stood at the wide end of the trunk and paced off the proper distance. The excess he chopped off.

Lightning had to help carry the log to the cabin. They walked down a short slope and deposited their burden in front of the nearly completed structure.

Stepping back to admire their handiwork, Cleve rubbed his palms together to remove tiny bits of wood that had stuck to his hands. He was rightfully proud of their new home. Long hours had been spent in its planning, and it had taken most of the spring to build it. In his opinion, there wasn't a finer cabin anywhere west of Missouri. His ma and pa would be right proud of him.

Second Son had been dubious at first. "We have no need of a wooden lodge," she had remarked when he first broached the subject. "Why not kill some buffalo and make a tipi as we always do?"

Cleve had gazed out over the broad valley they had laid claim to, nodding at the lake that had shimmered in the midday sun. "Because this is where we intend to spend the rest of our lives. This is where we're sticking down roots permanent like. So it's only fitting that we have ourselves a permanent home."

His wife had given him the sort of look wives always gave their husbands when they thought their men were not being sensible, but she had pecked him on the cheek and told him to go ahead, that it was all right by her.

That was Second Son. She might think him an idiot at times, but she would let him be an idiot to his heart's content if it made him happy.

As if Lightning could read Cleve's thoughts, the Cheyenne nodded to the west and said in thickly accented English, "It will be dark soon. Yet your wife is not yet back. Maybe we should go look for her."

"No need," Cleve responded, adding proudly, "Your aunt is one female who can take care of herself anytime, anywhere. We'll keep on working until it's too dark for me to use the ax. Then we'll have us some rabbit stew." He made for the top of the hill. "Don't fret yourself over Second Son. If she's not back by morning, then we'll worry."

At that very moment the object of their conversation was riding back to camp when she suddenly whirled toward the ridge behind her, a hand flying to her knife. She had grown careless. She had been so wrapped up in skinning the mountain goat and the painter that she had not been as vigilant as she should be.

The wilderness was no place for complacency. Too many wild beasts were abroad at any given hour of the day or night. Too many violent men roved the land in search of the weak and the unwary.

Second Son knew this better than most. Time and again she had been forced to defend her life or her virtue from those who had no regard for either. So she was greatly annoyed that she had let her guard down and put both herself and Shadow in jeopardy again.

Her anxiety, however, melted under the warm glow of profound happiness when she saw the lean figure who had nearly succeeded in sneaking up on her. Rather than draw the butcher knife, she smiled a radiant smile and declared, "Wolf Sings on the Mountain, what are you doing here?"

Billy-Wolf Bennett drew up short, dismayed that he had been discovered. Of late he had been trying to take his mother by surprise every chance he got. It had become a game with them, and more than a game. His mother tolerated it because he was honing skills that would serve him

well in the wild, skills that might one day mean the difference between life and death. "Aw, Ma," he grumbled,
"you found me out again. I'll never be able to count coup
on you."

"A true warrior never gives up once he sets his mind to
something," Second Son said, her dark eyes twinkling.

The boy came up and gave the warrior woman a fleeting hug, then quickly stepped back. Billy-Wolf did not say
so, but he felt awkward around his mother at times. He
disguised his feelings now by giving a little cough and nodding at the carcasses. "A mountain goat and a painter
both! Won't Pa be tickled. He sure does love painter
meat."

Second Son had noticed her son's reserve but did not
comment on it. He had been that way since they were reunited at Fort Hall many weeks ago. At first she had believed it to be the natural result of their lengthy separation,
but now she was no longer so sure. Often she wondered if
perhaps something she had done were bothering him.

Not a week ago Second Son had asked Cleve about it.
He had assured her that it must be her imagination, that
he had not observed anything out of the ordinary. But
then, her husband and her son were getting along just fine.

"Yes," Second Son answered. "Your father will be very
pleased." She gazed up at the ridge. "Did he come with
you?"

Billy-Wolf averted his eyes and poked at the ground
with a toe. "No. Lightning and him were still hard at work
on the cabin when I took off. You know how much he
wants to get it done."

Second Son pursed her lips. As a parent, she made few
demands on the boy. It was not the Cheyenne way to be
domineering. Her people preferred to let young ones learn
the lessons life had to teach at their own pace. Rarely were

children punished, and it was unthinkable for a parent ever to strike a child.

In this, Cleve disagreed. He had been reared by a rigid, God-fearing farmer who had attempted to mold the Bennett boys into his own image. Cleve had resented it while growing up and swore that he would never treat his offspring the same, but he still believed in "setting down the law" when their son became too rambunctious for his own good.

In that regard, she and Cleve were in harmony. Both agreed that Billy-Wolf should never stray far from their homesite without letting them know where and for how long he was going. There were just too many dangers. If something terrible befell him, they would have no inkling until it was too late.

Which prompted Second Son to now ask, "Does your father know that you came here? Did you tell him that you were leaving?"

Billy-Wolf poked at the ground again. "I reckon I forgot, Ma. Sorry." The truth was that he had not forgotten, that he had not told his pa because he had figured that his father would make him stick close and help out with the cabin. But he did not want to admit this.

The warrior woman was severely disappointed. Her son was lying to her. His memory was exceptional, better at times than her own and Cleve's. This was the first time in his thirteen winters that he had ever deliberately deceived her, and she hesitated, unsure of what to do.

Among the Tsistsistas, lying was not tolerated. Those who adopted the practice were looked down on and made to feel the shame of their deceit in a hundred subtle ways. A few moons of such treatment was usually enough to change the most hardened liar.

But this was Second Son's own child. Should she shame him, as she would any Tsistsista in this situation? Or should she let the matter pass for now and talk it over with Cleve later? The fact that Billy-Wolf would not look her in the eyes made up her mind for her. As a warrior, she had been trained to act whenever trouble presented itself. And this moment demanded action.

"I did not know you had been hit on the head recently," Second Son said tactfully. "You should have told me and I would have made an herbal poultice for you."

The boy glanced up in surprise. He had not suffered a head wound ever, and his mother knew it. "Hit on the noggin? What in the world are you talking about, Ma?"

"It is said that a strong blow to the head will make one forgetful," Second Son explained. "There is no other reason for you not to have told your father you were coming here." She made a show of inspecting his tousled hair. "So where is the bump? Where were you struck?"

Billy-Wolf was flabbergasted. He had not expected her to make an issue of his being there, and now she had caught him in his lie. He did not know what to do. Part of him wanted simply to admit the truth, but another part was afraid that if he did, his mother would think less of him. She was staring at him, waiting for his answer. Unable to make up his mind, he blurted, "My head is fine. I just forgot. All right? Don't you ever forget things?"

Second Son's heart fell. She had hoped to shame him into confessing, and instead he had compounded his lie by repeating it while looking her right in the eyes. Truly, this was a bad sign. To cover her dismay she turned and walked toward a stand of aspens. "I must make a travois to haul the meat. Would you please get the rope I keep in my parfleche?"

The boy was glad to have something to do. Anything to get off the subject they were on. He stepped to Shadow and rummaged through the two parfleches strapped on behind the saddle. With the coil of rawhide in hand, he re-joined his mother.

The warrior woman had found a small tree that suited her purpose. Squatting, she chopped at the slender bole with her butcher knife. She did not look at her son. His behavior had her so disturbed that she was afraid her eyes would give her feelings away.

To Second Son's knowledge, Billy-Wolf had never lied to Cleve. Nor did the boy act as reserved around his father as he had been around her. Something had gone very wrong between them, and for the life of her she did not know what it was.

As Second Son chopped, she mused. She thought back to the joyous times they had shared before Cleve got a hankering to go to California. The family had been whole then. Her son had treated her just as he treated Cleve.

Then came the journey, which had lasted far longer than she or Cleve had counted on and resulted in grueling hardships not only for them, but for their son as well.

Second Son had thought that leaving Billy-Wolf with the Burning Hearts was the right thing to do. He had lived with relatives and friends. It had been a chance for him to learn more of his Tsistsista heritage, a heritage he must pass on to his own children one day. And at the same time it had given the boy a measure of independence so he could learn to "stand on his own two feet," as Cleve had put it back then.

No one could have foreseen that everything would go so horribly wrong. The Burning Hearts had been attacked by a bitter enemy, but not an enemy of their own making. No, it had been a man who hated Cleve and Second Son who had wiped out her people as a means of getting re-venge on the two of them.

A day did not go by that Second Son did not think of the massacre. How could she not, when she had a daily reminder in the form of her scarred nephew? Every time she looked at Lightning's face was like having her own slapped for having been indirectly to blame for the slaughter. It was a heavy burden.

The aspen crackled as it tipped over. The top caught on another, so Second Son had to bear down with both hands to dislodge it. Billy-Wolf promptly jumped to help, adding his weight to hers, and in another moment the tree was down.

"Thank you," the warrior woman said softly.

Believing that the fib he had told had already been forgotten, Billy-Wolf was now in fine spirits. "What else is a son for?" he quipped. His mother did not grin, as his pa would have, but then she was not one to wear her emotions on her sleeve. The smile she had given him earlier was the first he recollected seeing in days.

A second aspen was felled in no time. The branches were trimmed off and the two poles were dragged out and set down near the carcasses.

Night was not far off. The sun had relinquished its blazing throne to darkening twilight. Already the first star had appeared to the northwest. The wind was picking up as it always did at that time of day.

Second Son worked faster. She took a half-dozen limbs, stripped them of shoots and leaves, then lashed them crosswise to the two poles. The branches were spaced close together so that the hides and meat could be placed on top and tied down.

Shadow was munching on the sweet grass. The mare perked up when Second Son began rigging the free ends of the two poles to either side of her Cheyenne-style saddle. After she was done, she had an adequate travois.

"I never saw you make one of these before," Billy-Wolf innocently commented.

Second Son saw no need to tell him that she seldom

had. Tsistsista society practiced a strict division of labor; certain work was done by the warriors, certain work by the women, and it was rare for the two to overlap. The women were the travois makers. They took considerable pride in their ability, and any woman who did an inferior job was not rated as much of a craftsman.

Because Second Son had been a warrior, she had done a warrior's work. She had hunted and tracked and gone on raids. She had stolen horses and scouted new country and defended the village when it was attacked. But she had not made blankets. She had not helped deliver babies. She had not crafted a travois.

"We must hurry," Second Son mentioned as she carefully climbed onto the mare. She eased her leg over the projecting pole on the off side so as not to snag it.

"I left Blaze on the other side of the ridge," Billy-Wolf said. "I'll go fetch him." Off he bolted, like a young wolf yearning to test its legs. He tore up the slope at a swift lope and raced over the crest.

Pride welled up in Second Son. Despite his recent strange behavior, Wolf Sings on the Mountain was growing into a strapping young man. In another few winters he would be of age to take a wife according to Cheyenne custom, provided he wanted to, of course. Once he did, he would move out on his own.

The thought was unsettling.

Two or three years sounded like a lot of time, but it wasn't. Time had a habit of flying by so fast that it was gone before a person realized it had slipped through their fingers. And the older a person became, the faster it flew.

Second Son wanted to use the time she had left with Billy-Wolf to be as close to him as she had once been. She wanted her son to be at ease around her, to always be honest with her as he had been before their separation. In effect, she wanted things to be as they had been.

But was she being practical? Second Son asked herself. One of the many lessons life had taught her was that there was no going back again. One could not relive the past. As Cleve liked to say, it was water over the dam, and no amount of wishful thinking could bring it back again.

Still, she could try. The idea grew on the warrior woman as she rode over the ridge. Her son waited for her astride the fine stallion that had carried him all the way from the plains.

Beside the horse stood the boy's other faithful four-legged companion, Snip. The yellow mongrel was in its prime, as stout as a redwood and as fiercely loyal to its master as any dog alive. Snip whined and wagged his tail in greeting.

"Ho, dog," Second Son said. She watched when Snip moved over to the travois to sniff at the bundles in case he decided to savor a morsel of raw meat. But Snip had been well trained. He did no more than nose around a little and then returned to her son's side.

They rode to the south in single file, Billy-Wolf in the lead. In his right hand he held the new Hawken his father had traded for at Fort Hall the preceding winter. Wedged under the belt around his waist was a flintlock pistol, while on his right hip nestled a hunting knife. He also had his own ammo pouch, powder horn, and possibles bag. In every respect except size he was the living image of a typical mountain man.

Second Son came to a decision about the time the sliver of moon rose above the jagged mountains. "Billy-Wolf," she called out.

The boy tensed. Dutifully, he wheeled Blaze and rode back to his mother. While he did not let on, he dreaded the prospect that she would again broach the subject of his lie.

"I have been thinking," Second Son began. "It will be

another two or three days before your father is done with the cabin. After that, he plans to build a small stable and a corral. And he mentioned making furniture. All that will keep him busy for several weeks yet."

Billy-Wolf said nothing. He did not know where this was leading but assumed his mother was about to request that he help out more instead of spending every free minute off gallivanting.

"This past winter we barely survived because we have no food stored up for hard times," Second Son went on. "I would like to go north into the deep forest to hunt elk. We can dry the meat so it will last us a long time, and make pemmican of whatever we do not use for jerky."

"We?" Billy-Wolf said in delight.

"Yes," Second Son confirmed. "Just the two of us. How would you like that?"

Before the boy could answer, both horses stopped cold and Snip let out a throaty growl. Mother and son glanced in all directions, seeking the cause. It turned out to be closer than they thought.

From a thicket twenty yards away had come the rumbling cough of an agitated grizzly.

chapter
4

Rakes the Sky with Lightning arched an eyebrow and regarded the flask being handed him with a skeptical air. "What would my aunt say if she were here, Yellow Hair?"

"We're grown men, aren't we?" Cleve Bennett responded testily. "We can do as we damn well please." He scanned the valley before he remarked, "Besides, she isn't here and probably won't be for a while, so we might as well treat ourselves. We have it coming. We put in a hard day's work."

Lightning could not argue there. Yellow Hair pushed both of them much too hard for his liking. His aunt's husband had not yet learned to live as the Tsistsistas did, taking each day as it came, taking each job that had to be done one at a time and doing the work at a proper pace.

With whites, everything was rush, rush, rush. All work had to be done in the shortest time possible, and then the next job was taken up with hardly a spare moment to relax. Always bustling about, as if the world would come to an end if they did not complete all that had to be done before the sun set. It was a crazy way of living, and seemed to explain why so many of the whites Lightning had met were not quite in their right mind.

Sighing, the Kit Fox warrior tipped the silver flask to his mouth. He had never tasted whiskey before and did not know what to expect. Certainly he was not prepared for the incredible burning sensation that seared his throat. For a moment he thought that he had swallowed liquid fire. Sputtering and wheezing, he lowered the flask as moisture rimmed his eyes. It was all he could do to breathe. To his amazement, his aunt's husband burst out laughing.

"Aren't you a sight!" Cleve declared good-naturedly, slapping a thigh. "It serves you right for guzzling it whole hog. The trick to downing good liquor is to sip it. Take your time. Isn't that what you're always telling me to do?"

Lightning could but nod. His mouth seemed incapable of forming coherent words. The burning persisted even though he swallowed again and again to clear his throat.

Cleve took the flask, drank deep, then smacked his lips. "Now me, I was brought up on 'shine. The pure stuff brewed back in the hills. So this whiskey they peddle at the fort is more like water than the real article." He clapped his nephew on the back, trying not to laugh at the warrior's red face and damp cheeks. It brought back memories of the time he had snuck off with a few friends to buy a jug from Old Man Jenks. That had been his first drink, and he had wound up on the ground coughing and shaking as if he were having a fit.

To Lightning, it made no sense for any sane person to put such terrible-tasting liquid into their bodies. Whiskey tasted a lot like horse urine smelled. "I do not want any more," he was finally able to croak.

"Don't give up so soon," Cleve said. "It has to grow on you." He offered the flask. "Trust me. After a few more swallows, you won't care what it tastes like."

Even though Lightning had no real desire to do so, he accepted the container out of politeness and took a tiny swallow. This time the burning was less intense, the taste not nearly as disgusting. He also noticed a peculiar warmth spreading through his stomach. It was very pleasant, like the sensation a man felt when he knelt beside a hot fire on a cold day. He took yet another swallow.

Cleve leaned back against the front wall of the cabin and surveyed the sparkling stars. It was his intention to add a porch at a future date, after everything else had been done. "I reckon now you know why some Indians call it firewater. Back home, folks call it coffin varnish, snake poison, and bug juice." The big man chuckled. "They all fit."

Lightning grunted. He took another swallow, then another. The more he downed, the warmer his abdomen became. And now he felt an odd lightness in his head that he had never experienced before. It was most baffling.

"Hey, quit hogging it all for yourself," Cleve said. Taking the flask, he puckered, then drank some and frowned. "I haven't had really decent whiskey in ages. Too bad nobody around here has a still."

"A what?" Lightning asked. The warmth continued to spread, giving him a giddy feeling. And was it his imagination, or were the stars blurry?

The free trapper went on at length about how whiskey was made back in the green hills of Missouri. He told about fermenting corn mash and letting it age in wooden barrels. He also mentioned how another drink he happened to be fond of, rum, was made from sugarcane or molasses. Presently he glanced at the warrior and was surprised to see Lightning grinning at him. It was the first time the Cheyenne had grinned since the death of his wife. "What is so funny?" he asked.

"You white men," Lightning answered. He had been drinking the whole time Yellow Hair had been talking, and the flask was about empty. His whole body was warm, his tongue felt as thick as his wrist, and everything he looked at had a fuzzy glow.

"What about us?"

"You are never happy with the way things are. You must always change them to suit you. You take metal and wood and make guns. You take metal and stone and make fire." Lightning shook the flask. "And you take corn and make this awful drink." He shook his head. "Whites are never satisfied to leave things be. One day that will bring about your ruin."

"Is that a fact?" Cleve said, chortling. His friend had not spoken so many words at one time in months. It was a good sign. It meant the whiskey was doing what Cleve and Second Son and Billy-Wolf had been unable to do, namely to get the warrior to unwind a little, to start enjoying life again.

Lightning nodded, then took one more sip. For some strange reason, he began to feel like he had the time his beloved wife pinned him under their buffalo robes and tickled his sides until he begged for mercy. The remembrance made him laugh.

A feather could have floored Cleve. He was so pleased that he went inside, searched through the pile of belongings stacked in a corner, and produced another flask, which was only half-full. Carrying it outside, he eased down beside the warrior. "This is the last of it. I was keeping it hid for a special occasion, but what the hell!" Removing the stopper, he drank greedily.

Lightning did not notice. He was adrift within himself, remembering, flitting from one treasured memory to another as a butterfly flies from flower to flower. As if it were only yesterday, he recalled the first time Twisted Leg had let him kiss her sweet lips, the first time he had seen the breathtaking beauty of her naked body, and that glorious sunny day they had bathed together in a shallow river pool.

Twisted Leg! Lightning's mind shrieked. How I miss you!

The warrior finished the last of the whiskey and gently set down the flask. It was good, he reflected, this firewater. It helped him remember things he had shut out for far too long.

Resting his head against the logs, Lightning continued to allow his mind to drift. Suddenly he was back in their lodge, listening to Twisted Leg hum as she prepared their supper. He glanced at her, on her knees by the cooking pot, a vision so lovely that it brought a lump to his throat. So immersed was he in the memory that he did not realize Cleve had addressed him until a hand nudged his arm.

"Did you hear me? Are you sleeping? Or was that teeny amount of whiskey too much for you?"

"What?"

"I asked if you had noticed that we're one shy. A certain rambunctious sprout and his dog are missing."

It took a monumental effort for Lightning to focus on the present and to understand Yellow Hair's words. As they finally sank in, he tensed and declared, "Wolf Sings on the Mountain is not here! We must go find him!" His words sounded odd to his ears, as if they were slurred.

Cleve was smiling. "Hold your horses, partner. There's no call for us to go rushing off. I happen to know that my naughty son and that mangy cur snuck off shortly after we had our midday meal."

"Yet you let them go?"

The big man made a tipi of his fingers under his bearded chin. "I thought of calling Billy-Wolf back and giving him a good scolding. But he was heading north. I figure he went to find his ma." Cleve frowned. "The two of them haven't been getting along all that well lately. It might be nice for them to have some time alone."

This was news to Lightning. He struggled to get his mind to function and asked, "What you mean, they not get along?" The warrior realized that he had not spoken proper English and blamed it on the firewater. Over the past winter he had worked hard to master the white man's tongue, speaking it every chance he got. While he was not as fluent as his aunt, he took pride in his accomplishment. It was a difficult tongue.

"I'm not rightly sure about the cause," Cleve said, "but Billy-Wolf has been acting a mite put off by Second Son. I think she's worried that he holds a grudge for her being away so long, but if that were true, he'd be mad at me, too. Hell, he'd be madder, since going to California was my notion to begin with."

"Do you want me to talk to him?" Lightning offered. It was no secret that the boy thought highly of him. Wolf Sings on the Mountain had stayed with Twisted Leg and him until the massacre, and the two of them had grown quite close.

Cleve pondered the notion. "No, I reckon we'd better let Second Son and Billy-Wolf work this out themselves."

"As you wish." Lightning leaned back, relishing the tingly feeling that continued to fill him. He upended the empty flask and gave it a shake. "Too bad you not have more whiskey," he said, his tongue now feeling the size of his thigh.

"Like it, do you?"

"Very much," Lightning admitted.

Very much indeed.

Billy-Wolf Bennett's first impulse on hearing the cough of the grizzly was to get away just as quickly as he could. He lifted Blaze's reins and went to slap his legs against the stallion's flanks, then stopped, aware that his mother could not possibly outrun a bear with that travois strapped to her mare. It would slow Shadow down and make them both easy prey.

The boy was not about to desert her. He raised his heavy new Hawken, tucked the smooth stock to his shoulder, and thumbed back the hammer.

"Do not shoot unless it charges us," Second Son advised. She had brought her makeshift lance, but she was not foolish enough to use it on a grizzly except as a last resort.

Grizzlies were the undisputed lords of the wilderness. No other animal dared stand up to them. They were enormous brutes capable of rending a man to ribbons with a single swipe of their massive paws. Some male grizzlies grew to be seven to eight feet high when erect on their hind legs and to weigh only slightly less than a full-grown bull buffalo.

The last thing Second Son wanted was for one to come after them. Snip started to growl again and she hushed him with a harsh word. Suddenly the thicket shook with the passage of a large body. The wind was blowing from the northwest to the southeast. Since the thicket stood to the southwest, there was a good chance the bear had not caught their scent but had only heard them. If they kept quiet, it might simply lose interest and wander off.

It was then that Shadow nickered.

At the sound, the bear uttered a grating growl. Once

more the thicket shook, and this time a huge head poked into the open with its large nose upturned to catch the breeze.

Neither Second Son nor Billy-Wolf twitched a muscle. Both knew that bears had a keen sense of smell but poor eyesight. Snip, thankfully, froze with his hackles raised. The horses stood stock-still, as if sensing the peril they would be in if they moved.

The grizzly grunted and lumbered farther into the open, exposing its powerful front shoulders and the sloping hump above them. It kept sniffing loudly.

In a rush of horror Second Son realized why. It was not their scent that interested the bear, it was the all-too-fresh smell of blood and raw meat wafting from the travois in all directions. The bear had caught a whiff of the dead goat and cougar.

Billy-Wolf leaped to the same conclusion moments later when the grizzly shuffled fully into plain sight and stared in their direction. The boy had no way of knowing if it would attack or not. But he couldn't sit there and wait for it to make up its mind when his mother would be the one in greatest danger if it did.

Billy-Wolf took matters into his own hands. Wheeling Blaze to the west, he applied his heels. The stallion took off as if its tail were ablaze.

Instantly the bear did the same. For so immense a creature it could move with astounding speed. Over short distances grizzlies were the equal of horses, and this one was no exception. With startling rapidity, it gained on the boy and Blaze.

Second Son was appalled by her son's action. It flew in the face of all reason. She assumed that fear had sparked his flight, and it filled her with shame. As he turned, she cried out, "No!" but he ignored her. So did the bear. In moments they were lost in the darkness.

The warrior woman chased after them, relying on the clatter of the stallion's hooves and the roaring of the bear to guide her. She could not go fast with the travois burdening the mare, yet neither could she afford the time it would take to climb down and cut the mare free. By then her son and the grizzly would be so far ahead that she might lose them.

Up ahead, young Billy-Wolf fled for his very life, his body bent low over the stallion's broad back. The bear was so close that when he glanced over his shoulder he could see its white teeth flash like the fangs of some gigantic monster.

Blaze came to a slope and took it on the fly. For a fraction of a second the horse slowed as it started to climb, and the grizzly almost caught up. Its iron jaws snapped shut, missing the stallion's hindquarters by inches.

Billy-Wolf had half a mind to try to shoot the bear. He even began to twist around, when it dawned on him that he should save the shot for when it was really needed.

Grizzlies were notoriously hard to kill. Their skull bones were so thick that lead balls glanced off them. And their bodies were so dense with muscle and fat that it sometimes took up to a dozen shots to bring one down.

The stallion's sturdy legs drove into the ground at breakneck speed. It pulled ahead a few yards and held the lead to the crest of a wide tableland crowned with grass and stands of trees.

Once on level ground, Billy-Wolf could goad the horse to its limit, and beyond. He lashed it with the reins, raked it with his heels.

The grizzly vented a roar of sheer frustration as it steadily fell farther behind. Doggedly, it continued to follow, even though it was obvious it would never catch up.

Billy-Wolf Bennett grinned and straightened. He had done it! He had saved his mother and given the bear the slip. His pa would be right proud of him. Slowing to a trot, he rode on until he was sure the brute had given up. The last he saw of it, the grizzly was standing and staring after them with what could only be described as a hangdog expression.

The thought made Billy-Wolf stiffen. In all the excitement, he had totally forgotten about Snip. Looking down, he discovered the dog had not left the stallion's side. He exhaled in relief and said, "Good fella."

The preceding year Billy-Wolf had lost his other dog, Jase, to a different bear, and he could not stand the idea of losing Snip, too. Evidently the yellow mongrel remembered the harrowing incident well, for it had not tried to tear into this grizzly as it had the one that killed Jase.

Circling to the north, Billy-Wolf stayed alert. He fought shy of every stand of trees he passed. On completing his loop, he reined up to scour both the tableland and the slope below him. The bear was nowhere in sight.

Satisfied that he had given the beast the slip, Billy-Wolf descended. He heard his mother coming a long time before he saw Shadow materialize out of the night. "Ma!" he called out, smiling, thinking that she would be highly pleased by his ruse.

Second Son was nearly beside herself with anxiety. Combined with that was her lingering disappointment over her son's cowardice. On seeing him, she snapped, "Do you have any idea how foolish you just were? You could have been killed! Running off like that was not the act of a true warrior!"

Taken aback by the uncharacteristic outburst, Billy-Wolf reined up. "But, Ma—" he started to protest.

"We will talk later!" Second Son interrupted, gazing beyond him. "That bear may come back this way and we do not want to be here if it does." So saying, she turned the mare in a wide loop, watching the travois every step of the way to ensure that it didn't hit a boulder or tip.

Cowed into silence, the boy trailed behind. Never before had his mother raised her voice to him in so angry a manner. Here he had figured that she would be grateful that he had lured the bear away, but she was not. He shook his head in bewilderment. Bitter resentment flared, but he suppressed it. She was his mother. No matter what she did, he had no right to be angry at her.

Yet, as time went by, Billy-Wolf could not keep the bitterness at bay. His pa would have praised him for a job well done, not lashed out as if he had committed a crime. It seemed to him that his mother had been unduly harsh. She had no call to be treating him as if he were a child when in a few short years he would be on the verge of manhood.

In mutual silence, mother and son rode briskly southward.

The warrior woman was too upset to risk saying more on the subject. In the span of one evening her boy had lied to her and displayed cowardice, despicable traits her people did not countenance.

Second Son was hurt and confused and at a loss about what to do. Being a warrior, a person of action, she was accustomed to dealing with problems as they arose in the best way she knew how. But the truth was that as far as being a parent was concerned, she relied heavily on her husband's advice.

They were an oddly matched pair, the warrior woman and her giant white husband. Where he was big and blond and outgoing, she was short and dark and reserved. Where he tore into life with hearty gusto, she accepted what came her way with stoic calm.

In many respects they complemented one another. What one lacked, the other possessed. Through compromise they had learned to mesh as one, to mold their two backgrounds and cultures into a robust whole.

As parents they shared responsibility for their son. Cleve had taught the boy all there was to know of white ways; Second Son had done likewise with Tsistsista customs.

But there was no denying that Cleve had a talent for getting the boy to open up about things that were bothering him, a talent Second Son lacked.

Second Son wished her husband had been there when their son bolted. She did not know how she was going to tell him. Cleve was a proud man, excessively so, some might say. He would no more accept cowardice in their offspring than she had.

At long last the pair gained the crown of a low foothill at the north end of the valley the Bennett family had claimed as their own, and in the distance sparkled the light from a lantern Cleve had placed in the window of their cabin. Second Son felt her heart grow warm as she hastened toward the large lake that lay northwest of their homestead.

Billy-Wolf was not nearly so glad to be back. His pa would be annoyed at him for having snuck off. He tried to think up an excuse that would forestall his father's anger but could not.

Despite the late hour, Second Son expected her husband and nephew to hear their approach and rise to greet them. When she drew rein beside the four other horses tethered to the side of the building, and still no one had appeared, she immediately grew wary.

Trappers at Fort Hall had warned the Bennetts to be on the lookout for hostiles.

To the east lived the dreaded Blackfeet and their allies in the Blackfoot Confederacy, the Piegans and the Bloods. All three tribes killed white men on sight.

To the south dwelled the Bannocks, who were not

averse to taking white scalps if they believed they could do so with impunity.

Off to the west lived various coast tribes, few of which were overly friendly to whites. Some made slaves of those they captured. Others did much worse.

So the Bennetts always had to be on their guard. They never knew from one day to the next when their tranquil paradise might be visited by a roving war party.

Second Son held her lance level at her waist as she approached the cabin door. She doubted there was cause for apprehension. For one thing, the cabin had not been burned to the ground and the other horses were still there. For another, Snip had shown no alarm. But she was not one to take chances.

The door hung partly ajar. The warrior woman was almost to it before she heard the rumbling from within. She pushed with a toe, and as the door swung in, her nostrils were assailed by a foul odor she remembered only too well. It was one she would just as soon forget.

"Is everything all right, Ma?" Billy-Wolf called out softly.

In the act of entering, Second Son drew up short when her left foot bumped an object that skittered against the jamb. Bending, she picked up a silver flask and raised it to her nose. "No, son," she answered, their strained relationship forgotten for the moment. "It is not."

chapter

— 5 —

Rakes the Sky with Lightning opened his eyes and promptly regretted it. Bright light seared them, making him blink and bite his lip to keep from crying out. As if that were not bad enough, his head pounded to the beat of a score of drums and his mouth felt as if moss had grown in it while he slept.

The Kit Fox warrior went to rise, but his vision spun and his stomach churned. Overcome, he sank back down. His arm bumped something beside him. Moments later he heard a groan, so he turned his head to isolate the source. Moving proved to be his third mistake. The drums beat so loud that he thought his head would explode.

Cleve Bennett blinked at the midmorning sun. He

raised up high enough to see the cabin ten feet away, then sank down with a louder groan and smacked his dry lips. "Lord. I know I was out of practice, but this is downright embarrassing."

"Yellow Hair," Lightning said, "I think your firewater has killed me."

The big man chuckled. "No. The way you're feeling is the way a man always feels when he's so drunk that he can't tell his hind end from a tree stump. It'll pass, my friend. Trust me."

"That is what you said to do last night," Lightning chided. It took forever for his sluggish mind to grasp the full implications of the rest of Cleve's words. "Drinking a lot of whiskey always makes a man feel as if he were dead?"

"Afraid so. You're getting off lucky. I've seen many a gent so sick they could barely stand. Had a cousin of mine back on the Little Sac in Missouri ruin his Sunday-go-to-meeting clothes on the night before his wedding because he didn't know when to stop. The poor guy puked his guts out all over himself. Phew! Talk about stink!"

"Yet men drink anyway?"

"All the time. Some, like my cousin, take to it like a fish to water."

The meaning of that comment was lost on the Tsistsista. So far as he knew, fish did not *drink* water. They lived in it. He had to remind himself that whites had many strange sayings to go with their equally strange customs. Such as drinking firewater.

"Now it's my turn to ask a question," Cleve said. A hunch had come over him, and if he was right, he knew he was in for a heap of trouble. "Do you have any idea how in blazes we got out here?"

"That is a mystery," Lightning confessed. "I remember you carried me inside. Maybe you were so drunk, as you call it, that you carried me back out again for some reason."

"I wish." Cleve could forestall the inevitable no longer. Sitting up, he determined that Shadow and Blaze were picketed beside the cabin, and muttered half to himself, "I wonder how it feels to be scalped alive."

Lightning misunderstood. "I would never take a knife to your hair. Do not worry. I am not mad at you."

"It wasn't you I was thinking of," Cleve said as he stood. He had to take a few steps before his balance returned. The door was closed. Squaring his broad shoulders, he worked the wooden latch and plastered a welcoming smile on his face.

The cabin was empty.

Cleve scratched his chin, then moved around to the side. The horses looked at him, but he ignored them and walked to the rear corner. Second Son was back there, all right, slicing thin strips of meat from a haunch and draping them over a rack to dry in the sun. "Morning, dearest!" he greeted her as he strolled into the open. "I'm glad you made it back safe and sound."

Second Son did not look up. She had heard their muffled voices and the creak of the door and had known he would venture around back. "Are you?" she asked coldly before she could stop herself.

It was as if Cleve had been slashed by a bullwhip. Only two or three times had she ever used that tone on him, and each time he had done something appropriately harebrained to deserve it. But he didn't see where indulging in a little liquor qualified. It wasn't as if he guzzled the stuff day after day. "I take it that you're a mite put out with me."

"No, I am a lot put out with you." Second Son was so angry that she cut too deep into the haunch and had to wrench the knife out.

For the life of him, Cleve could not understand her re-action. "Are you mad because I let your nephew drink a little more than he should have? Is that why you drug us outside to sleep it off?"

"Rakes the Sky with Lightning has nothing to do with this," Second Son said. She jabbed the gory knife at him. "You, Cleve, are to blame. I took you outside because I could not stand the smell."

Cleve stepped closer, his arms outstretched. "I really didn't drink all that much. Honest. It's just that it had been so long since the last time, I couldn't hold it like I used to. It won't happen again, I promise." He stopped, his brow knitting as her last statement registered. "The smell? It wasn't that bad."

"It was enough."

"My brains are mush today. I just don't follow you."

Second Son bowed her head. "It was enough to remind me of our first rendezvous."

"What about it?" Cleve said, and wanted to bite his tongue off when the full significance hit him like a ton of firewood smack between the ears. It all came back in a rush of images, memories so disturbing that he had not re-called them since the day they happened.

Billy-Wolf had been but a baby. Cleve had taken his new family to the annual rendezvous on the Green River to trade peltries, meet old friends, and make new ones. While there, he had gotten so drunk that he could not stand.

Second Son had gone into the camp to buy some goods, their son strapped to her back in a cradleboard. On her way back to their tipi, as she wound through the brush, she had been jumped by a pack of drunken trappers. She had fought as best she could but was hampered by the cra-dleboard and her fear for Billy-Wolf.

For the first time in her warrior life, Second Son had

been beaten. The trappers had battered and bruised her and pinned her to the ground to have their way. They would have, too, if not for a preacher who stumbled on the scene and saved her from the lustful vermin.

And where had Cleve been all that time? Passed out in their lodge, so soaked with liquor that he could barely think straight. Dear God in heaven! he now scolded himself. What had he been thinking of last night when he pulled out that flask? He hunkered in front of his wife and winced at the pain her features reflected. "I'm so damn sorry."

The warrior woman nodded. She believed him.

Cleve wanted to take her in his arms and comfort her, but he knew how she disliked displays of affection. That was part of her nature. She was, without a doubt, the toughest woman he had ever met. No, more than that, she was the toughest *person*. Which, in a sense, had contributed to this whole misunderstanding.

It had been so long since the rendezvous that Cleve had assumed she had forgotten all about it, as he had. His wife was so adept at hiding her feelings, he tended to take it for granted that events did not affect her as much as they did most folks. He should have known better. No matter how hard she seemed on the outside, deep down she was still a human being with feelings like everyone else, feelings she tried to bury but that were bound to crop up now and again.

Even knowing all this, Cleve could not help but think that there might be more to her anger than she was letting on, that maybe something else had triggered her unusual behavior.

Cleve Bennett would be the first to admit that women were a profound mystery to him. They always had been and they always would be. He liked to laugh at men who claimed they understood women, because any man who made the absurd claim was making a jackass of himself.

Men and women were just too different. That was the plain and simple truth. They thought differently. They acted differently. They had different bodies. In effect, they were like two sides of the same coin. But unlike a coin, which could be melted down so that the two sides blended into one, men and women would always be opposites.

It made figuring out a woman's true feelings awfully hard. Cleve had it even harder than most because he had to figure out a woman who didn't think or act like any other woman he knew of.

Second Son was a *warrior*. Everything she did, her every thought and action, stemmed from that fact. That didn't mean she thought like a man, either. Being a warrior was more a state of mind than a matter of being male or female. No Tsistsista would deny the fact that while Second Son was a woman, she was also one of the best damn warriors in the tribe.

It gave Cleve one more factor to take into account when trying to read her feelings. One more factor to confuse an already perplexing situation. No wonder thinking about it sometimes gave him a powerful headache.

Now, watching as she composed herself, and her iron will once more asserted itself, Cleve decided to change the subject. He brought up the first thing that popped into his head, asking, "How did things go between Billy-Wolf and you yesterday?"

Second Son turned to the goat haunch and resumed her work. She was ashamed of her momentary weakness and grateful to have something else to discuss. "He lied to me," she said bluntly.

"What?"

"He told me that he forgot to tell you he was going. We both know better."

"Likely story is right," Cleve huffed. "But he's not as smart as he thinks. He doesn't know that I saw him sneak off. I could have called him back, but I didn't."

About to drape a thin slab of meat over the rack, Second Son looked at her man. "Why not?"

Cleve shrugged. "I figured the two of you could use some time together to mend fences. If I'd called him back, I would have had to make him stay to punish him."

"Mend fences," Second Son repeated the phrase. Like Rakes the Sky with Lightning, she was often baffled by the many figures of speech the white men used. She liked this one, though, having seen fences in Missouri the time Cleve took her to meet his folks. It fit.

"Yes," Second Son agreed. "We do need to mend fences. That is why I would like to go away with our son for a while, up north to hunt elk."

"Just you and him and no one else within hundreds of miles?" Cleve caught on immediately. "Yep. That should do the trick. I expect he'll open up to you in no time."

His approval pleased her immensely. Smiling, Second Son reached out and lightly touched his cheek. There were times, like this, when her husband was so sweet that she wanted to take him in her arms and pour out her love. Then there were other times when he was so aggravating that she wanted to take him by the throat and throttle some sense into him. She wondered if all women had the same problem with their husbands.

"When do you want to leave?" Cleve inquired.

Second Son tapped the haunch, shifted, and pointed at the bundled hides she had placed near the back wall. "In three days. It will take that long to dry all this meat."

The big trapper gave the bundles an idle glance, then shot toward one of them as if he'd been fired from a catapult. "Is this a painter hide I see?" he asked, beaming like a kid who had just been handed a jar of hard candy.

"It is," Second Son said, grinning. Her husband's fondness for panther meat was second only to his fondness for his family. Nor was he alone. Most trappers rated cat meat as the tastiest around, better than bear and buffalo put together. "I thought I would treat you tonight."

"I'll do the cooking," Cleve responded. "It's only fair, since you did the hunting." He licked his lips and caressed the hide as if it were her leg. "Wait and see. I'm going to fix myself the thickest, juiciest steak any man ever bit into." A dreamy look came over him and he moaned in anticipatory ecstasy.

His expression was so comical that Second Son laughed. Why was it, she mused, that men were so attached to their bellies? Food was food. Yet they treated it as if it were the next best thing to life itself.

Just then Rakes the Sky with Lightning walked around the corner, both hands pressed to his head and his complexion a sickly pale shade.

"What is the matter with you, nephew?" Second Son asked, although she knew full well. She used English, since Lightning was still learning the tongue and needed all the practice he could get.

"My head is broken."

"Do not expect me to feel sorry for you."

Lightning did not see why she was being so hard on him when it was not his fault. "Your husband did this to me. He told me that I would like whiskey. That it would make me feel good."

"And if he told you that jumping off a cliff would also make you feel good, would you do it?" Second Son countered with a meaningful glance at her husband.

Cleve inwardly squirmed. Here all he had been trying to do was to get her nephew to relax a little, and look at the trouble he was in. Once more he elected to talk about something else. Rising, he scanned the valley and asked,

"Where's that boy of ours? I should sit him down and explain a few facts of life."

"He took Snip and went hunting," Second Son revealed. She hesitated, wanting to tell Cleve about the bear incident but reluctant to do so in front of Lightning.

"Well, in that case, I might as well get to work." Cleve rubbed his big hands together. "In a few days the outside of the cabin will be done. Then I start on the corral and stable."

The rest of the day passed quietly. The men worked at felling and trimming trees while the warrior woman made jerky and pemmican. Billy-Wolf showed up about the middle of the morning with two dead rabbits, and Cleve put him to work chopping saplings for the corral.

An hour before sundown the free trapper called it quits and got a fire going. He whistled gleefully as he cut the painter meat Second Son had butchered into steaks large enough to fill a grizzly. Soon the tantalizing aroma of the roasting meat filled the air, and Second Son had to admit it smelled delicious. She had eaten an extra helping of rabbit stew at midday and did not think she was hungry enough for steak, but her growling stomach proved her wrong.

There in the picturesque valley, under the sparkling stars, with a cool breeze bending the grass around them, the Bennett family and their kinsman gathered around the fire and gorged themselves on a feast fit for royalty. In addition to the meat, Second Son had gathered roots that reminded Cleve of sweet potatoes. They had some rabbit left over to garnish the steak, and the sweet stems of flowers for added flavor.

Billy-Wolf ate with relish. The day had turned out nicely, much to his surprise. His father had given him a talking-to, but had not punished him for sneaking off. And the trip north was still on. He looked forward to exploring new country, but he was nervous about being alone with his mother after the way she had acted the day before. Twice during supper he caught her studying him on the sly, which added to his unease.

The next two days were much like the first. Second Son finished drying the meat, the men added the final logs.

On the evening before they were to leave, Cleve helped her pack all she and Billy-Wolf would need for their journey: plenty of jerky, some coffee, flour, and a cup of sugar, ample ammunition and black powder, flints, a fire steel, a small trade ax for chopping firewood, a spare knife, blankets, and more.

Afterward, the two of them took a stroll, hand in hand, under the starlit sky. Now that the time had come, Cleve did not like the idea of parting. For all his confidence in his wife's prowess, he knew only too well the many dangers the pair might face. It troubled him to think that he might never see them again.

Yet the big man did not let on. He put on a brave front, smiling and reminding Second Son of their courting days, when they had been so shy around each other. Presently they came to the lake and Cleve turned to her, looping his brawny arms around her slender waist.

"You be careful up north, you hear? I don't want anything to happen to either of you."

"And I do?" was her impish reply.

Cleve stared deep into her dark eyes and felt a familiar yearning in his heart and a stirring in his loins. "I know I don't say it nearly as often as I should, but I love you more than words can say." Bending, he kissed her, and the kiss lingered much longer than he had intended, in part because her ardor matched his own.

"Be careful," Second Son said when they broke for air. "Do not start something you cannot finish."

His low laugh rolled across the water. "That'll be the

day." He glanced at the cabin, debating whether they could or not. Lightning was still feeling poorly and had already turned in, while their son was getting his things together for the hunting trip. It should be all right.

Second Son did not need much intuition to know what he had in mind. Ordinarily she would have put him off. She did not like to make love out in the open, where anyone or anything might stumble across them. But this night was different. This night she wanted him as much as he was forever wanting her.

Over the next hour many sounds arose in the vicinity of the serene lake. From the woods along the shore came the hoots of owls and the squeal of rodents caught in their steel talons. Fish splashed the surface. Ducks quacked every so often. Geese and brants honked.

Mixed in with the sounds of the wild were other, softer sounds, sounds not normally heard by any of the many creatures that came to the lake nightly to drink. There were groans and moans and fluttering sighs. There were gasps and grunts and low mewling cries.

At length Cleve and Second Son made their way back, their arms around one another, their sweaty bodies brushing together as they walked. "Was it me, or was that special?" he asked in a childlike voice.

Her answer was another long kiss. When they straightened, Cleve grinned and said, "I sure hope the two of you find some elk quick. I'm liable to catch my death if I have to take a dunk in that cold lake every damn night."

Lightning and Billy-Wolf were both asleep. Cleve and Second Son turned in and slept soundly, locked in a tight embrace under a heavy buffalo robe in a front corner of the cabin.

As usual, the warrior woman was the first to awaken. Well before the sun crowned the eastern sky with golden glory, she was up and at the lake, filling the coffeepot. Her husband was becoming spoiled; he could not start the day without his two cups of scalding coffee.

Second Son faced to the east. The first faint flush of dawn tinged the horizon. She raised both hands on high and greeted the new day as befit a Tsistsista warrior. When she was done she took the pot to the cabin and soon had the fire rekindled.

Tendrils of acrid smoke drifted upward. At the side of the house, the horses stirred. In the distance deer grazed. Much farther off, close to the foothills, a small herd of shaggy mountain buffalo had appeared. Out on the lake a large fish soared in a high arc, then struck the water in a glittering spray.

Second Son surveyed the valley from end to end and inhaled deeply. The air was crisp and fresh and clean.

Yellow Hair had been right, she mused. This was the perfect place to set down roots, as he called it. Game and water were abundant. Wood was theirs for the taking, and the horses would not lack for forage. Best of all, they had the valley and the surrounding region all to themselves. Cleve often called it their "little paradise," and she had to agree.

Soon Billy-Wolf shuffled outdoors. Still half-asleep, he rubbed his eyes and yawned. "Morning, Ma. Today is the big day."

"Are you ready?"

"Am I ever," the boy said excitedly. "I have my possibles bag full to the brim. And Pa gave me the folding knife that his own pa gave him to take along."

This was interesting news to Second Son. Cleve was extremely fond of that knife. "You must not lose it."

"Don't fret. I aim to watch over it like a hawk."

A strapping figure filled the doorway. "What in tarnation is all the racket out here? A man can't get a few extra minutes of sleep if his life depended on it."

Father and son hugged and went to wash up. Not a minute later Lightning emerged, a bounce in his stride. "I can think without my head hurting," he announced. "Never again will I let the white man's firewater pass my lips."

"See that you do not," Second Son said earnestly. "Those who make a habit of it are never the same."

The next hour passed swiftly. Everyone was unusually quiet during breakfast and the cleaning up afterward. Cleve hovered over Second Son as if vying to be her second shadow. The parfleches and packs were strapped onto the sorrel. As the warrior woman went to mount Shadow, Cleve impulsively embraced her and pecked her on the lips.

Her back rigid, Second Son rode off, leading the packhorse. Billy-Wolf was all smiles and looked back several times to wave and holler. She was more subdued. On gaining the crest of the first hill to the north, she reined up to gaze back out over their private paradise.

"Something wrong?" Billy-Wolf asked.

"No, son," Second Son replied. She did not bother to mention that she was wondering if they would ever set eyes on the valley again.

chapter
6

Thanks to Cleve's wanderlust, Second Son had seen more of the vast wilderness that covered half the continent than any member of her tribe. She had stood on the shore of the Pacific Ocean as rolling surf swished around her moccasins. She had traveled the length of the mighty Columbia River. She had traveled the width of the Rockies and set her eyes on too many lesser mountain ranges for her to count. She had beheld natural wonders galore, but they all paled in comparison to the breathtaking majesty of unexplored western Canada.

The rugged wilds were magnificent. High peaks extended northward for as far as the eye could see, many gleaming with blankets of ivory snow. Lush green valleys separated them, valleys richer in game and grass than any the warrior woman had ever seen. And everywhere there were mountain lakes as cold as ice and crystal-clear streams.

Second Son could not help but marvel. This new land conformed in every respect to the image she'd always had of the Other Place, the spirit land where the Tsistsistas went after dying. From the time she had been old enough to sit up, she had listened to the elders of her tribe tell of the wonderful land on the other side, where the hunting was always excellent and there was never any winter. No one went hungry there, no one knew cold or hurt or fear. It was where all true warriors went to live forever, and Second Son looked forward to making the journey one day.

For now, she was content to explore this spectacular new domain with her young son as they meandered slowly but steadily northward.

Every day brought fabulous new surprises.

Once it was a score of roosting bald eagles scattered around a particularly large lake. Mother and son stopped and watched the eagles dive for fish and execute dazzling pinwheels high in the sky.

Once it was a herd of mountain buffalo so vast that Second Son and Billy-Wolf had to wait in a ravine for over three hours before the last straggler had passed.

Another time they came on a jagged cliff dotted with scores of moving white dots. They had drawn closer and sat, entranced, as the mountain goats leaped across gaping crevasses and traversed ledges no wider than the palms of their hands.

They lost all track of time. Second Son spotted signs of elk several times but made no attempt to track the animals down. She was enjoying this interlude with her son too much. She did not want it to come to an end. And much to her relief, Billy-Wolf was just as happy.

In a way, they had peeled back the past two years and reclaimed the close bond they had shared before the California nightmare. They were truly mother and son again. For a whole week and a half they did not bicker once. They rode when they felt like it, stopped when they felt like it, ate when the urge struck them.

Then came the evening when they camped beside a wide stream so clear that they could have counted every pebble lining its bottom.

Billy-Wolf speared four fish for their supper. He was proud of his accomplishment, it being only the second time in his entire life he had attempted the feat. As he sat watching the flames lick at the fish, basking in the glow of his mother's smile of approval, he thought of that other night not that long ago. The night he had unwittingly earned her disapproval.

Second Son saw the cloud that unexpectedly came over his features. She was tempted not to say anything. It had been her secret dread that something would arise to mar their hunt. But ignoring a problem was not part of her nature, no matter what the consequences. "Are you all right, Wolf Sings on the Mountain?" she asked.

"We need to talk, Ma," Billy-Wolf said solemnly. "There's something that has been bothering me and I need to get it off my chest."

"I am listening."

Billy-Wolf placed his hand on Snip's neck and fanned his courage. "Do you remember that night right before we left, when we ran into that grizzly?"

"I will never forget it."

"Then maybe you'll tell me why you got so riled when I tried to lead that darned bear off? I thought I was doing the right thing, what with you hauling a travois and all. But you tore into me as if I'd been as bad as could be."

The warrior woman let his full meaning sink in before she answered. "You led the bear off so it would not attack me?"

"Sure. Why else do you think I did it? I'm not real partial to having a griz make wolf meat of my ma," Billy-Wolf declared. He looked down at Snip and gave the dog a pat, and suddenly his mother's arms were around him and she was holding him closer than he could ever remember her holding him before, so close that he could barely breathe. Startled half out of his wits, he blurted, "Ma?"

Second Son did not reply. Her emotions were awhirl. Strong feelings of motherly love combined with keen self-reproach had rendered her mute.

How could she ever have doubted her own flesh and blood? she wondered. How could she have jumped to the conclusion she did? She had never done anything like that before.

Others might scoff. Others might claim—as Cleve no doubt would put it—that she was making a mountain out of a molehill. But they did not understand. Her mistake brought her judgment into question.

For someone who prided herself on her clear thinking and self-control, it was a serious oversight.

She had not had faith in her one and only son. What sort of mother was she?

Second Son stepped back. She paid no attention to Billy-Wolf's look of amazement. "I am sorry I doubted you. It will never happen again."

Flustered, the boy said, "Goodness gracious. You have no call to apologize. You haven't done anything wrong."

Haven't I? the warrior woman thought as she took her seat. She gazed idly into the flames. At the back of her mind stirred the same gnawing specter that had been troubling her for many days. Only now it was not as vague. It was as if a memory were trying to surface. A memory long buried.

The very next instant it gushed up out of her in a painful rush.

It had happened long ago. She had seen but thirteen winters.

Second Son was seated beside another fire. This one burned in the lodge of her uncle, Standing Bear. Her favorite aunt, Buffalo Hump, was mending one of his torn buckskin shirts.

Second Son's youthful face shone with excitement. "You know him. His name is Thunder Hawk. My mother says he comes from a good family and would make a fine husband one day."

Buffalo Hump lowered her bone needle and the shirt. "And what do you say, little one? You are the one he has shown an interest in."

"I am not yet ready to share a lodge with a man. But when I am, I could do worse."

The Tsistsista matron was silent awhile. She ran a hand across her gray hair, then said, "You would be wise to never take a man as your own. If you do, it will be the biggest mistake of your life. Heed my words. You will live to regret it."

"What? Why?" Second Son exclaimed.

"Because you will make a terrible wife and a worse mother."

This was Buffalo Hump speaking. A woman Second Son admired second only to her own mother. A loving aunt who had her best interests at heart. A wise counselor who had never given her bad advice.

Second Son did not know what to say. Dismay and confusion overcame her. She very nearly rose and bolted from the lodge, but that would have been the height of bad manners.

"Listen to me." Buffalo Hump offered a reassuring smile and placed a kindly gnarled hand on the girl's wrist. "Try to understand." Placing the beaded shirt aside, she pointed at the knife on Second Son's hip and the quiver and bow on her back. "Do you know of any other women of the Burning Hearts who go around as you do, with weapons?"

Immediately Second Son went to answer but was silenced by a finger.

"No, you do not. And why is that? Because out of all the women in our band, you are the only one who walks the path of a warrior. It is rare for a woman to do so. In my memory, which is long, I know of only one other who did. Her name was Badger Woman, but everyone called her Badger. She lived many years ago."

Despite her inner turmoil, Second Son listened intently. She had heard a few stories about Badger when she had been very small, and they had keenly kindled her curiosity. So much so, that on hearing them she had first entertained the idea of being a warrior herself. "Tell me of her. Please."

The matron did not do so immediately. She closed her eyes awhile, and when she opened them they mirrored an immense sadness. "Most of the older Burning Hearts know of Badger, but few know, as I do, that she was not born a Tsistsista. She was a Sans Arc, taken on a raid when she was less than half your age."

The fire crackled softly. Second Son rested her elbows on her knees.

"It was Big Hail who took her into his lodge. He gave her the name Badger Woman because as he raced from

the Sans Arc village with arrows flying around him, his
warhorse nearly stepped on a badger and threw him."

Among the Burning Hearts, Buffalo Hump was re-
vered for her honesty, generosity, and precise memory. It
was said that she remembered everything that had ever
happened to her or that she had ever learned. Second
Son knew that the details she was hearing were actual
facts.

"Big Hail and his wife were fond of the girl. They
treated her well. They brought her up as they had their
own daughters. Yet she was different from the start."

"Different how?"

"Like you, she wanted nothing to do with dresses and
dolls and cook fires. Like you, she would rather be out
with the boys learning to hunt and track and make
war."

This confirmed what Second Son had heard as a child.
She grinned in satisfaction.

"By the time Badger came of age, no one looked at her
as a woman. She was a warrior. She went on raids. She
counted coup. She proved herself time and again. When
the names of the bravest Burning Hearts were mentioned, hers was always among them," Buffalo Hump dis-
closed.

Second Son hung on every word.

"Badger had her own lodge, her own horses. In the
councils she was given a seat of honor. She took a wife,
and the two of them lived as man and woman."

Here was news so incredible that Second Son gaped.
She had to ask to have it clarified. "Badger took a *woman*
for her wife?"

The question seemed to distract Buffalo Hump from her
train of thought. She blinked, then said, "Yes. Forked
Rope was her name." She paused. "Anyway, one day
Badger went on a raid against the Sans Arcs, her own peo-

ple. She killed two of them and came back with six new horses. Everyone was proud of her, but there were some who noticed that she was troubled."

"Why?"

"Be patient. All will be made clear." Buffalo Hump's voice lowered. "For a long time Badger was bothered by something but she would not say, not even to Forked Rope. Then, two winters after the Sans Arc raid, she announced that she wanted to pay her former people a formal visit. She wanted to see if her mother and father and brothers were still alive."

Outside, the wind whipped past the lodge, rustling the smoke flaps overhead.

"Everyone warned her against it. They told her that she was now Tsistsista. That the Sans Arcs would regard her as an enemy. Big Hail and his wife talked to her in private. But it did no good. Badger was determined to go." The matron clasped her hands. "A meeting was arranged through the River Crows."

"The Crows?" Second Son repeated in surprise.

"They were not our enemies at the time, as they are now. And they also happened to be on friendly terms with the Sans Arcs. So it was agreed that Badger would meet with her Sans Arc father and her brothers at Fire Rock, the rock that was turned black the summer the prairie burned."

Second Son had been there once. She remembered a solitary boulder over eight feet high, located near a small stream lined by cottonwoods.

"The whole village came out to see Badger leave. Big Hail and four others would not let her go alone. They rode off at first light with Badger leading the six horses she had taken in that raid plus two others of her own. Many of us were very worried for her. Forked Rope could not stop crying."

The wind gusted even harder.

"It was six sleeps before Big Hail and the four warriors came back, alone. Everyone gathered around to hear their story. I was a small girl at the time, but I remember every word." Buffalo Hump took a breath. "Badger had been happy on the ride to Fire Rock. She had joked with the others and tried to make them laugh."

Suddenly the fire sputtered, kicking embers into the air. Buffalo Hump and Second Son made sure none posed any threat before the story was continued.

"They came to a low hill south of Fire Rock and scouted the area. Three warriors waited near the rock, but Badger could not say if they were her father or her brothers. Big Hail begged her not to go down. She would not listen."

How Badger met her fate was common knowledge, but to Second Son it was as if she were hearing it for the first time.

"Big Hail and the others could do nothing but watch helplessly as she rode up to the three Sans Arcs and greeted them. Words were exchanged, although what was said no one could tell. Badger moved closer and offered the horses as a gift. One of the warriors took them."

In her mind Second Son pictured everything.

"Then another Sans Arc, one much too young to be her father, moved his horse near her and reached out to embrace her. It seemed to Big Hail and the others that she was very surprised by this and tried to push him away. But he grabbed her and held her fast, and suddenly another one rushed to help him while from out of the trees rode close to thirty Sans Arcs."

Buffalo Hump bowed her head. Second Son did not prompt her to go on. She knew the older woman would do so when she was ready.

"Badger was thrown to the ground. Before she could get to her feet or pull her knife, she was riddled with arrows, so many that Big Hail said she looked like a porcupine. One of the Sans Arcs cut off her hair. He waved it in the air and did a dance. Then the whole band went after Big Hail and our men, but the Burning Hearts had strong horses and were able to get away."

"That was a sad day for the Tsistsistas."

"Child, you do not know how truly you speak. I mourned greatly when I heard the news, as many did. Forked Rope went into her lodge and would not come out for many sleeps. Finally someone noticed a smell. Bear Walking went in even though the flap was closed and she would not answer his call." The last statement was uttered in a whisper. "Forked Rope was dead. She had taken a knife and opened a big vein in her leg, then had lain down on her robe with her hands folded across her chest as if she were merely going to sleep."

In the course of this narrative, Second Son had forgotten about the reason her aunt had brought it up to begin with. Now she was reminded when Buffalo Hump wagged a finger at her and spoke sternly.

"You are just like Badger in your ways. One day you will be a warrior every bit as worthy as she was. And because of this, you must give up every thought of marriage and motherhood."

"But why?" Second Son asked once again.

So much talking was making Buffalo Hump weary. She patted her niece's hand before saying, "I know my words seem hard, but I say them out of love to spare you greater hardship. You will be a warrior woman. You will live as a warrior, do all the things that warriors do. And since most of the time warriors are men, that means you will be doing all the things that men do. You will be living like a man even though you are a woman. Do you follow my path so far?"

"Yes."

"Look at me. Or look at your mother. We are women. We are wives. We do not dress as men or act as men or do the same things men do. We cook and sew and tend the sick and gather plants and look after our children when they are young. In our way, we are as essential to the upkeep of a family as our husbands, but our ways are not their ways." Buffalo Hump paused. "Does a warrior do any of those things I just mentioned?"

"No," Second Son admitted, and a chill rippled down her spine.

"Then who will do them in your lodge if you take a man as your husband? Will he cook and sew and cure hides? Will he go to the river to fetch water? Will he go with the other women to collect roots or berries? No, never. Not since the beginning of time has a man done such a thing."

"But the *heemanehs*—" Second Son began lamely.

"Do not count. You could not marry one because they only like other men." Buffalo Hump grew solemn. "If you marry another warrior, you will bring much sadness down on yourself. You cannot be a wife and a warrior both. As for children, how can you raise little ones when you will be away so much of the time hunting and raiding? Will you carry your baby with you into battle? Can you fight or steal horses with a cradleboard on your back?"

No one had ever pointed out the conflicts a warrior woman faced so clearly before. Second Son's heart was heavy with sorrow. She refused to give up her dream of becoming a respected warrior like Badger one day. Yet, at the same time, deep down within her, part of her also longed to have a man she could call her own and children who would grow up to carry on Tsistsista ways.

Buffalo Hump took gentle hold of her hands. "I am sorry to upset you. I love you as I love few others. But now you see why I told you not to marry. It is not that there is anything wrong with you. It is the life you have chosen. No woman can be a wife and a mother and a warrior all at the same time. It is not done."

Second Son made no response. But within her a tiny voice called out as if from the depths of a deep hole in the ground, *You are wrong. There must be a way. There must!*

"There must!" Second Son said aloud without realizing she was doing so, and suddenly she was back in the present, seated by the fire with her son an arm's length away and the horses grazing nearby.

Billy-Wolf had been troubled by his mother's long silence. He did not know what to make of it, or of her troubled features. It was so unlike her. As far back as he could recollect, she had always been the rock of the family, the one who never grew flustered, who took everything that came along in stride. On hearing her outburst, he glanced up. "What was that, Ma? I didn't catch it."

"I was talking to myself," Second Son said. The fish were done, so she picked up one of the two slabs of bark she had collected earlier and transferred a simmering pair onto it. These she handed to her son, conscious of the curious slantwise look he gave her.

The delectable odor reminded Second Son how hungry she was. She ate with relish. As she chewed, she thought about Buffalo Hump. It was strange that words spoken so many winters ago should come back to bother her now.

Why now? she asked herself. Was it because Billy-Wolf was the same age she had been when she had the talk with her aunt? Or had his behavior triggered the memory without her being aware of it? Whatever the case, it would bother her no longer. Now that she knew why she had been so upset around him, she would no longer be so. Buffalo Hump had been wrong. It was possible to be a wife and mother and warrior. She had been doing it for thirteen winters; she would keep on doing it until her son was fully grown and off on his own.

The mind was a peculiar thing, Second Son noted. Sometimes it did as it wanted with no regard for the person who called that mind her own. Why that should be so, she could not say.

The warrior woman faced her son. He was eyeing her as if she were someone he had never seen before. Smiling, she clapped him on the back as Cleve was prone to do and stated, "I am all right. You have no need to worry."

"I'm not—" Billy-Wolf started to say, and froze when a haunting cry wafted to their ears from far to the north.

Second Son felt her own blood chill.

It was a cry like no other. It rose as high as the piercing shriek of a hawk, then fell as low as the menacing growl of a wolverine. It wavered. It echoed. It was part human, yet less than human. It was bestial, yet more than the howl of any beast known to man. It silenced every other creature within earshot. Bouncing off the high peaks, it receded into the remote distance and died to a thin whine.

The hair at the nape of Billy-Wolf's neck stood on end. "What in tarnation was that?" he breathed.

"I do not know," Second Son answered honestly. She had never heard such a sound before. Her son's anxiety was so plain that she made light of it, adding, "But whatever it is, we have nothing to fear. You have your Hawken and I have my lance and Lightning's bow." She nodded at the mongrel. "And with Snip here, no animal or man can sneak up on us. We are as safe as we would be back in our valley."

"I hope so," Billy-Wolf said, his ears cocked in case the cry was repeated. Thankfully, it wasn't.

All they heard was the howl of the wind, reminding them how very alone they were.

chapter

— 7 —

The next day began pleasantly enough.

Second Son was in fine spirits now that she knew what
had been bothering her all this time. She went to the
stream as soon as she woke up. At the same spot where
Billy-Wolf had used her lance to catch the four fish the
evening before, she searched the shallows from the bank
and spotted more.

Stringing Lightning's bow, she drew an arrow and
nocked it. The next step required skill. As any hunter worthy of the name knew, fish were never where they appeared to be. The water distorted both their size and their
position. Aiming right at the fish guaranteed a miss.

There was a trick to it. For someone with a lance, the

trick involved slowly dipping the tip of the weapon into the water and sliding it ever so carefully toward the fish until it was close enough for a quick, short thrust.

A bow user relied on a similar technique, as Second Son did by bending until the barbed point of her shaft went under. By comparing the angle of the arrow to that of the fish, and by keeping in mind that fish were always a little higher in the water than they seemed to be, she was able to put her first shaft squarely through the middle of a big one. It twisted and dived but the water was too shallow for it to escape. A deft flip of her arm and it was flopping on the bank.

The rest of the fish scattered except for one that hugged the bottom in the shadows. Her next arrow tore through the center of its head, pinning it.

Rekindling the fire took no time.

The odor of the roasting fish brought Billy-Wolf around. He sat up, his mouth watering, and gave his mother an ear-to-ear smile. They had stayed up late talking after hearing the strange howl, and by the time he slipped under the blankets, he had been convinced that she was her old self again.

"Morning, Ma," Billy-Wolf said. "You're up early."

"We have a busy day ahead of us," Second Son said. "It is time we gave thought to why we are here. Yesterday we passed plenty of fresh elk sign. There are many in this area, so it should not be hard for us to find one."

The boy sighed. So much for loafing around as they pleased. He should have known it would not last forever.

"If we can kill one by sunset, we will spend the next four days drying the meat," Second Son remarked while rotating the fish.

"I can hardly wait," Billy-Wolf said dryly.

The sarcasm was not lost on Second Son, but she offered no comment. She remembered Cleve's advice, given shortly before they left, to take what the boy did "with a grain of salt." "All parents go through this. I can remember my grandpa saying that kids reach an age where they try their best to drive their folks crazy. From about thirteen to sixteen is the worst, although Old Man Webber claimed that once kids shed their diapers the headaches begin."

Second Son had been fascinated. Tsistsista children would never ever do anything that reflected poorly on their parents. They were reared to always be well behaved.

As if Cleve had been privy to her thoughts, he went on, "Much as I hate to say it, there's another fact you have to keep in mind. Our boy is part white. And if he takes after me, we could be in for a hard time. I seem to remember doing one or two things which made my folks want to tear out their hair. My backside stung for days after."

With that in mind, Second Son let the sarcasm pass. She ate quickly and had the packhorse ready when Billy-Wolf finished. They mounted and forded the stream where a gravel bar jutted halfway to the other bank.

To the northwest reared towering peaks covered with snow. The slopes below were heavily forested. Elk would rest up there during the day, so that was where she bent Shadow's steps.

The air was cool, the sky bright blue. Birds chirped gaily. Wildlife, as always, was everywhere.

A winding route brought them to a bench that afforded a breathtaking vista of the country they had passed through. They watched a golden eagle glide on the currents before taking to a game trail. A steep slope led to a barren spur, and there, newly embedded in the earth, were the tracks of a bull elk and three cows. The animals had walked out of an adjacent copse, turned onto the trail, and climbed.

The warrior woman did likewise. Her mare was as sure-footed as a mule and half the time required no guidance on her part.

A series of slopes led them to a spiny ridge dotted with fir trees. They were quite high by now. Seen through the green growth, the stream they had spent the night beside resembled a tiny blue ribbon.

Billy-Wolf was enthralled. The land stirred him to the depths of his soul. The north land had a certain grandeur that he lacked the maturity to put into words. He promised himself that when the time came for him to go off on his own, he would remember this place and come back here to plant his own roots.

The appearance of a fish eagle, or an osprey, as the whites called it, signaled to Second Son that they were nearing a large body of water. She was proven right when they topped the next ridge and discovered an extensive tableland dominated by the biggest lake they had seen so far.

Billy-Wolf sucked in his breath. He had encountered few osprey before, and the sight of dozens soaring and diving and wheeling in graceful pinwheels dazzled him. Their strident calls, a whistling *k-yewk, k-yewk, k-yewk*, rose in a constant chorus. As he drew closer he could see that they were smaller and sleeker than bald eagles, and much faster. It amazed him how they looped and spun and banked so sharply.

One of the larger birds suddenly hovered as still as a hummingbird, its bent wings barely fluttering. Then it streaked straight down to the water. Its forked talons hit with an audible smack. When it rose, a struggling fish was clenched tight. The osprey winged to a huge stick aerie.

"I sure would like to rest here a spell," Billy-Wolf mentioned.

Since the sun was almost straight above them, Second Son assented. She followed the elk tracks down to a rocky stretch of shore where the elk had paused to drink. The trail led on around the lake, but she reined up.

"Can I go exploring?" Billy-Wolf asked. A nod sent him on his merry way, his Hawken in hand. He bounded in the opposite direction as the elk, letting off excess energy in a burst of speed.

Tracks were abundant. Deer, mountain goat, black bear and grizzly, painter and lynx and bobcat, wolves and foxes and raccoons and more, they had all come to the lake at one time or another. The prints held little interest for him until he sprang onto a low, flat boulder and coiled to leap from there to a log.

Between the two, on a strip of soft ground that extended from the lake to the woods, were recently made tracks that stood out like the proverbial sore thumb.

They were human footprints.

Billy-Wolf stopped so abruptly that he came close to losing his balance. Hunkering, he studied the many impressions as his pa and ma had taught him to do. He counted six Indians, all men, all with long strides, indicating they were tall.

Inserting two fingers into his mouth as Cleve had shown him, the boy cut loose with a whistle that put those of the ospreys to shame. He beckoned when his mother looked and she came on the fly, an arrow notched to her bowstring.

The peace and tranquillity they had savored for close to two weeks came to an end the instant the warrior woman set eyes on the footprints. Potential enemies were abroad. From now on, she had to be more on her guard than ever.

"What tribe are they?" Billy-Wolf asked. "Do you know?"

Second Son had been trying to determine that very thing. No two tribes fashioned their moccasins exactly alike. The shapes of the heels and toes were always different, as was the style of stitching.

The Pawnees, as Second Son knew, preferred moccasins that flared wide across the ball. The Crows wore footwear with a distinct crescent shape. Widest of all moccasins were those worn by the Arapahos. Second Son was familiar with each, as she was with those of the Lakota, the Kiowa, the Comanche, and the Blackfeet.

The footprints the warrior woman now studied were a complete mystery to her, unlike any she had ever seen. She memorized them for future reference, noting the exceptionally wide heels and the evidence of cross-stitching around the bottom.

"I do not know this tribe," Second Son told her son. "They might be friendly, but we will not take it for granted. We will avoid them."

"Was this a hunting party, you reckon?"

"Or a war party." Second Son ran her fingertips over one of the prints. "These were made not long after the sun came up. So they should be far from here by now."

Billy-Wolf had never had reason to doubt his mother's wisdom. If she said it was so, then it was. He relaxed, thinking they were out of immediate danger. "I can go on exploring, then?" he inquired.

Second Son scoured the stretch of forest into which the tracks disappeared. Ospreys were perched in their big nests and smaller birds flitted about in the underbrush. Nothing else was evident. It should be safe. "Do not take long," she cautioned.

The boy grinned and went on with his carefree frolic. Anything of interest merited inspection, whether it was the spoor of a grizzly, the tracks left by a pair of wolves, a dead fish that had been partially eaten, or the charred stump of a tree that had been blasted by lightning long ago.

The tree was high up on the shore, close to the woods. Billy-Wolf held his Hawken in the crook of his left elbow as he ran his right hand over the smooth stump. When he pulled his arm back, he discovered his palm and fingers were solid black. He needed to wash.

Shifting, Billy-Wolf was about to hasten to the lake when the faintest of noises, a soft scrape, fell on his ears. He glanced into the pines just as a sparrow took wing from a thicket. Assuming the bird to be to blame, he went down to the lake and dipped his right hand in the frigid water.

Something—Billy-Wolf could not say what—made him pivot on a heel and peer deep into the trees. He had the strangest feeling that he was being watched. It was so strong that his breath caught in his throat. Yet, though he squatted there for over a minute, there was no sign of life other than birds. Snip did not growl once. Shrugging, Billy-Wolf stood. He had let those tracks rattle him, he scolded himself. Not a smart thing to do. Anyone who jumped at shadows had no business being in the wilderness, as his pa had mentioned more than once.

The boy retraced his steps to where his mother sat on a knob of earth that afforded her an unobstructed view of the lake. He suspected that she had been keeping an eye on him the whole time without being obvious about it. It warmed his heart to think of her constant devotion and foresight. If he turned out to be half the warrior she was, he'd be a man to reckon with.

"The elk went west," Second Son said, nodding, "into those fir trees. We will bring down the bull."

"Why not a cow?" Billy-Wolf asked. "There are three of them, which means we're three times as likely to drop one."

"At this time of year?"

Billy-Wolf did not see what that had to do with anything and stated as much.

"The cows may be heavy with calf," Second Son explained, and shared the words of wisdom her own father had once shared with her. "A wise hunter never kills more game than is needed. That means never killing two when one will do, or never killing a big one when a smaller animal has enough meat on it to suit your needs."

The boy had heard all this before. "I know. Pa and you and Lightning have told me a hundred times."

"And we have also told you that creatures must be allowed to breed or they will die out. Look at what has happened to the beaver in the Rockies since the coming of the white men. Very few are left."

The boy nodded. It was a favorite topic of his father's, and yet another reason they had settled north of Fort Hall, where beaver were plentiful.

"Always remember, my son," Second Son said. "All creatures must be allowed to breed or the cycle of life will be broken. The elk calf we spare today might feed a starving family many winters from now."

Mounting, they rode westward, hugging the water's edge. This was deliberate on Second Son's part. It gave her more time to react if something, or someone, came at them from out of the woods.

Judging by the size of the strides the elk had taken, which amounted to no more than an arm's length, the wapiti had held to a slow gait, browsing as they went.

The trail led gradually upward. Firs reared on all sides, shutting off much of the sunlight. Uneven shadows dappled Second Son and Billy-Wolf as they climbed.

Second Son had attached a leather cord to her lance and slung it across her back. In dense forest a bow was better. It allowed for greater range and accuracy. She held an arrow notched at all times since she never knew when they would come on their quarry.

Billy-Wolf, eager to be the one to drop the bull, kept a

thumb on the hammer of his rifle. They had gone perhaps a quarter of a mile when that bothersome feeling returned, the sensation that he was being watched. It made his shoulder blades itch. Twisting, he scanned the firs and the brush, without result.

Ahead appeared a huckleberry thicket covering a full acre or better. The berry bushes were interspersed with islands of tall grass.

Acting on a hunch, Second Son skirted wide to the left, staying well back in the trees and far enough from the thicket that the clomp of their mounts' hooves would not be heard.

Behind a row of pines she drew rein, slipped off, and looped the reins to a tree. She did the same with the sorrel's lead rope. It was a simple precaution in case there was a lot of commotion when they spotted the elk. She did not want the horses spooked into running off.

The boy's face glowed. He was at that age where he thrilled to the excitement of the hunt. The reason for it, the necessity of preserving meat for the winter and to have thick hides to use for clothes or robes, was nowhere near as important. He nodded when his mother touched a finger to her lips, then fell into step behind her.

The huckleberry bushes were about four feet high. The grass, weeds, and other bushes were much higher. Second Son moved quietly around the perimeter until she located a trail containing fresh elk tracks.

Ducking low, Second Son penetrated the huckleberry growth. A turtle could have gone faster than she did. She would move one foot silently forward, pause to look and listen, then move her other foot. At this stage she was not going to let the elk get away if she could help it. All it would take was one misstep, one fleeting moment of carelessness.

Elk, deer, and other prey were accustomed to being

hunted. Their lives were in jeopardy every minute of every day. As a result, they were always wary. As if to compensate them for their place in the food chain, nature had equipped them with extraordinary eyesight, hearing, and sense of smell so they could readily elude predators.

Elk were some of the wariest animals alive. They were quick to melt into the shadows at the slightest hint of a threat. And despite their great size, they could move as quietly as ghosts when they needed to.

The warrior woman reached a bend and paused to peek around it. The next leg of the trail was clear. She started to go on, then caught a pungent whiff and halted. Glancing down, she saw animal droppings almost at her very feet.

Elk were one of very few creatures that left different types of droppings depending on their diet at the time. When they migrated to lush lowland areas, they left large flattened chips. But when high up in the mountains, where their diet was much the same as that of deer, their droppings consisted of dark pellets similar to deer droppings, only much larger.

Second Son was staring at a pile of the latter. Each was more than an inch and a half long, indicating an elk of considerable size, most likely the bull.

Confirmation came in the form of urine markings. Females always sprayed behind them, males urinated directly underneath. These markings showed that it had indeed been the bull.

Bending, Second Son gauged the texture of the droppings by picking up a pellet and squeezing. It was slick and mushy and still warm inside. The bull had gone by not very long ago.

Second Son pointed the pile out to her son, who grinned and nodded. Stepping over the spoor, she moved along the trail, her eyes sweeping from side to side. The elk were bound to have made beds for themselves and would be resting until evening, when they would rise and forage.

Another turn made Second Son slow. Suddenly, from the depths of the thicket, came a low snort. She froze, focusing on a wide island of grass at the very center of the tract. The elk were in there.

The wind was blowing from the wapiti to them, so Second Son need not worry about the animals detecting their scent. She stayed still for quite a while, though, on the off chance that one of the animals had heard them.

Billy-Wolf was impatient to go on, but he held himself in check. His parents had taught him that the key to being a successful hunter was patience, patience, and more patience. He found it hard sometimes to stay still for hours on end, but he was getting better as he grew older.

At last Second Son advanced. She scouted the trail in front of her to avoid twigs and dry grass. The many twists and turns slowed them down. In due course they came to the final straight stretch leading to the grass at the center.

The Burning Heart warrior squatted. She held the bow with the string partially drawn. When the opportunity to shoot came, if it did, she would be lucky if she had a clear shot, let alone ample time to aim.

Billy-Wolf dogged her steps. It abruptly occurred to him that he had neglected to cock the Hawken, and now it was too late. The loud click would carry to the elk and they would flee. There was no recourse but to wait until he was about to fire.

Second Son stopped when the grass rustled and shook. She thought that she glimpsed a patch of tan hide. Once the shaking ceased, she stalked closer, the bow high so she could sight down the shaft. She was within ten feet of the grass when she spied several sparrows in the huckleberry bushes.

There were three of the little birds, hopping from branch to branch. They did not appear disturbed. Yet it would not take much to scare them into taking noisy wing, which might be just the thing to make the elk run off.

Second Son stayed where she was, waiting the sparrows out. They continued to flit about for quite some time. She was glad when the male uttered a single chirp and flew off. The females were swift to streak after it.

The grass stood silent as Second Son crept close enough to touch it. No sounds issued from within. Parting the stems with the tip of her arrow, she sought some trace of the animal she had glimpsed. Apparently it had gone deeper in. Slowly straightening to her full height, she surveyed the stand from one end to the other. She saw no elk.

Billy-Wolf took his mother's cue and rose. On realizing the wapiti, as some settlers called them, were nowhere in sight, he stepped to the left without paying attention to where he placed his foot.

The resultant crack of a twig was like the retort of a small pistol.

Four enormous forms reared up out of the grass. Nostrils flaring, ears upright, the animals sought the source of the noise. It took them but moments to spy the Tsistsista and her son, and in unison they wheeled to race off.

Second Son needed a few moments of her own to identify the bull, since it had shed its antlers and one of the cows was almost as big. As she brought her bow to bear, the massive male turned. Too much vegetation intervened for her to let fly. Taking several long strides into the grass, she hastily aimed and released the arrow.

The bull squalled when the shaft sank deep into its body, but it did not slow down. Moving almost too quickly for the eye to follow, it sped out of the grass and crashed into the huckleberry bushes.

Instantly Second Son gave chase, notching another shaft

on the run. She angled to the right so she would have a better shot.

Billy-Wolf, meanwhile, was sprinting flat out to the left to do the same. He cocked the Hawken, swept around a thick clump to keep from tripping, and halted where the grass ended. The bull was twenty yards away, swiftly gaining speed even with the arrow protruding from between its ribs.

The boy took precise aim, lining up the front bead with the rear sight as his father had taught him. Holding his breath to steady his arms, he mentally counted to three, then stroked the trigger. The Hawken belched smoke and lead.

A heartbeat later the bull's front legs buckled. It fell heavily and rolled onto its side. Snorting wildly, legs thrashing, the elk tried to regain its footing but could not. A spreading scarlet stain marred its hide.

Second Son halted to await developments. It was risky to get too close to a dying animal, since at the moment of death even the most timid of creatures might turn on the one who had shot it. And elk were hardly timid. Generally they shied away from people, but they were big enough and powerful enough to trample a careless human to death quite easily. Which made her all the more alarmed when her son unexpectedly ran around in front of the bull and drew his pistol to finish it off. "Billy-Wolf, no!" she cried, too late.

The stricken elk lurched to its feet and bore down on the startled boy.

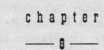

chapter

8

There is an old saying to the effect that at times our lives hang by threads.

At no time was this more true than when Billy-Wolf Bennett stood rooted in place as over one thousand pounds of sinew and bone bore down on him.

Grown elk were as fleet as horses, sometimes even more so. This one was almost on the boy in the blink of an eye. He had no time to take aim. He could not dive to the right or the left and hope to get out of the way. Nor could he just stand there and let himself be bowled over.

Billy-Wolf had one option left to him and he took it. He flattened onto his belly and threw both arms over his head to ward off heavy hooves.

It seemed as if thunder boomed. The very earth shook. Off to one side Snip barked wildly. Through narrowed eyes the boy saw flailing hooves sweep toward him. He tensed for the torment to come; to his astonishment there was none. The hooves pounded past on either side, kicking dirt into his face but leaving him unscathed.

Spinning around, Billy-Wolf raised the pistol again. But another shot proved unnecessary. The bull took two more steps, then collapsed again, this time to lie utterly still with crimson rivulets oozing from its nose and mouth. The ball had caught it in a lung.

A hand fell on the boy's shoulder and he was yanked to his feet to find himself staring into the eyes of his indignant mother.

"Were you trying to get yourself killed? Or was that your clever way of taking a close look at the belly of an elk?"

Billy-Wolf stared at the dead animal. "I shouldn't have rushed in close like that, huh?"

"I would not make a habit of it if you want to live to what your father calls a ripe old age."

Second Son willed her nerves to calm. For harrowing seconds she had thought that her sole offspring would certainly die. It reminded her yet again of how deeply she cared for her son, and how grateful she was for this precious time they were enjoying together.

Most women would have indulged in a lavish display of hugs and kisses to show their relief that their child had survived his close call. But not Second Son. She was a warrior. Instead, she gave him a playful cuff on the shoulder and said gruffly, "See if you can fetch the horses without getting yourself killed."

"Yes, Ma," Billy-Wolf said, and dashed off. He crammed the pistol under his wide leather belt, then remembered that his rifle was empty. Halting, he reloaded, carefully measuring the proper amount of black powder in his palm before pouring it down the muzzle. He used the ramrod to tamp the ball and patch down.

It took some doing for the boy to navigate the maze and find his way to the point where they had entered the thicket. Taking his bearings by the sun, he hurried toward the spot where they had left Shadow, Blaze, and the sorrel. But as he neared the row of pines, he was mystified to see no trace of the horses. He looked all around. It was just possible that he was wrong. But no, on noting the landmarks, there could be no doubt.

Billy-Wolf jogged on past the pines. Clear as day in front of him were the tracks the horses had made and an oval of cropped grass where the mare had grazed.

He distinctly remembered tying the stallion's reins to a limb. And he also recalled his mother making sure Shadow and the packhorse would not wander off.

Bewildered, Billy-Wolf examined the area. He saw where the three horses had headed off into the brush to the south. He went to trail them but caught himself when for the third time that day he had the sensation of being watched by unseen eyes. At that same instant Snip faced due south and growled deep in his chest.

An overpowering urge came over Billy-Wolf. More than anything he wanted to get out of there, and get out of there quickly. "Come on, boy," he urged softly, back-pedaling so he could watch the undergrowth. He pushed through the pines. Once in the open, he turned on a heel and lit out as if the hounds of hell were after him.

Second Son, meantime, had slit the elk's throat to bleed it. She inspected the bull from head to tail and was pleased to find everything in good order. Sometimes a hunter went to a lot of trouble only to find an animal sickly or old and feeble, the meat not worth the effort.

This bull was in its prime and would feed her family for many moons.

The patter of flying feet alerted Second Son that something was amiss before she spied her son weaving through the huckleberry toward her. She rose to meet him.

Billy-Wolf was almost out of breath. "It's the horses," he rasped, and then had to suck in air and run right back out again, huffing and puffing in his mother's wake.

The warrior woman lost no time reaching the pines. The welfare of their mounts was second only to their own. If anything happened to the horses, they would be stranded, left afoot, far from the valley they called home.

In itself that was not a calamity. They were competent hunters. They could live off the land. But being on foot exposed them to dangers they could otherwise outrun. And the journey back to Cleve, a matter of days on horseback, would require many weeks of hard walking.

In a glance Second Son read the sign. Stepping a few yards to the south, she sank to one knee beside a partial print. The style of moccasin was identical to those her son had found at the lake. It had to be a member of the same unknown tribe.

Billy-Wolf had not noticed the print earlier. "Our horses have been stolen!" he declared. "Do you think it's the bunch of warriors from down yonder?"

The suggestion was upsetting. It meant that she had been careless, that the band had shadowed them since they left the lake without her catching on. "We will soon find out," she said. "Come."

Hefting his Hawken, Billy-Wolf followed his mother into the forest. Snip loped at his side, head low to the ground, sniffing.

The next moment the foliage closed around them.

•   •   •

Cleve Bennett was fit to be tied. He stormed out of the cabin, paused with his malletlike hands on his hips, and glared at the world as if daring it to defy him. "Damn it all!" he bellowed. "I know I had more! They have to be around here somewhere!"

Seated on a stump near the partially completed stable, Rakes the Sky with Lightning regarded his aunt's husband with amusement. Lightning did not know why it was, but white men liked to rail at empty air. They yelled. They shook their fists. They cursed as only white men could. And to what end? To get themselves red in the face and short of breath.

Cleve walked toward the Tsistsista. "It's the story of my life. If something can go wrong, it will. Now what are we going to do?"

"I do not see why you are so upset, Yellow Hair," Lightning said. "The next time we go to the fort, you can buy or trade for more."

The big trapper jabbed a thick finger. "But we need those nails now! Why do you think I've been breaking my back since Second Son left? For my health?" He stepped up to the stable and patted a log. "I want to get everything done before she gets back so we can give her a homecoming she'll never forget. She'll be tickled pink."

The warrior could think of many things that would delight his aunt, but a log lodge for horses was not high on the list. He said nothing, though.

"We don't have any choice," Cleve declared. "I could finish without nails, but I want to do it proper so these buildings will still be standing long after our bodies are dust. One of us will have to go to Fort Hall."

"I want to," Lightning promptly volunteered.

"How come?"

The Kit Fox warrior did not have a ready answer. Part of the reason was that although he thought of Cleve as a brother and liked his company, there were times when he wanted to be by himself. And although Second Son had stressed that her home was Lightning's home, the warrior never truly felt comfortable there. He would rather live as a Tsistsista should, in a buffalo-hide lodge.

There was one additional factor. For some time Lightning had been feeling too cooped up. It was a familiar feeling, one he'd often felt after a long snowy winter on the prairie when he had been forced to spend most of his time inside. He wanted to get out and about. Go somewhere. Do something. This was the reason he now gave Cleve.

"I can understand," the other said. "I get that way on occasion myself." He nodded. "All right. I'll give you the money. Bring back all the nails you can get your hands on. Plus a few odds and ends we've been needing."

The warrior did not waste any time. Eager to be off, he threw his Cheyenne saddle and a pair of parfleches over the back of his bay and was ready to go. Since he had lent his bow to his aunt, he settled for taking his lance and butcher knife.

Cleve told Lightning what they needed, then offered to give him a rifle or a pistol. "Just in case you run into trouble."

Giving the lance a shake, the Tsistsista said in his own tongue, "The weapons of my people have served me all my life, Yellow Hair. I will not start using the white man's now."

"Suit yourself," Cleve responded. He then insisted that Lightning take ample jerky. "It'll save you from having to rustle up a lot of game while you're on the trail." After handing over the bundle, he said, "I'll do all that I can while you're gone. Hurry back, you hear?"

"I will," the warrior promised. Swinging onto the bay, he gave a toss of his long black hair and urged the horse into a trot.

"Take care!" Cleve called. It bothered him a little, not going himself. By rights it was his job. But he had so much work to do that he was reluctant to lose the time it would take to travel to the post and back. And, too, the man in charge of Fort Hall was a personal friend and knew Lightning. The warrior would be well treated.

Satisfied that he had done the right thing, the big trapper shouldered his heavy ax and headed for the stand where he had been felling trees. There were still five or six hours before sunset. He could get a lot done in that time.

The last Cleve saw of Lightning, he was a distant stick figure on the horizon.

Second Son was a shadow among shadows as she paralleled the tracks of their mounts and the packhorse. Her every nerve was raw. The slightest of movements drew her gaze. The faintest of sounds caused her to stop and listen intently. She saw jays, ravens, and chickadees. She heard finches, a bluebird, and a grosbeak. Not once did she glimpse or hear the men responsible for stealing their animals.

Billy-Wolf Bennett's nerves were stretched as taut as piano wire. He was worried, but for his mother, not himself. He knew his mother all too well, knew that she would stop at nothing to get the horses back even if it meant tangling with an entire band of hostiles.

Snip glided along next to the boy, sniffing every so often.

The three of them were almost to the bottom of a long incline when Second Son halted and whispered barely loud enough for her son to hear, "Do you see him?"

See who? Billy-Wolf was about to ask, when he happened to notice a spruce tree about sixty feet off to the southeast. Thanks to the angle of the sun, a tall figure crouched on a thick limb a third of the way up the trunk was outlined against the green background. If the sun had not been just right, they would never have spotted him.

Billy-Wolf was smart enough not to stare. He pretended not to see the man while roving his eyes back and forth. Few details were apparent other than that the warrior held a long bow and wore a shirt with long sleeves. "What do we do?" he whispered back.

"Circle around and take him by surprise," Second Son proposed. She went on, deliberately ignoring the tree and the warrior. When they had gone far enough to convince her that the warrior could no longer see them, she swung wide to the left. From then on, they stayed low and never left heavy cover.

It was a painstaking chore, working their way around without making any noise.

At last Billy-Wolf saw the exact tree ahead. The lower limbs hid the man from sight. He glanced at his mother, who used sign language to direct him to one side while she bore to the other. At her signal, they sprinted to the bole and pointed their weapons straight up to cover the warrior. Only no one was there.

Billy-Wolf spun, his back to the trunk. He had a terrible hunch that their enemies had known what they were up to all along, and that they had been played for fools.

Second Son was also frustrated by their failure. Whoever these strange Indians were, they were as skilled at woodlore as she was, perhaps even more so. If that was the case, the outcome was a foregone conclusion. She did not mind for herself so much as she did for Wolf Sings on the Mountain. She had always expected to go down fighting one day. Her son, however, deserved to live. He had his whole life ahead of him.

"What now?" he asked.

The warrior woman hunched over, gestured, and darted to the west. She held to a brisk pace for hundreds of feet.

Reaching an earthen bank, she dropped onto her side below the rim, then raised her head high enough to see their back trail. Almost immediately she spied a number of vague figures slinking through the forest. The hunters had become the hunted.

Billy-Wolf saw their pursuers, too. He fought down a wave of dread and lifted the Hawken to take a bead, but his mother put her hand on the barrel and shook her head. He understood. It was best he save the lead for when they really needed it.

Sliding to the bottom of the bank, Second Son veered into the brush, keeping it between her and the warriors. The horses would have to wait. Her first priority was to get Billy-Wolf to safety. Then, and only then, would she go after the animals.

They pushed on rapidly. Second Son did not know how many were after them. She thought there were four, but there might be many more. Whenever she paused to look back, they were still there, never gaining ground, never losing any. It perplexed her.

Presently a deadfall barred their path. Fallen trees choked the earth for as far as Second Son could see in both directions. She bore to the right to go around, her son close behind, Snip last.

Suddenly two more figures appeared up ahead. Second Son immediately stopped and raised her bow. As if they were unearthly specters, the pair vanished. To their rear the rest stayed just out of arrow range.

"What in the world are they up to?" Billy-Wolf wondered.

"I wish I knew," Second Son answered. They had been cut off in front and could not go back. Since few in their right mind ever tried to cross a deadfall, it was apparent that the band wanted them to cut into the vegetation to their right. Why? So they would blunder into an ambush from which there was no escape?

Second Son was not about to play into their hands. A Tsistsista warrior was taught at an early age that the key to victory in battle was always to do that which the enemy would not expect.

In this instance, Second Son swung toward the deadfall and plunged in among the fallen trees and dead brush. A shout of outrage from the pair up ahead verified her reasoning.

Billy-Wolf saw warriors converging from several directions at once. It was obvious that they would overtake him before he covered ten more feet. Automatically, he whipped the Hawken to his shoulder, worked the hammer, and fired at the foremost man, who dropped.

Something else happened. Something amazing. At the booming blast of the rifle, every last warrior disappeared; one moment they were there, the next they weren't.

Second Son had stopped. She saw the men go to ground and moved to her son's side to protect him, since the warriors were bound to rise up again and charge before Billy-Wolf could reload. Yet none did. There was no sign of them at all.

The boy had never reloaded so fast in all his days. His fingers were a blur. "I had to shoot," he apologized. "They would have been on us if I didn't."

"I know, son," the warrior woman responded, proud that he had seen fit to stand his ground and fight back. In less than a minute he was ready to shoot again. She indicated the deadfall and said, "They do not want us to go in there. So that is what we will do. You first."

"But—"

"Go," Second Son said sternly.

Most of the felled trees were firs. They had all been

downed at the same time, evidently by a tornado-force wind, most probably a Chinook.

During warm lulls in the middle of winter, roaring windstorms shrieked down out of the north, snapping saplings as if they were so much kindling, flattening reeds and grass and brush, and raising dust clouds that could be seen for miles.

Billy-Wolf had experienced Chinooks before in the southern Rockies. Once he had been blown clean off his feet, nearly dashing his brains out on a boulder.

Never had the boy beheld devastation like this. Tree after tree had been broken off near the base. In row after row, layer after layer, they lay in uneven ranks, all with their tops pointing to the southeast. Some had shattered on impact, littering the ground with jagged logs. As if that were not enough, thick brush was rampant.

Cleve had always advised Billy-Wolf to fight shy of deadfalls, no matter what. His father liked to tell a story about a certain free trapper who brazenly tried to take a shortcut across a deadfall near Long's Peak and was never heard from again.

Billy-Wolf knew a tall tale when he heard one. But, as with most of his pa's stories, it contained a kernel of truth.

Deadfalls were deadly places. A single misstep could cost a person a busted limb or a broken neck. Horses would not enter one unless made to. Nor were elk or deer willing to risk a broken leg. And because it was too easy for predators to trap prey among the jumbled mass of deadwood, most of the smaller animals stayed away as well.

It was as if they had stumbled on an eerie tract of forest where all the creatures had died out. Billy-Wolf scanned the dark tangle and did not like what he saw. Everywhere there were shadowy pockets and recessed nooks. None of the dead trees had leaves; their skeletal limbs poked into the air like accusing fingers. No breeze penetrated, so the air hung deathly still.

"Keep going," Second Son directed when her son slowed down. Every so often she would stare over a shoulder, but the warriors did not reappear.

It was hard work, clambering up and over tree after tree. Ten yards into the deadfall they could no longer see the forest behind them. Bending, stooping, twisting, they wormed their way steadily farther into the maze.

Suddenly Snip stiffened and growled.

To their rear excited jabbering had erupted, the voices of many men upraised at once.

Billy-Wolf listened but could not make hide nor hair of the language. "What tongue is that?" he asked.

"One I have never heard before," the warrior woman said. To her, it sounded as if the members of the band were arguing over whether to come in after them. "We must go faster," she instructed.

A particularly massive trunk reared in front of them. Billy-Wolf leaped, attempting to snag a branch that proved to be too high. Moving to the side, he sought another way over. Shortly, he discovered where part of the trunk had crumbled on impact, allowing enough space for them to crawl under. "This will have to do," he said softly.

Squatting, Billy-Wolf poked the Hawken through the cavity, then scrambled on his hands and knees over a half-dozen bent and twisted branches that tore at his buckskins. Once safely on the other side, he stood and kept watch while his mother and Snip came through.

The shadow of the trunk shrouded them, creating an illusion of twilight when there were actually several hours of daylight remaining.

They continued on. Second Son had to keep an eye on her quiver as she climbed over and under tree after tree. She did not want to lose a single arrow.

Time seemed to stand still. The warrior woman and her son penetrated fully halfway into the deadfall before pausing to rest. Billy-Wolf was winded and in need of water. He noticed a small puddle of rainwater that had collected under a felled fir and went over to determine if it was safe to drink.

The hubbub of voices had long since dwindled. Second Son wanted to believe that the warriors had given up, but she knew better.

"Say, Ma?" Billy-Wolf said, his features reflecting puzzlement. "You should take a gander at this." He had knelt beside the puddle. "I don't know what to make of it."

"What have you found?" Second Son wanted to know. Walking up behind him, she glanced at the mud ringing the puddle, figuring that he was mystified by a track.

Sure enough, there was a print, a footprint that appeared to be human, yet much more than human.

And whoever or whatever had made it had been by that spot less than five minutes ago.

chapter

9

Rakes the Sky with Lightning wore a broad smile. As well he should. For the first time in many sleeps he was on his own, with a dependable horse under him, the sun in his face, and the wind at his back. It was almost, but not quite, good to be alive.

Lightning had been riding for several hours at a steady gait. When on horseback, he liked to think, and at that moment he was thinking of his future. Or, more appropriately, his lack of one.

Once, everything had looked so bright. He'd had the loveliest wife in the Burning Heart village. She had been heavy with their first child and the pregnancy was going well. They had owned several fine horses, a spacious lodge.

He had been a highly respected member of the Kit Fox society. Life had been sweet and rich, with each day better than the last.

Then came the massacre, and practically everyone Lightning had cared for and everything he had valued had been destroyed. His wife, their unborn child, their lodge, his relatives and friends, everything. On top of that, he had been burned and horribly scarred.

For the longest time Lightning had wanted to die. He had not eaten. He had refused to drink. If not for Wolf Sings on the Mountain, he would have gone to join his wife in the Other Place.

The boy had stubbornly forced food down his throat, had made him drink whether he wanted to or not. His body had mended despite his best efforts, and in due course he had been restored to a semblance of his former self.

That had been many moons ago, yet Lightning still did not feel whole. Where his heart should be, there was a yawning black pit. Where once he had been filled with a keen zest for life, he now felt partly dead inside. And that part of him that was alive had grown so cold toward everyone and everything except his aunt and her family that he had taken to believing he was no more than a walking dead man waiting for the right moment to keel over.

A silly notion, Second Son might say, yet he could not help how he felt.

The bay suddenly nickered. Lightning glanced up and set eyes on a huge four-legged form moving through woodland to the southwest. The brown coat, high hump, and lumbering gait identified the creature as surely as if it stood in front of him.

A crooked smile twisted the Tsistsista's lips. An idea born of acute despair and profound loneliness caused him to slant toward the trees. The beast heard him coming and slowed. It shuffled to the tree line, its ponderous head up-raised to sniff the air.

Lightning halted when he was close enough to see the bear's eyes fixed balefully on him. Laughing at his inspiration, he waved the lance and launched into his death chant.

The young male grizzly reared onto its hind legs as if to see him better.

Raising his voice to a strident pitch, Lightning chanted his lungs out. The prospect of soon seeing Twisted Leg flushed him with joy. He expected the bear to tear into him at any moment, but it stood there on its thick hind legs regarding him as if it could not quite credit its senses.

Then Lightning finished his chant. Thrusting the lance into the air, he shouted, "Hey! Hey! Hey, bear! Come and kill me!"

As if the animal understood him, it dropped onto all fours again. But instead of snarling and charging, it spun around incredibly fast for its bulk and sped off through the forest.

"What are you doing?" Lightning cried, outraged. "I want you to attack me, not run away!" Goading the bay into a gallop, he gave chase, threading recklessly through the trees. "Come back, bear! Come back!"

The grizzly wasn't listening. It flashed into dense brush and was gone. Lightning had to rein up at the edge to keep from harming the bay. He rose as high as he could but did not see any sign of the brute. Hoping against hope that it was circling around to come at him from behind, as grizzlies sometimes did, he sat there for the longest while.

At length the Kit Fox warrior frowned and resumed his journey to Fort Hall. Once again life had denied him that which he wanted more than anything. Once again life had mocked him.

How else could he explain stumbling on the only grizzly bear alive that happened to be a coward?

The track was half again as long as an average man's and a third again as wide. There were five toes, as with any human print, but each toe was capped by a curved claw. A dozen small holes showed that the soles had been covered with knobby bumps. And on both sides were shallow scrape marks, as if bony spurs grew out the sides of the foot.

"No man made this," Billy-Wolf said in apprehensive awe. Another partial print was three feet away. "Look at the stride of this thing. It's real tall, whatever it is."

Second Son was more concerned about the fact that it was there in the deadfall with them. Any creature with claws like that was not a plant eater. She raked the tangle of trees from top to bottom, seeking clues to its whereabouts. There were none. Just those two footprints and that was all.

Billy-Wolf stepped to the second track and looked all about. "Where do you reckon it went from here? Did it sprout wings and fly off?"

Nearly six feet past the last track was another large prone tree, the top third broken off. Second Son bobbed her chin at it and speculated, "It jumped to that trunk and climbed on over."

"That far, Ma?" Billy-Wolf said skeptically. "I don't see how it could have. It would need a running start and it was just walking."

Second Son did not debate the point. There was only one place the creature could have jumped to and not left more tracks. It seemed impossible, but she accepted the evidence of her own eyes and got on with the more important matter of saving their hides. Motioning for her son to bear to the right, she scanned the top of the tree in case the creature lurked up there waiting to pounce.

Snip picked that moment to turn to the left, where the tree blended into briars run wild. The dog snarled, the hairs on its neck rising, and made as if to dash into the undergrowth.

"No, boy!" Billy-Wolf scolded. "Stay!" Taking hold of the scruff of Snip's neck, he hauled the mongrel after him. Snip growled and tried to break free, but Billy-Wolf was not going to let go no matter what.

Her bow bent, an arrow touching her cheek, Second Son retreated, not once taking her gaze off the briars. It was disturbing to think that whatever had made those tracks was in there, maybe watching them. She did not think it would show itself. Yet suddenly the bushes trembled as if to a stiff breeze and a couple of thin branches seven feet off the ground parted ever so slightly.

For a fleeting moment dark, bestial eyes blazed at the warrior woman with an inhuman hatred. They appeared to be lit by inner flames that burned as brightly as a campfire.

Then the branches shifted and the moment was gone.

Second Son had no time to release her shaft. She trained it on the spot where the eyes had appeared as she backed away, but they did not show again. Something told her the creature was still there, though. Watching. Just watching.

Snip would not stop growling and striving to break free until they reached the end of the tree and moved to the other side. Once he could no longer see the briars, he calmed down.

The warrior woman let the bow relax and turned westward. It was critical that they get clear of the deadfall before whatever she had seen decided they should be its next meal. Hustling her son along, she wound through the downed firs rapidly.

Several times Snip glanced back and growled softly, as if he sensed that they were being shadowed. But the dog stayed by their side.

It was with great relief that Second Son saw the edge of the forest only sixty feet off. She hiked herself up onto a log, slid over, and turned to ease the mongrel to the ground after her son gave Snip a boost to the top. As she straightened, she saw high weeds not four strides from her son sway back and forth. "Hurry!" she coaxed, grabbing his hand as he pulled himself up and virtually yanking him to the ground beside her.

Billy-Wolf whirled and brought up the Hawken. He did not know what his mother had seen, but he figured his life was in imminent danger, judging by the flicker of anxiety he saw in her eyes. Nothing was coming after them, though. All he saw were trees and weeds.

"What was it, Ma?"

"Run."

"What?"

"Run," Second Son said, and gave him a push to get him going. The creature was in those weeds, she was sure of it, just as she was sure that unless they got out of there quickly it would attack. She could not say how she knew. She simply did.

Billy-Wolf had long since learned to obey his parents without question. In times of crises their survival often hinged on split-second decisions, so when he was told to do something, he did it.

On being directed to run, Billy-Wolf fled for his life. He did not linger to ask her why he had to run or what she might have seen back there. He ran as fast as the tangle of trees and vegetation allowed, Snip keeping pace at his side.

Second Son covered them with her bow. The weeds

shook, but the creature did not appear. Then she caught a glimpse of something big and dark and hairy moving low to the ground to the right, moving so swiftly that if she had blinked, she would have missed it. She swung to face the beast and lost sight of it.

The tree line was close now. Very close. Billy-Wolf smiled and vaulted a low log. He'd had enough of dead-falls to last him a lifetime.

It had taken them longer than Second Son had counted on to cross. By this time the sun hung low in the sky and inky shadows were spreading across the landscape, devouring every patch of sunlight.

The warrior woman and her son clambered over the final few trees and straightened. They waited, weapons ready. But whatever was in the deadfall stayed there.

At a nod from his mother, Billy-Wolf backed into the trees. Once the brush hid them, they turned and jogged westward into ever-deepening twilight. A fiery arc rimming jagged peaks was all that remained of the sun. It would not be long before total darkness claimed the countryside.

And that worried Second Son. The creature in the deadfall haunted the shadows, a common trait among nocturnal predators. With the advent of night the thing would roam the wilds seeking prey. If it could track by scent, it would hunt them down. She needed to find somewhere to take shelter, somewhere the creature could not get at them without being seen.

For long minutes the pair traveled. The arc faded. Presently the trees thinned at the bottom of a grassy slope. Erosion had worn a deep gully down its center. Boulders dotted the bottom, some in clusters as high as the gully rim.

Second Son entered the mouth and ascended. She had not gone all that far when an interesting arrangement of boulders drew her attention.

At some point in the past an immense slab of rock had been washed down from higher on the mountain and wedged against the side wall, partially embedding itself. Other, smaller boulders had in turn been washed up against it, forming an uneven circular wall. There were many gaps and openings but few large enough to admit anything bigger than Snip.

Bending to the largest, Second Son poked her head inside. There was an open pocket with enough room for several people. The air was musty. No snakes or small animals called the place home, so she slid in and knelt. "Send Snip through."

Billy-Wolf had to squat behind the yellow dog and shove before Snip would obey. Enclosed spaces grated on the animal's nerves. When confined to a tipi or cabin for any length of time, Snip invariably grew terribly restless and would pace and whine for hours on end if not made to stop.

Second Son sat with her back to a boulder, facing the opening. She rested her bow across her thighs and loosened her knife in its sheath. Mustering a smile, she said, "This is not so bad. It will keep out the wind."

"I sure could use a bite to eat," Billy-Wolf mentioned. His stomach had been rumbling off and on since they struck the deadfall. He draped an arm across Snip's back and made himself comfortable. "Tomorrow we go after our horses, I take it?"

"We do," Second Son agreed. Or, rather, she would. Their adversaries had proven to be more formidable than most, so she deemed it best to go alone. She held off telling her son since he was bound to make a fuss.

Make a fuss. Second Son chuckled at the turn of phrase. She had been with Cleve so long that she now used many of the same phrases he did without realizing that she was doing so. And she had caught him doing the same, using Tsistsista sayings she had taught him.

That was what happened when a man and woman lived together for so long. They started to talk like one another, think like one another. The two became one.

"What's struck your funny bone?" Billy-Wolf asked. A great fatigue had come over him, seeping into every muscle in his body. He stifled a yawn.

"I was thinking of your father."

The boy had been doing the same earlier. Had his pa been there, they would have held their own against the war party. His ma was as tough as any person he knew, but with Cleve at her side she was unbeatable. "There's something I've been meaning to ask you, Ma, for a long time. Why exactly did you marry Pa?"

Young ones had a habit of asking unforeseen questions. Second Son should have been used to it by now. But this one caught her off guard, given their circumstances, and she responded, "Why do you want to know?"

"I'm just curious, is all. You keep telling me that one day I'll take the right woman as my wife, so I'd better know what to look for." Billy-Wolf paused. It was near to pitch-black in their hideaway and he could barely make out his mother's features. "I asked Pa the same question once."

"What did he say?"

"He married you because you were the only woman who ever whipped him at wrestling."

Second Son could not help but laugh. Those had been grand days, when Cleve and she first met! She had been drawn to him from the moment she set eyes on him, but she had been too proud to admit as much. As it turned out, he had been attracted to her but had figured he didn't stand a prayer of winning her since she was a warrior.

Cleve had lived with the Burning Hearts for many moons, then gone his own way. Their parting had been formal. She had tried to act as if it were of no consequence, but her heart had not given her a moment's peace. At her brother's urging, she had gone after Cleve. And in ritual mock combat she had triumphed over him and made him her wife.

"Did you really whip him?" Billy-Wolf wondered.

"Yes," Second Son confirmed, "but at the time he was laughing so hard that Snip could have pinned him."

"So why did you pick him as your husband? Why Pa out of all the men you knew? Why a white man when you could have had your choice of any of the Burning Heart warriors?"

"Who told you that?"

"Lightning. He said that you were the talk of the tribe there for a while. 'Most every single man in the village wanted you for himself, but you being a warrior and all made it hard for them to court you."

Outside their shelter the wind had increased. Second Son listened awhile to assure herself all was well before saying, "I have always walked my own path. And I hope that you will do the same, Wolf Sings on the Mountain. Never let others tell you how you must live. Do what is best for you."

"Was Pa best for you?"

The warrior woman nodded, then realized Billy-Wolf had probably not noticed in the dark. "Yes. It is hard to put into words. But when we were together I was happier than I had ever been. And when we were apart, I hurt here." She thumped her chest.

"Is that love?"

"It is one of the signs. There are others." Second Son slid closer to him so they could talk in a whisper. It would not do to give themselves away. "I was very fortunate.

Some Tsistsista women do not have the freedom I did. They marry men their fathers pick for them."

Billy-Wolf was going to comment on that practice when Snip raised up, sniffed a few times, and bristled.

"Something is out there!"

The wind was all Second Son heard. Moving to the wall of boulders, she peered through a gap. The dirt bottom and sides of the gully were a pale contrast to the background of night. She could not see above the opposite rim, but the trees below the gully mouth were visible.

"Anything?" Billy-Wolf asked, pressing his face to a different opening.

Above them several wide boulders were wedged tight, forming a partial roof. A pebble clattered against the one nearest the rim and Second Son looked up to see a shadow flit across a narrow opening. She swung the bow to shoulder height, but whatever it was had gone.

"It's that thing, isn't it?" Billy-Wolf asked breathlessly. "The animal that made those strange tracks?"

A piercing shriek rose from the rim above. Snip voiced a challenging howl, which elicited a louder shriek. A rock or a paw thumped loudly on top of the flat slab.

"It wants in here to get us but can't figure out how to enter," Billy-Wolf guessed.

There was a loud thud outside, as if a heavy body had dropped from the rim to the bottom of the gully. Second Son looked out but did not spot the mystery beast. The wind abruptly died. In the ensuing quiet they both could hear something sniffing at one of the cracks to her right.

Snarling, Snip flung himself at the crack and went into a frenzy of snapping and barking. Billy-Wolf leaped to pull the dog back.

Second Son turned to assist. As she bent, a black hairy paw shot through a gap directly above her and claws bit into her left shoulder. Before she could tear herself loose, she was slammed into the wall and the paw slipped around her neck, choking off her air and her voice. She let go of the bow and grabbed the paw with both hands to prevent those wicked claws from shredding her throat. To her amazement, the paw was not a paw at all. It had a thumb and four fingers.

The warrior woman pushed against the thing's arm. A claw nicked her skin, but she was able to hold the rest at bay. She glanced down, thinking her son would help, but Billy-Wolf was so busy restraining Snip that he had not noticed her plight. Nor had he heard the bow fall. The dog was making too much noise for him to hear anything.

Second Son smelled an overpowering stench. She nearly gagged. Locking her elbows, she bent her knees, slipping below the creature's reach. It howled and clawed wildly, its claws clacking against the boulders.

Twisting, Second Son drew her butcher knife. She thrust upward as the arm started to withdraw. The blade sliced into the back of the hairy hand, provoking a roar of outrage. The thing jerked its arm clear and smashed a fist against their shelter.

Meanwhile Billy-Wolf had pulled Snip over against the flat slab. The dog was nearly beside itself. Lips drawn up, teeth exposed, Snip strained to get at their attacker. It was all the boy could do to hold on.

A shadowy figure filled the largest opening. Second Son kicked dirt at it and the creature jerked back. Grabbing the leather cord that held the lance in place across her back, she cut through it in two slashes, pivoted, seized the lance before it could fall, and spun with the weapon leveled to confront the monstrosity.

A hairy head appeared. Second Son had a brief impression of long, straggly hair, big teeth, and those baleful eyes. She stabbed at its chest, but she was nowhere near fast enough. The thing sprang to the rear, out of sight.

Second Son crouched a few feet in front of the opening, the lance cocked at her shoulder for a death stroke. She braced for another onslaught while her son tried to quiet Snip.

A howl split the night. But it was a gust of wind, not the creature.

As time went by and the thing did not reappear, Second Son edged closer to peek out. If the creature was out there, it was well hidden. She scooted over to join her son, speaking soothing words for Snip's benefit. The dog had ceased barking but would not stop growling.

"That was too close for comfort," Billy-Wolf declared. "Do you think it will come back?"

"We will know soon enough," Second Son said. She retrieved Lightning's bow and her arrow and set them in front of her. Now all they could do was wait.

Billy-Wolf put a hand on top of Snip's wide shoulders and pressed, compelling the dog to lie down. His insides were fluttering like the wings of a butterfly but he was not about to show it. "I have this feeling we're in for a long night," he commented.

Second Son agreed. Deep down, she suspected that the worst was yet to come.

chapter
— 10 —

As if to prove the Burning Heart warrior wrong, the night passed uneventfully. She stayed awake until the quiet hour right before the dawn, when she could no longer hold her leaden eyelids open. Wolf Sings on the Mountain tried his best to stay up with her, but shortly after midnight he leaned back against the slab and was fast asleep the moment he closed his eyes. Snip slumbered next to the boy's leg.

The first faint glow of approaching daylight brought Second Son around. She let her son sleep. He would need all the rest he could get.

Moving to the opening, she studied the gully, the rim, the forest below. The way down seemed clear. She wondered about the creature and hoped they would not run into it again. Twice they had been lucky. It would be foolish to count on fate being so kind a third time.

The sun crowned the eastern mountains with golden glory. Bright rosy rays filtered in through the many gaps and openings. One fell on Snip, causing the yellow dog to blink, then sit up and yawn noisily. The yawn in turn woke up Billy-Wolf, who sat bolt upright and scooped up the Hawken from his lap.

"We are safe, my son. The beast did not come back."

"Sorry I dozed off," Billy-Wolf said sheepishly, rating himself a failure for having done so. He'd wanted to stay up all night with her to prove that he could and show her that he was more mature than she suspected.

"We both did," Second Son said to put him at ease. "Now let us go find water and game. If you are as hungry as I am, we can eat a whole buffalo."

The boy smiled. "I'm afraid you'll have to get your own, Ma. I could eat a bull by my lonesome."

It reminded Second Son of the elk they had slain. Cautiously crawling out, she slowly straightened and arched her spine to relieve a kink in her lower back. From the woodland rose a chorus of bird cries. The feathered denizens of the forest were welcoming the new day as their kind had been doing since the dawn of time.

Low clouds covered the slope above and the mountains to the north. To the south the sky was clear. The air was cool and held a tinge of moisture.

Second Son climbed to the opposite rim to verify that they were alone. As things had turned out, they had done all right. Not only had they withstood the hairy creature, they had eluded the war party.

Much to her regret, however, the horses were long gone. Shadow had been with her for many years and was as

much a part of the family as Snip. She also regretted having lost her saddle and the parfleches, neither of which
were so easily replaced. It had taken her weeks to make
the saddle and half as long to fashion the large buffalo-
hide bags.

At least they were still alive.

Billy-Wolf and the dog climbed up beside her. "So
where do we go to rustle up breakfast? That hollow yonder
might be good for deer."

"Are you forgetting the elk you shot?" Second Son
started down the slope. "If the warriors did not find it, and
if a bear or big cat or wolves did not catch its scent during
the night, we will have all the meat we can eat."

"That's a lot of ifs," Billy-Wolf remarked, but he went
along anyway. His mother was not one for letting prime
meat go to waste.

They fought shy of the deadfall by a wide margin. Second Son was on the lookout for tracks but saw only those
of animals. Once the sun had risen, the birds quieted.
Other than an occasional gust of wind and the chatter of
squirrels, the woodland was silent.

Rather than approach the huckleberry patch from the
same direction they had left it, Second Son circled around
to the north. No buzzards circled overhead, which was a
good sign. She crept forward and came to the patch of
high grass where the elk had bedded down. Just past it, lying where it had fallen, was the dead animal.

Amazingly, the bull was mostly intact. Ravens or jays
had been at the eyes and pecked them clean out. And a
small animal had gnawed on the nostrils and the lower
lip.

Billy-Wolf walked up to the animal and rested a hand
on his butcher knife. "Breakfast," he declared. "I can
hardly wait."

Snip had been testing the air since they entered the

huckleberry. Second Son assumed the dog had caught the scent of the elk's dried blood and thought no more of it. But now the yellow dog put its big front paws on the bull and stared fixedly at a row of huckleberry bushes flanking them.

Puzzled, Second Son did the same. Shock rippled through her as the bushes suddenly came to life, disgorging three tall warriors, who hurled themselves at her and her son. She had the lance in her right hand and drew back her arm to throw it, but as she did a callused hand clamped on her wrist, stopping her. A heartbeat later a bony shoulder caught her low in the back, knocking her to the ground.

"Ma!" Billy-Wolf bellowed, forgetting his own plight for fear she had been harmed. He took a single step toward her, then saw Snip launch himself at one of the warriors and be batted aside by a powerful sweep of a war club.

Another hostile reached the bull and leaped over it to get at Billy-Wolf. The boy swung the stock of the Hawken up and around, smashing the warrior full in the mouth. The man fell back across the elk. Billy-Wolf instantly pointed the rifle at a second foe, tugged on the hammer, and fired.

At that very second, an onrushing attacker slammed into Billy-Wolf from the side. He was sent sprawling onto one knee. The shot, he saw, had missed. Without delay he clawed at the pistol under his belt. Two swarthy figures were on him before he could draw.

Second Son had been dazed by the blow to her back. Her vision cleared just as her son went down fighting and the lance was wrenched from her grasp. Someone clamped down on her shoulder. She was roughly pulled to her feet. But as she rose, she tensed and slipped her knife from its sheath. A quick shift on her heel and the deed was done, the blade buried to the hilt in the man behind her. His tattooed face contorted in torment, he tottered backward, his palms pressed to the gaping wound.

Whirling, Second Son voiced her war cry and threw herself at the men on top of her son. They both heard and looked up. The nearest managed to raise an arm to block the downward sweep of her knife. She crashed into him and they went down together.

The warrior ducked under a swipe that would have opened his throat from ear to ear. He made no move for his own knife but instead flung both arms around her waist to hold her in place.

To Second Son the tactic seemed stupid. Her knife arm was free, and she swept it on high to plunge the blade into his exposed back. Fingers closed on her forearm. She glanced up into the smirking features of another adversary, who bent her arm so far back that she thought the bone would break. His intent was plain. Either she dropped the knife or he would snap her limb. She reluctantly released the hilt.

Second Son still had the bow and her arrows in the quiver on her back, but they might as well be on the moon for all the good they did her. She resorted to the close-fighting techniques she had honed in personal combat. A knee into the groin of the warrior holding her waist was sufficient to make him let go and stagger to the side. This freed her to swivel on her hip and drive her foot into the left kneecap of the man who held her arm.

There was a sharp crack. A howl burst from the warrior's throat and he hopped backward, clutching his leg.

Second Son came up off the ground in a blur. Another warrior barreled toward her, grabbing at her neck. She slipped under his arms, grabbed one, bent, and heaved. The man flew up and over her shoulder and sailed over six feet to smash down in the huckleberry bushes.

Suddenly Second Son saw her knife lying close by. She took a step and lunged, but her hand was short of the hilt when moccasins materialized beside her and something rammed into the base of her skull. Her legs buckled. A swirling black cloud engulfed her mind.

The last sight she saw was the ground rushing up to meet her face.

The last emotion she felt was keen regret at having failed her son, and the certainty that she would never see the man she loved ever again.

Cleve Bennett had felled two trees already that day and was drawing back his ax to chop into a third when he heard the horses picketed by the cabin nicker. Lowering the ax, he moved to the edge of the stand. It occurred to him that he had been careless in leaving his rifle behind. If hostiles decided to pay the homestead a visit, he'd be liable to lose his hair. And a lot worse.

From his vantage point Cleve could see Socks, his gelding, and one of the other animals. Both were gazing intently at the high grass that bordered the rear of the cabin. That did not bode well.

Forty yards separated the stand from the building. Cleve leaned the ax against a trunk, took a breath, and exploded from cover. Legs pumping, he raced for the door, half expecting to see painted warriors rear up out of the grass at any moment.

Socks looked at him and stomped the ground, a clear sign the gelding was agitated.

Cleve wanted to kick himself for becoming too complacent. He tried to tell himself that it was understandable. After all, they had occupied the valley for months and not seen another living soul. No other trappers, no friendly Indians, or any hostiles. It was only natural that he had begun to take their safety for granted, tucked away as they were in their little slice of paradise.

Yet he knew better.

Anyone who let down their guard in the wilderness inevitably paid for their folly.

The big man was almost to the cabin. Socks had swung to the east and seemed to be listening. Cleve heard nothing, but that was not unusual. Horses had better hearing than humans. If enemy warriors were slinking through the grass, the horses would be the first to know.

It was too bad that Snip wasn't there, Cleve reflected. The dog had the best hearing of all of them and would let Cleve know right where the invaders were.

In another moment Cleve gained the sanctuary of the cabin. He wasted no time cramming two pistols under his belt and making sure his Hawken was loaded. Throwing an ammo pouch and powder horn over his shoulder, he hastened back outside to the front corner.

As yet no Indians had appeared. Cleve crouched, his thumb resting on the hammer. He tried to tell the exact location of the hostiles by the direction the horses were looking, but to his bewilderment one was staring to the right, one to the left, and Socks gazed straight ahead. Were there hostiles all over the place? Or was there another explanation?

The wind, which had been blowing from the northwest to the southeast, momentarily shifted, as winds often did in the high country. It brought with it a faint rank odor.

Cleve held his breath before he breathed in too much of it. Backing away from the corner, he exhaled slowly and shook his head in amusement. "A damned polecat!" he muttered. "All this fuss over a stinking skunk!"

Relieved, Cleve looked around. The silence and lack of activity struck him like a physical blow. He hadn't realized until that very moment how utterly lonely it was there without his wife and son and Lightning.

The big man missed Second Son and Billy-Wolf terribly. He had tried to take their absence in stride, tried not to worry, but the truth was that he harbored a troubling premonition that all might not be well with them. Facing northward, he glumly regarded the stark peaks that framed the sky. Where were they at that very moment? he wondered. Were they safe? Were they *alive*?

There were times when Cleve thought he was plumb crazy for living out in the middle of nowhere as he did, exposing his loved ones to all sorts of dangers. But then he would see buffalo grazing nearby and a bald eagle soaring high in the sky and chickadees frolicking in a tree and maybe a large fish would leap up out of the lake, and he'd know beyond a shadow of a doubt that this was the life for them. The only life that would make them happy.

Cleve had never much liked big towns and cities. He remembered the time his pa had taken him to visit kin in New Orleans. All those people rushing around like chickens with their heads chopped off was enough to give a sensible man a case of the hives. Most of them, he had learned, lived in cramped quarters the size of bread boxes. He never had understood how folks could stand to be cooped up like that.

No, give Cleve the wide-open spaces. Give him fresh air and plenty of game for the table and clean water to drink. Give him the freedom to do as he pleased when he pleased, with no arrogant politician looking over his shoulder to say this or that was wrong. He would never settle for anything less.

Rising, Cleve headed back toward the trees. Only this time he took the pistols and the rifle. He might be harebrained at times, but he seldom made the same mistake twice.

Halfway there Cleve paused to again stare at the distant peaks. It would be another week or two before Second Son and Billy-Wolf returned. He could hardly wait. Lightning would be back well before then, and with a lot of hard work they could finish the stable before his wife showed up. He did so want to surprise her.

Sighing, Cleve Bennett thought to himself, Godspeed, my wife, wherever you are, and went on about his work.

Miles to the south, Rakes the Sky with Lightning was almost to the top of a spiny ridge when a gunshot brought him to an instant stop. It came from the other side. He slipped off the bay, then glided to the top, the lance at his side. From behind a waist-high boulder he peered down into a narrow valley.

Within earshot of the ridge gurgled a ribbon of a stream. Beside it, lying with its head arched and one leg bent under its body, was a dead black-tailed buck. Surrounding the slain deer were nine warriors, one with a smoking fusil.

They were variously dressed, some in leggings, some in buckskins, a few in breechcloths. Only two had trade guns; the rest were armed with traditional bows and lances and war clubs. Their style of hair, worn for the most part parted on the side with thick braids hanging just behind the ears, identified them as Blackfeet, the scourge of the northern plains and the Rockies.

Lightning had no doubt they were a war party on the prowl. The Blackfeet regularly patrolled their territory and were never kindly disposed toward those who had no business being there.

In a way the Kit Fox warrior admired them. They were one of the few tribes powerful enough and willing enough to resist the influx of whites and the wholesale slaughter of the game on which they depended for their very lives. If the Burning Hearts had been more like the Blackfeet, he mused, perhaps his wife and friends would not have been wiped out.

Not that sympathizing with the Blackfeet would do Lightning any good if they got their hands on him. They would kill him on sight. And while he wanted to die, he would not let them count coup on him. To do so would dishonor his wife's memory.

Lightning resolved to work his way around the ridge and give them a wide berth. Backing down the slope, he took the reins in hand and carefully led the bay lower. When he was positive the Blackfeet would not be able to hear, he swung up and trotted eastward. He did not give much thought to whether that was wise. If he had, he would have remembered that the Blackfeet heartland lay to the east.

On coming to the end of the ridge, Lightning slowed to a walk. Ahead lay a wide grassy strip, then a wider one of sparse trees. He had to keep his eyes peeled. If the war party spotted him, even though they were on foot and he was on horseback, they would give chase and try to bring him down.

Lightly tapping his heels, the Kit Fox warrior edged out past a projecting finger of rock. The grass was so high that he could not see the stream or the Blackfeet. He hoped that meant they couldn't see him, either.

Hugging the bay's broad back, Lightning made for the cottonwoods. He was glad he did not have any eagle feathers in his hair. The streaks of white were bound to give him away.

All went well until the Cheyenne warrior came to the middle of the grass. Then he was jolted to hear low voices to his left. Shifting, he beheld a line of seven more Blackfeet warriors at the very moment the leaders beheld him. Their reaction was to vent war whoops and spring forward. His was to goad the bay into a gallop and swing onto the off side so he would be less of a target.

An arrow cleaved the air inches above the bay. A fusil boomed, but evidently the shot missed the mark. The Blackfeet spread out, bounding after him like ravenous wolves after a stricken fawn. From the west came answering cries as the other half of the war party closed in from that direction.

Lightning was caught between the two. Lacking a rifle and a bow, he could not hope to pick any of them off from a distance. To fight them, he would have to get close enough to use the lance, and doing so would spell his doom, since he could never prevail against such overwhelming odds.

Another arrow clipped the bay's flying mane moments before the horse sped in among the trees. Lightning pulled himself up and lashed the reins. Behind him the Blackfeet were in full-throated uproar. He was not very worried, though. He had a more than adequate lead.

Lightning's confidence was shattered seconds later when he swept around a cluster of saplings and saw even more warriors in front of him. They were spread out in a half circle, their plan clearly being to cut him off.

Instantly the Kit Fox warrior reined to the left. A tree trunk took a lead ball meant for his head. Another deflected a barbed shaft. He ducked, weaved to the northeast, and promptly had to weave back again when several Blackfeet appeared ahead. It was as if they were sprouting up out of the ground. No matter which way he turned, there they were.

Lightning could hardly hear himself think for all the bloodthirsty whooping and hollering. He galloped between a pair of cottonwoods spaced so closely together that he scraped both legs. Angling sharply to the east, he made a beeline for the plain beyond. Once in the open he could give the bay its head and leave the war party far behind.

The Blackfeet had other ideas. From three directions they swooped toward him, as fleet as the deer they had slain, a shower of arrows preceding them.

A score of yards were all that remained and Lightning would be in the clear. Unexpectedly, a brawny Blackfoot darted into his path from the north. The warrior had a war club poised to strike. Lightning clasped the lance to his side, leaned forward, and speared the point into the man's chest above the heart. So forceful was the thrust that the tip sheared completely through the Blackfoot's body and jutted out his back.

The Blackfoot crumpled without a word. His weight dragged the end of the lance with him, nearly unhorsing Lightning. The Tsistsista tugged hard to pull the lance free, but it was wedged between ribs.

An arrow whizzed by Lightning's cheek, reminding him that he had no time to waste. Frowning, he let go of the lance and galloped on, his sole weapon now the long knife hanging at his hip.

The last of the trees appeared. Lightning glanced over a shoulder and saw the woods swarming with furious warriors. There were fifty if there was one. He should have known. Blackfeet war parties frequently numbered in the dozens. He faced forward and was confounded by the sight of two more blocking his escape. Apparently they had been off hunting small game. One held a pair of bloody rabbits. Both were as surprised as he was.

Lightning was on them before either could jump aside. He made no effort to slow down. At a full gallop he guided the bay into the man on the right even as he flicked his left foot out and caught the other Blackfoot full in the face. The two men went down, stunned.

The way open was before him. The perfect chance to

flee had presented itself, the very chance he had been waiting for.

Instead of taking it, Rakes the Sky with Lightning reined up in a flurry of flying grass and dirt. He was off the horse before it stopped moving. All too aware of the war party swarming through the woods toward him, he bent over the warrior he had run down.

The man had been armed with a fusil, which lay a few feet away. Lightning picked up the rifle, then hastily stripped off the Blackfoot's leather ammunition pouch and powder horn. The warrior groaned and feebly clutched at him, but Lightning swatted the arm aside, rose, and fled.

Arrows and lead cleaved the air like a swarm of riled hornets. Shafts thudded into the grass on all sides. Somehow Lightning reached the bay and vaulted up. A flick of the reins was all it took to spark the horse into resuming its flight.

The Blackfeet were beside themselves with indignation. Many kept on shooting long after the Kit Fox warrior was out of range. The fleetest chased after the bay for hundreds of yards before they gave up.

Soon Lightning gained the far side of the valley. On a knoll in plain sight of the Blackfeet he shook the fusil overhead and yipped in triumph to taunt them. Then, smiling broadly, he journeyed on to the south.

For a brief span Lightning had forgotten all about his wife and unborn child. For those precious moments he had been his old self again, fired with a zest for life and a thrill for combat. But it did not last. It could never last, not while she had gone on and he was still there.

The warrior thought of the fond memories he'd had of her while he had been under the influence of the firewater and he regretted not having more so he could relive those memories again.

An idea hit him. He patted his pouch and heard the coins Cleve had given him jingle.

Maybe.

Just maybe.

What harm could it do?

chapter

— 11 —

Someone had thrown Second Son into a deep hole. She could see the top high above her, a pinpoint of light that did not seem to get any closer even though she climbed and climbed and climbed. From the dark walls enclosing her issued low, grating growls. She recognized them. She had heard them when the creature with the blazing eyes attacked Wolf Sings on the Mountain and her.

The beast was hiding in the dark, biding its time, waiting for the right moment to reach out and slash her to ribbons.

Second Son climbed faster. She moved her arms and legs in a frenzy. Yet it proved futile. The pinpoint of light grew no larger.

The growling, though, became louder. The creature was drawing closer and closer. She looked around and thought she saw its glittering orbs fixed on her, thought she saw pale fangs and hooked claws. In a final, desperate effort she threw herself at the light, but she was too far down. She could not reach it. Her body plummeted back into the hole, falling end over end, over and over, until, with a jarring impact that shattered every bone in her body, she struck bottom.

And suddenly Second Son was wide-awake, staring up into a lake-blue sky. It took a moment for her sluggish senses to come to grips with the fact that she was bound hand and foot and trussed to a long pole being carried by two sturdy warriors. The growling she believed she had heard was actually their muted conversation, and that of their companions.

My son! was Second Son's next thought. She craned her neck to see in front and in back. Ahead limped the warrior she had kicked in the knee. Behind her were three more members of the band, one with a crudely bandaged shoulder, another with a bandaged chest who walked unsteadily, and a third man whose lips were split and puffy. In front of the last man shuffled Billy-Wolf, his head bent, his arms tied behind his back. As near as she could tell, he was unhurt except for prominent bruises.

"A Tsistsista warrior does not hang his head in the presence of his enemies," Second Son declared.

Billy-Wolf glanced up and beamed for joy. He had thought that his mother was severely wounded. She had been so limp and pale for so long that he had feared she was close to dying. "Ma! You're alive!"

"As are you," Second Son stressed, "and where there is life, my son, there is always hope."

At a bellow from the warrior in the lead, the procession halted. He stalked back and glared down at the warrior woman. A thick finger was jabbed into her face. He spoke gruffly, accenting his demand with a ringing slap to her face.

Second Son had been in agonizing pain from the moment she came around. Her head drummed to the beat of her pulse and it felt as if she had a lump the size of an eagle egg on the back of her head. The slap compounded her torment, lancing her with spikes of anguish that tore through her from head to toe. She gritted her teeth to keep from crying out. Under no circumstances would she give her enemies the satisfaction of seeing weakness.

"Ma!" Billy-Wolf cried.

The warrior with the injured knee hobbled over to the boy and gave him the same treatment. The blow rocked Billy-Wolf back on his heels. He nearly fell. Recovering, he emulated his mother's example, clenched his teeth, and glared.

The trek was resumed.

Second Son closed her eyes and waged an internal war to suppress her pain. In a short while she had herself enough under control to take stock. The first thing she noticed was that Snip was missing. She remembered the dog being hit by a war club during the battle, and feared the worst. Now she understood her son's sorrow. Their captors would pay dearly. She made herself a promise that if she ever got the chance, she would wreak vengeance on the one who had slain the loyal dog.

Next Second Son studied the warriors. She had never encountered their like in any of her many travels.

They were all tall, which in itself was unique. Every man had a tattooed face. Their hair was long, parted in the middle, and tied at the back to form a flowing tail. Their garments were like buckskin but not buckskin; she did not know what they were made of. Oddly, the shirts fell to a point below the waist in front and in back.

Every man wore a knife sporting an antler hilt. Most had short axes with copper blades. The exception was the brawny warrior with the war club. All of them had slung quivers containing long bows made from birch. Their arrows had three feathers fastened with sinew. Among them had been distributed her own and Billy-Wolf's weapons. The leader held the Hawken as if it were a delicate flower that would break if dropped.

Their language was a mystery. Second Son listened but could not make any sense of their jabber. Not a single word was familiar. She wondered if they knew sign language.

Before long the party came to a clearing and halted. A whinny fell on Second Son's ears and she twisted to find Shadow, Blaze, and the sorrel tied to stakes. The warrior whose lips had been split untied the three horses and looped a lead rope over the head of each. Soon they were under way again, the animals at the rear.

Their line of travel, Second Son noticed, was due north. She also observed that the warriors acted nervous. Frequently they cast anxious glances into the forest, and the slightest unusual noise was cause for them to halt and listen until they were convinced it was safe to go on.

The only explanation Second Son could think of was that the war party was passing through the territory of another tribe and did not want to be caught. She had to admire their wariness. It was no wonder they had been able to shadow her for half a day without her catching on. They had honed the ability to move stealthily to an art.

The sun hung high in the afternoon sky. Second Son caught Billy-Wolf looking at her and smiled encouragement. She had meant what she said about having hope. So long as she was alive, she would never submit.

The thin leather cord binding Second Son's wrists and ankles chafed her skin terribly as time went on. Her ankles began to bleed. She tried many times to shift her weight to relieve the torment, in vain.

Toward sundown the warriors picked up the pace and made for a rugged mountain to the northeast. Second Son suspected that they wanted to reach a specific spot before night fell. As twilight spread over the countryside, they came to a ravine. Up it lay a shallow cave at the base of a smooth cliff. From the charred bits of wood lying near the left-hand wall, Second Son gathered that the war party or hunting party or whatever it was had stopped there before.

A small oval spring provided ample water. The warriors all drank, then permitted Billy-Wolf to quench his thirst. Second Son they ignored. She was dumped at the back and left there, tied to a pole. None of the warriors spoke to her. None brought her any of her own jerky, which they passed among themselves. She was treated as if she did not exist.

Billy-Wolf was angry. They had untied his hands so he could eat, but he felt no gratitude. He caught the leader's attention, motioned at his mother, and gestured to show he wanted to give her some of his own jerky. The leader's curt response needed no translation. Billy-Wolf decided that if they refused to give her food, then he would not eat, either. He cast the jerky to the cave floor.

The leader did not like that. He stalked over, favoring his bad knee, and clenched his fists as if to strike. Then a strange thing happened. One of the others made a comment that prompted the irate leader to stare at the Hawken, which he had leaned against the wall near the fire. Slowly his anger melted away and his fingers uncurled.

Billy-Wolf did not know what to make of it. He was flabbergasted when the man picked up the jerky, gave it back to him, and indicated he could take the piece to his mother.

Second Son was likewise mystified. The faces of the rest of the men were inscrutable, but it was not hard to see that they attached special significance to the rifle. She gratefully took a bite when her son stepped to her side and held the jerky to her mouth.

"How are you holding up, Ma?"

The concern in Billy-Wolf's eyes touched Second Son deeply. "I am fine," she answered. Which was true to a degree. The headache and her chafed limbs were trifles. No true warrior would give them a second thought. "How are you?"

"All they did was cuff me around some," Billy-Wolf answered. "Then they took all my weapons and trussed me up." He bent lower to whisper, "But they're not as smart as they think they are. They didn't get everything."

Before Second Son could learn more, the warrior whose lips were swollen as thick as his thumbs turned to them and growled a few words while raising a finger to those swollen lips. His meaning was transparent. No talking.

In silence, Second Son ate the rest of the jerky. She smiled up at her son when she was done. He gave her a sly wink and grinned as he returned to where the warriors wanted him to sit. His expression reminded her of when he had been a little boy, and he would dash up to her all excited about something he could not wait to tell her.

Their captors huddled around the fire. The constant buzz of their low voices filled the cave.

Second Son saw one of them go to the horses and run a hand over Shadow's back and sides. She thought that he was merely admiring the mare. But then he began lightly pinching Shadow's flanks and belly as if gauging how much meat the animal packed on its sturdy frame. Second Son became alarmed. It occurred to her that the warriors might be from a tribe that routinely ate horseflesh, as the Apaches were reputed to do.

The warrior woman was glad when the man gave Shadow a final pat and walked back to the fire. He pointed at the horse and made a remark that sparked a general discussion. Once again she tried to understand them but could not. Catching her son's eye, she silently mouthed, "Sign language," and nodded at the tattooed warriors.

At first Billy-Wolf did not know what she was trying to tell him. He formed his lips as she was forming hers but could not decide if she was using English or the Cheyenne tongue. And her repeated nods at their captors only confused him further. He shrugged to show her that he was at a loss.

Thwarted, Second Son tried something else. She wriggled her fingers, then nodded at the warriors. It was the best she could do with her wrists tied so tight.

Billy-Wolf was upset with himself. He wriggled his fingers but still failed to comprehend. He glanced at the warriors, who were jabbering away in their alien language. One of them happened to gesture, and in a burst of insight Billy-Wolf divined his mother's request. Clearing his throat, he said loudly in English, "Hey, you there. The ugly one with the bad knee."

The warriors fell quiet and turned their attention on the boy.

"Do you savvy sign language?" Billy-Wolf slowly asked. At the same time he posed the question in sign.

First Billy-Wolf held his right hand up, palm outward, at shoulder height with the fingers and thumb extended. A wag of the hand signified the word "question." Next he pointed at the leader, then held his left hand flat with the back up and brushed the tops of his fingers with the fingers of his right hand. Reversing that motion, he held his right hand close to his mouth with the nail of his index finger pressed against the thumb and moved the hand forward while snapping the finger outward. Lowering his arms, he waited for a reply.

None was forthcoming. The warriors exchanged perplexed looks and regarded the boy as if he might not be in his right mind.

"I reckon not," Billy-Wolf said softly to himself. "Too bad."

Second Son was equally disappointed. With no way to communicate, their hardships were bound to be compounded. It was not much of a surprise to learn the warriors were ignorant of sign since she had met other tribes to whom it was unknown during her visit to California and her trek along the Columbia River.

On the prairie and in the Rocky Mountains it was another story. Every tribe from the Comanches in the south to the Bloods and Piegans in the north was familiar with hand language. If a Tsistsista met a Crow or an Arapaho, or a Lakota met a Pawnee or a Mandan, they could always make their thoughts known, even though their spoken tongues were so unlike.

Second Son leaned her head back and resigned herself to a long night. She could do nothing but lie there when two of the warriors made her son move over by the back wall and tied him again.

A guard was posted at the entrance. The rest stayed up telling tales until late. When one was ready to sleep, he curled up where he sat and drifted off.

After a while the only sounds were the crackling of the low flames, the popping of embers, and the loud snoring of the leader and the man with the hurt mouth.

Sleep eluded the warrior woman even though she was exhausted. She tried but her nerves would not let her. For hours she lay and stared at the smooth stone ceiling. She hated to think that so soon after mending fences with her son, they stood a very real risk of being separated or slain.

In due course her fatigue asserted itself. One moment Second Son was thinking about Cleve, the next she was sound asleep. She slept fitfully, tossing and turning as horrid images racked her brain.

The scuffle of soles on the floor brought Second Son back to the realm of the living. One of the warriors was awake, busy rekindling the fire. She tried to rise onto an elbow and winced as her arms and legs flared with prickling agony. The circulation had been cut off for so long that she could hardly feel them.

Refusing to give in, Second Son shifted her body closer to the wall, dragging the pole with her, and managed to swing her torso high enough to lean against it for support. The simple effort left her gasping.

Soon Billy-Wolf sat up. Having slept so little during their ordeal in the gully, and having been driven to the brink of collapse during their long march, he had enjoyed a good night's sleep and was well rested. The first thing he did was look for his mother and smile to show her everything would be all right. Her answering smile was feeble, and she was paler than he could ever recall seeing her. Billy-Wolf feared that her head was worse than she was letting on. It would be just like her to suffer in silence.

Second Son tugged at her bonds, trying to loosen them enough so her blood would flow freely again. Her fingers and toes tingled so badly that they hurt. She was beginning to gain a little slack in the cord around her wrists when a shadow fell across her and she glanced up into the spiteful eyes of the warrior she had kicked in the knee.

The leader was not in the best of tempers. He grabbed her left wrist and shook her violently, then slapped her hands and threw her down.

Billy-Wolf pushed upright, swayed, then caught himself.

He started to hop around the fire. "Leave her alone, damn you!" he demanded. "Keep your hands to yourself!"

Another warrior reached out almost casually and caught hold of the boy's legs.

The next moment Billy-Wolf pitched forward. His elbows and knees bore the brunt of the fall. He saw the leader kick his mother. Shrugging off the pain, he raised up high enough to jab his hands at the leader and say, "So help me God, mister, I'm going to kill you before this is done."

The man with the hurt knee limped toward him and this time might have struck him had not one of the others cried out. Four of the warriors were gathered around the sixth man, who had not yet woke up. One of them shook him gently, but the sleeper did not open his eyes. The leader eased to the floor, then pressed a hand to the prone man's neck.

Second Son recognized the one who would not awaken. It was the man she had stabbed. His bandage was stained red with dried blood and a few scarlet drops had dried under his nose. When the other five turned glowering faces in her direction, she knew the man had died during the night.

The skinniest of the warriors snapped a few words at her and started to rise while drawing his copper knife. The leader stopped him from coming any nearer. But if looks could kill, Second Son would not have lived another moment.

Unnoticed, Billy-Wolf had crawled close to his mother so he could defend her if she were attacked. He placed his bound hands close to the top edge of his wide belt, to the right of the buckle, and idly slipped the tips of his fingers underneath to touch his ace in the hole, the knife his father had given him.

The warriors held a council. Presently three of them

went off down the ravine. When they came back they carried enough poles and branches to construct a travois. While they worked, the other two wrapped the body in a blanket and performed a ritual over it.

Second Son and Billy-Wolf were left alone. The boy leaned to the left, and when their shoulders bumped, he whispered, "I don't want you to worry, Ma. I'm going to get us out of this fix. You wait and see."

"Do nothing which will arouse their wrath," the warrior woman cautioned.

"So long as they keep their paws off you, I won't start anything," Billy-Wolf promised. A quick check revealed that none of their captors were staring at them. He patted the belt and went on. "When the right time comes, I'll cut you free and we'll light a shuck for the deep timber." Billy-Wolf smirked and answered the question her eyes conveyed. "I still have Pa's folding knife."

The news cheered Second Son immensely. "If they ever leave us alone, waste no time using it."

Once the ritual had been completed, the leader and the other warriors carried their slain fellow out of the cave and deposited him near where the travois was being fashioned. In half an hour the work was done. The warriors then dragged the travois over behind Blaze and attempted to lash it to the paint.

Billy-Wolf snickered. Blaze had never hauled a travois in his life and was bound to act up. He nearly laughed aloud when his horse gave a mighty shake and the two warriors stumbled back. One tried again to raise a pole to Blaze's back and had to spring aside or be bitten.

But the boy's mirth changed to horror when the man reached for his short ax. "No!" he cried. "Don't hurt him! Tie the travois to the mare!" He wagged his arms at Shadow. "The mare!"

A brief argument broke out. The leader decided the issue by going up to Shadow and slapping her on the rump. Presently the travois was attached and the dead man had been tied down.

Camp was quickly broken. The fire was extinguished.

Second Son did not like the thought of having to spend another day dangling from the pole. So she was pleasantly surprised when her feet were untied and a warrior indicated that she should walk. Curling her legs, she endeavored to stand but got no further than her knees when her numb legs gave out on her and she fell onto her side.

Impatient to be off, the warrior prodded her with a toe.

"Can't you see she's trying, you polecat?" Billy-Wolf growled. His own ankles had also been freed and he was walking in small circles to restore the flow of blood.

The leader entered. Without ceremony, he stepped to Second Son, hauled her erect, and shoved her toward the opening. She staggered wildly. Her feet felt as if they were still bound. Contriving to land on her knees, she reached behind her and rubbed her calves. She forgot about the leader for the moment, so she was caught off guard when his hard hands gripped her from behind, yanked her upright, and pushed.

Once again Second Son's legs were unable to bear her full weight. She took three swift faltering steps and collapsed. The skinny warrior who had wanted to stab her laughed.

Out of the corner of her eye she saw the leader coming toward her for a third time and also saw Billy-Wolf crouch as if to throw himself at her tormentor. To keep her son from making a mistake they would both regret, she steeled her will and straightened.

It took all the strength Second Son could muster, but she stood under her own power. The leader blinked, then nodded, grunted, and gestured for her to follow three warriors who had already headed out. She complied, haltingly at first.

Every step made her stronger. Each additional stride pumped more blood into her limbs. Soon she could walk without fear of tripping over her own feet.

Billy-Wolf wanted to be close to his mother, but he was ushered to the back of the line, second to last, as he had been the day before. He walked ahead of the warrior leading Shadow but behind the one leading Blaze and the packhorse. It occurred to him that he could jump up on Blaze before any of their captors were the wiser, tear the lead rope loose, and escape to the forest. But if he did, he would have to leave his mother behind, and that he would never do.

At the mouth of the ravine the leader turned to the north. He had looped a leather cord around the Hawken and slung the rifle across his back.

Second Son never stopped trying to loosen her wrists. Staring at the foreboding slopes that loomed before them, she could not help but wonder where they were headed. Even more important was the crucial question: What would happen to them when they got there?

chapter

—— 12 ——

Rakes the Sky with Lightning regarded with amusement the fusil resting across his muscular thighs. Just days ago he had told Yellow Hair that he never intended to use the white man's weapon, yet here he was with one.

He'd had no choice but to take it. The other Blackfoot had been armed with a club, and the Kit Fox warrior needed a weapon that could kill at long range if he was to make the journey to Fort Hall and back safely.

The rifle was different from the ones Yellow Hair and Wolf Sings on the Mountain carried. Where theirs was heavy, this one was quite light and easy to wield. The barrel was shorter than that of a Hawken. The wood was very plain.

Lightning liked the smoothness of the stock and the cool feel of the metal barrel. He had been told that a fusil could drop a buffalo with a single shot and he was eager to try the gun out.

Of special interest was a brass side plate in the shape of a twisted animal. Lightning could not decide if the creature depicted was a snake or a spirit beast. The scales were huge, the head more like that of a horse than a serpent. Whatever the case, he couldn't stop rubbing his fingers over the figure.

About the middle of the morning Lightning was unable to contain his curiosity any longer. On a hill he reined up and slid off the bay. He had seen Yellow Hair and Wolf Sings on the Mountain shoot their guns so many times that he was confident he could fire the fusil.

He was about to uncap the powder horn when it struck him that the rifle might already be loaded. There was only one way to find out. Thumbing back the hammer, he placed the stock against his shoulder as he had seen Yellow Hair do and slipped his finger through the wide trigger guard.

Now all he needed was a target. Lightning surveyed the adjacent slopes but saw no game worthy of the name. A warrior did not shoot sparrows. Finally he settled on the scarred stump of a tree close to the bottom of the hill on which he stood.

Lightning pointed the barrel as he had always seen Yellow Hair do. The gun seemed to be lined up properly, but he had the nagging feeling that he was doing something wrong. Then he recalled the time many winters ago when he had watched Yellow Hair teach his cousin how to shoot. Yellow Hair had tapped the tiny bead of metal at the end of the barrel and told his cousin that it must always be fixed on the target.

Lightning did so now. He tingled with excitement as he

took a deep breath, which Yellow Hair always did, although Lightning had no idea why, and jerked on the trigger.

It was as if Lightning's shoulder were kicked by a horse. There was a tremendous blast and a cloud of smoke belched from the muzzle, which swept upward and nearly hit him in the forehead. Simultaneously, the stock slammed backward so hard that it turned him half around.

Lightning gaped at the fusil in awe. To think that such power was at his command! All the times he had seen a rifle used, and he had never realized! No wonder so many Indians favored them instead of bows.

The choking cloud of smoke shrouded his head. Lightning coughed and swatted at the acrid tendrils, then strode down the hill to see if he had hit the tree. Hunt though he might, he could not find a hole. He had tried his best but missed.

Climbing back to the top, Lightning pondered what had gone wrong. For one thing, he knew that he had held the fusil too loosely. A firm grip was needed so the barrel would not buck. His other mistake, he suspected, was in jerking on the trigger. Yellow Hair always squeezed gently.

Another test was called for. Lightning uncapped the powder horn, held his left hand under it, and hesitated. How much black powder was he supposed to use? Yellow Hair was an expert and could measure the exact amount at a glance. Unfortunately, the warrior had never paid much attention to how much that was.

Lightning did know that if a man used too much powder, the rifle might burst. So to be on the safe side, he poured about enough to fill an acorn shell down the barrel. From the ammo pouch he took a ball and patch. The former he wrapped in the latter. Then, employing the ramrod housed under the barrel, he gently tapped the ball down until it could go no farther.

Lightning was excited. This time he would do it right. He aimed most carefully, wedged the stock tight, held his breath, and gently applied pressure to the trigger.

There was a blast, but not as loud as before. There was smoke, but nowhere near as much. And, to the Kit Fox warrior's consternation, the lead ball flew about four strides and plopped to the earth like a stricken bird.

Walking over, Lightning stared at the ball in baffled irritation. He had not added enough black powder. The tree was five times as far as the ball had traveled. That must mean, he reasoned, five times as much powder had to be added.

Which is what he did. Quickly, because he was eager to get done and be on his way, he rammed the ball and patch down, then went through the motions of aiming. He was confident that this time he had done everything perfectly. Smiling from ear to ear, he fired.

At the thunderous retort, the fusil smashed against him with so much force that Lightning teetered backward, tripped over a clump of grass, and landed on his backside. So much smoke choked the air above him that when he breathed in, he thought his lungs had been seared by fire.

It reminded him of that awful day when the Burning Hearts had been massacred. It brought to mind the nightmare he had endured when he had been caught in the midst of the raging prairie fire ignited when the village had been set aflame. Unconsciously, Lightning placed a hand on the scarred half of his face and shuddered.

Coughing and sputtering, the Kit Fox warrior regained his composure, leaped to his feet, and hustled toward the bay. He'd had enough of target practice for one day. Maybe for all time. How anyone could shoot a fusil properly was beyond him. He had been right all along.

Guns were for white men.

• • •

High in the Canadian Rockies reared a tableland luxuriant with plant growth. It was ringed by ragged peaks sheathed by drifting clouds. Thick forest covered the steep bordering slopes.

At the east end of the tableland rippled an icy mountain lake that fed into a swiftly flowing river. As Second Son and Billy-Wolf were ushered along a well-worn trail toward the lakeshore, they spotted structures and figures.

It was the third day of their captivity. Since dawn the warriors had grown increasingly animated, leading the warrior woman to deduce that their village was near. An hour ago they had come on the trail, which bore countless footprints.

Billy-Wolf fought to conceal his apprehension. He'd heard many a story about tortures inflicted by the Blackfeet and Sioux and others, and he did not relish the notion of suffering the same. Taking inspiration from his mother, he put on a brave front, his head held high, his chin jutting in defiance. When his time came, he would try his utmost to die as his pa was always telling him a man should.

An odd fact impressed Billy-Wolf as they neared the dwellings. If this had been a Burning Heart village, he would have heard the sounds of girls laughing, of boys playing, of women singing and men chanting. But not here. Not a single laugh wafted on the breeze. Not a single woman so much as hummed. An unnerving pall of deathly silence hung over the village.

Second Son studied the encampment closely. She was very curious to learn what sort of people her captors were. It would give her a clue about the treatment she could expect.

The lodges were much like those of the Tsistsistas. Frameworks of poles had been arranged in circles and each tied at the top. Then huge hide covers were draped around the frames. The skins were from an animal about the size of an elk but otherwise different. Second Son guessed that as many as sixty hides or more went into the making of a single cover. She noticed smoke holes at the tops of the lodges, just as there were on Cheyenne tipis. Here and there stood tripods from which hung large bags.

The people of the village were busy at various tasks. Some cleaned hides. Others were hanging hides on racks to dry in the sun. One person was busy stretching beaver pelts over small wooden frames. Near the lake some were sewing strips of birchbark together and covering the seams with hot pine pitch mixed with animal fat. A few young boys were making bows and arrows.

Second Son was about to enter the village when a striking fact became evident. Other than the boys, the ones doing work were *women*. She saw warriors talking, warriors playing a game with small chips of wood, and warriors lounging about with nothing better to do. But every single female, from the very youngest to the oldest, toiled at some labor.

None of the women or girls stopped work to greet the new arrivals. Several looked up. That was all. The majority went on about their business as if acquiring captives were of no interest whatsoever. With one notable exception.

Second Son saw a young girl glance at her. She saw curiosity light the child's eyes and the girl rose to come over. A harsh word from an older woman, her mother perhaps, stopped her, and with a sideways glance at several nearby men, the girl hastily went back to work on the hide she was scraping.

The party halted as warriors came from all directions. Every last warrior in the village gathered to welcome them. But the welcome quickly turned sour, thanks to one man.

Second Son noticed him immediately. He came out of a lodge and stared with cold dark eyes at her, at her son, at the horses, and finally at the warriors who had taken them captive. Last of all his stern gaze alighted on the travois and his features became as hard as flint.

He came toward them. Of all the warriors, he was the largest. Broad of shoulder and slender of hip, he carried himself with an air of authority. His knife was bigger than any man's there. His ax sparkled in the bright sunlight. As he approached, warriors saw him and moved out of his way, opening a path.

The hubbub of voices died. All eyes were fixed on the newcomer.

The warrior with the injured knee, the same one who had led the returning band and shoved Second Son around at his whim, now visibly tensed and treated the newcomer with obvious deference. Bowing his head, he said, "Mattonabee."

Second Son found the chief's eyes fixed on her. She saw no warmth there, no friendliness. If anything, there was hostility and thinly veiled contempt.

"Takwugan," Mattonabee responded, then growled a series of questions that Takwugan dutifully answered. Other queries were addressed to the men who had accompanied Takwugan.

Billy-Wolf found himself the object of the chief's attention. It made his gut churn, but he didn't flinch. He had a very bad feeling about what might happen next; he'd seen how the man had looked at his mother.

Mattonabee walked to the travois and unraveled the blanket sufficiently to see the face of the dead warrior. He rested a hand on the man's shoulder, intoned solemn words, then suddenly stepped right up to Second Son.

The warrior woman held her ground. She met his gaze, refusing to be cowed as were his own people.

Touching his wide chest, the chief said, "Mattonabee. Chipewyan." He pointed at her and arched his eyebrows.

She understood instantly and replied in her own tongue. "Second Son. Tsistsista."

"Tsistsista?" Mattonabee repeated. He examined her from head to toe. His right hand plucked at the fringe on her buckskin shirt, then at her hair, then, without warning, lowered to her left breast and cupped it.

For a heartbeat Second Son was riveted by commingled shock and outrage. No man was permitted to touch her there except Cleve. Twice white men had taken liberties with her; one she had gutted, the other she had relieved of his manhood. Other than the drunken trappers who had tried to rape her at the rendezvous, no man had ever laid a hand on her with impunity.

This time would be no different.

Second Son could not use her arms since they were bound behind her. She jerked away from the chief's hand, then stepped in close and arced her knee at his groin. At the last instant Mattonabee shifted. His inner thigh bore the impact. She pivoted and was going to kick him in the knee when two Chipewyans leaped to their leader's aid and seized her.

Second Son desisted. But the look she gave Mattonabee left no doubt as to what she would do if he tried to touch her again. Most of the warriors appeared astonished at her temerity. Strangely, the chief himself was not flustered in the least. He merely grunted and faced Takwugan.

A long talk ensued. Second Son was released, but the two brawny men stood ready to grab her again if she acted up. She took the time to compose herself. Anger had no place in a warrior's heart in the heat of combat. It made a warrior careless.

Second Son took her mind off the outrage by surveying

the village again. She noted that it was smaller than it had first appeared, with less than a dozen lodges. There were only fifteen warriors, counting Takwugan and his party, and nine women. Boys and girls together totaled seven in all.

The numbers did not seem quite right. There should be at least as many women as men, and more young ones.

Suddenly a commotion broke out. Another warrior had shown up, a young man whose lean frame was covered by tattered pants and nothing else. He was virtually skin and bones. His hair hung in grimy strands. His bare chest was covered with scratch marks, as if he had wandered through a thicket and been slashed by countless thorns. His naked feet were filthy and bore many scars. He moved with a listless step, as if he were only half-awake. Going up to another Chipewyan, he appeared to ask a question. When the first man responded, the young warrior moved on to the next, and then the next, and on around the ring until he stood before the chief. Mattonabee's reply was curt.

Second Son stood firm as the flesh-and-blood apparition faced her. He posed the same query, his dilated eyes boring into hers in mute appeal. Having no knowledge of his tongue, all she could do was shake her head.

The young warrior shuffled to Billy-Wolf and asked him. The boy had never beheld such a sorry specimen of humanity. "I don't speak your language," he said in English. "I can't help you."

Uttering a pathetic groan, the young warrior moved off toward the lake, mumbling to himself. He sat down cross-legged close to the water and launched into a singsong chant while rocking back and forth.

Billy-Wolf felt sorry for the man, but there was nothing he could do. He had his own problems. At a word from the chief, four warriors surrounded his mother and him and ushered them toward a small lodge on the north side of the village. The flap was pulled back and they were shoved inside.

Second Son was pushed so hard that she fell to her knees. She twisted to glare at the warrior responsible. He merely laughed.

When the flap closed, the lodge was plunged in gloom. Enough light filtered in through the smoke hole for the warrior woman to discover that the floor had been covered with soft hides. Near the back the cover had been partly pulled back, exposing a bed of boughs. Lining the sides were someone's personal possessions: a folded shirt, several large skin bags, a robe, and a big copper spoon.

Billy-Wolf stepped to the flap and listened. Footsteps receded as the warriors departed. Scooting to his mother, he declared in a whisper, "Now's our chance, Ma! I'll cut us both loose and we can get out of here!"

"Shhhh," Second Son said, and gave a toss of her head toward the entrance.

The boy did not understand until the flap snapped open and a tattooed visage regarded them with suspicion. When the warrior was satisfied that they were not up to anything, he stepped back and lowered the flap.

"Did you think they would not post a guard?" Second Son asked her offspring. "Even if we slipped past him, in the middle of the day we would not get far before one of the others spotted us. We must wait for a better chance."

Billy-Wolf could not conceal his disappointment. "I just want to get out of here before we come to harm." He meant to say before *she* came to harm but changed his mind at the last moment. Taking a sniff, he commented, "This lodge is sort of musty. I don't think anyone has lived here in a while."

"No," Second Son agreed.

"Did I hear right? Are these people called Chipewyans?"

Second Son nodded while rubbing her wrists from side to side. The cord was beginning to slacken. Not enough for her to slip loose if she wanted, but enough to encourage her to keep trying.

"Have you ever heard of them?"

"No. But there are many tribes I do not know. A trapper at Fort Hall told your father and me that more tribes live in this north land than live on the prairie where we come from. Very little is known about them. The Tsistsistas never travel this far north. And these tribes have had few dealings with white men."

"What do you think they'll do to our horses?"

Second Son had been wondering the same thing. The chief had been particularly interested in the animals. And it had bothered her to see that there were no other horses anywhere in the village. These people evidently had no use for them, which made them expendable. She did not like to think that her mare would end its days in a stew pot.

Billy-Wolf ran a hand over the hides on which they sat. "What kind of skins are these? They're not deer or antelope, and they're sure not buffalo or bear."

"They come from an animal I have never killed."

The boy rose and moved around the perimeter, seeking a crack at the bottom through which he could look out. There was none. The lodge was well constructed, the hide covering thick. He guessed that was to keep out the winter cold.

Second Son moved closer to the wall and leaned back. She'd had hardly any sleep in days, and she was sore, bruised, and famished. Her thoughts strayed yet again to Cleve. She wondered what he was doing at that very moment. Chopping more trees? Building his stable? Or had he started on the corral? A mental picture of him swinging his big ax, his long golden hair shimmering in the sunlight, his muscular form moving in graceful rhythm, was enough to soothe her and perk the corners of her mouth.

Billy-Wolf took to pacing. The gnawing suspense of not knowing what their captors planned made him restless. He resisted an urge to pull out the folding knife and cut his hands free.

Needing something to do, Billy-Wolf went over and sat down next to his mother. "I want you to know something, Ma."

The warrior woman looked at him.

"No matter what happens to us, I want you to know that I love you with all my heart." Billy-Wolf paused. "You might not have noticed, but I was a bit nervous around you after you came back from California. I'm over that now. These past few weeks have taught me that you're the same woman you always were."

Second Son was all interest. "You did not think I was?"

Billy-Wolf did not respond right away. He needed to find the right words to express how he had felt so she would not misunderstand. "When Pa and you left, I was still pretty much a boy." She grinned, so he quickly amended his comment. "By that I mean that I never gave much thought to you being anything other than my mother."

"What else would I be?"

Embarrassment crept over Billy-Wolf. "I don't rightly know quite how to put this. But when you came back, it was like you were a whole new person. I saw you more as a warrior and a woman than I did my mother. That probably doesn't make much sense, but that's how I felt."

Second Son tried to remember how old she had been when she ceased regarding her parents through the eyes of a child.

"Every time I was around you I felt awkward," Billy-

Wolf went on. "I know that it was silly. But I didn't think I could measure up in your eyes."

"Measure how?"

"As a warrior. As a person." Billy-Wolf was more serious than she had ever seen him. "With Pa it's easy. He takes everybody as they come. But you don't open up to just anyone. You take a person's measure, and if you like what you see, then you're their friend for life." He shrugged. "I was sort of afraid that I wouldn't measure up. That you'd think less of me because I'm not just like you."

It was true. Every word. Second Son did judge others by their character. "Heed my words, Wolf Sings on the Mountain. You are my son. You measure up, as you call it, just by being you."

Billy-Wolf was going to say something, but at that juncture the flap was flung wide and into the lodge came the very last person Second Son ever expected to see in a Chipewyan village.

Fort Hall stood at the junction of the Snake and Portenuf rivers. Originally built by fur trader Nathaniel Wyeth, it later came under the ownership of the Hudson's Bay Company. Over a dozen company men manned the post at any given time.

Rakes the Sky with Lightning had visited the fort on several occasions with Yellow Hair. He knew the white man in charge, Courtney Walker. At a trot he wound down from the hills toward the sandy plain on which the outpost stood.

As usual, friendly Indians were encamped nearby. Lightning counted ten Flathead lodges near the Snake River and spied a sizable Shoshoni village strung along the Portenuf.

Sitting tall on the bay, the Kit Fox warrior slowly neared the gate. Although he was on friendly terms with the trappers and traders, he would not take a warm reception for granted. Ever since the massacre, he found it hard to trust any whites except Yellow Hair.

Cleve had told Lightning that the fort originally had been constructed from cottonwood trees set on end and sunk two and a half feet into the ground to form a stockade eighty feet square. Two bastions at opposite angles were put up to serve as sentry towers.

Later, when the Hudson's Bay Company took over, the log stockade had been torn down and replaced by the current adobe walls. Lightning did not see why the whites had made the change. What difference did it make if their oversized lodge was made of wood or dry mud?

A guard at the corner bastion noted the warrior's advent onto the scene with a stoic nod.

Lightning returned the gesture. He could feel the man's eyes on his back as he came to the gate and reined up. Within, all was quiet. Flatheads and Shoshonis mingled with company men, trading pelts, bartering for goods, or swapping stories. He became an object of interest when he entered, but everyone went about their business as soon as they marked him as friendly.

At a rail held up by two short posts Lightning halted. Other horses were tied there, so he dismounted, looped the reins, then opened one of his parfleches and rummaged for the pouch containing Yellow Hair's coins and the large empty bag.

The interior of the trading post was dark and smelled of scents foreign to the Kit Fox warrior. Since not much business was being transacted indoors, only two other men were present. One was the portly bald man who operated the store. The other was a grizzled trapper with a leather patch over one eye. They had been talking but hushed on seeing him enter. The white man with the patch moved aside so he could approach the counter.

"Hello there, chief," said the portly one in the peculiar clipped accent some of the Hudson's Bay men had. "Andrew Blevitt, at your service." Wiping a sweaty palm on his greasy wool shirt, he leaned on a pudgy elbow and regarded the warrior with a twinkle in his beady eyes. "What can I do for you today?"

Lightning gazed around the store, seeking nails.

"Speak English, buck?" Blevitt asked sarcastically. "Or are you another heathen who is as du—"

The trapper with the eye patch had been studying the Tsistsista closely. Suddenly he leaned over and smacked the trader's arm. "Here now, Andy! What the hell is the matter with you? Where are your manners? Don't you recognize Cleve Bennett's kin, Rakes-somethin'-or-other?"

Blevitt's twinkle faded. "Bennett's kin?" he repeated, then his eyes widened and he blurted, "Oh, damn. I didn't realize, Rakes. It's been months since you were in here last. No hard feelings, eh? I know how close Mr. Walker and Bennett are."

Lightning had never understood why so many white men saw fit to jabber like chipmunks half the time. He set the pouch on the counter and announced in his best English, "Yellow Hair sent me for nails."

"Nails, is it?" the trader said, gesturing behind him at a cabinet containing tiny drawers. "Well, what kind would your kinsman be interested in? Two-penny? Four-penny? Six? You name it, Andrew Blevitt has it."

The warrior was glad that Cleve had thought to include one with the coins. Opening the pouch, he held it up. "Like this."

"Eight-penny nails?" Blevitt said. "What's that crazy Yank doing, then? Building himself a fort of his own?"

"No. A cabin."

The trader glanced at the trapper and rolled his eyes, then turned to the drawers and opened one. "How many does he need?"

Lightning put the empty leather bag down. "He wants this filled."

"That's an awful bleeding lot," Blevitt said. "He does know that my policy is cash on the barrel or the equivalent in trade? I'm not a charity for every Yank trapper down on his luck, you know." He extended a hand and rubbed his forefinger and thumb together. "What that means in the King's basic English is that you had better have money or you get no nails."

The warrior was taking a strong dislike to the portly chatterbox. Upending the pouch over his palm, he caught the three yellow coins Cleve had sent with him. He took note when the trader stiffened and gawked. "Yellow Hair told me these are enough for the nails and other things he wants."

"Are they what I think they are?" Blevitt said. He went to take one but stopped. "May I, Rakes?"

The warrior nodded. He was astounded when the white man took a coin and bit down on the edge as if it were food to be eaten. The gleam returned to the trader's eyes, only now it was brighter, almost sinister.

"I'll be damned. Real damned gold. Where did·a bloke like Bennett get his hands on these?"

The Kit Fox warrior elected not to answer. He knew that Cleve had accumulated a parfleche full of such coins before leaving for California. Most were hidden somewhere back in Tsistsista country. Second Son once told Lightning that they had received them for beaver pelts. She had also warned him not to tell any whites, for they would kill to get their hands on the yellow metal.

Pulling the list from the pouch, Lightning gave it to the trader. "How long will it take you?"

Blevitt consulted the list. "Let's see. Powder, lead, some cloth, and odds and ends. I reckon I can have this all set to go inside an hour." He picked up the coins. "These are more than enough to pay for everything. Hey! That gives me an idea. Instead of making change, why don't I give you goods to make up the difference?" Stepping to a pile of neatly folded blankets, he rambled on, "How about all the Point blankets you can carry? No? Then what would you say to a shiny new ax with a steel head, or maybe a new butcher knife?"

"Just the nails and those things," Lightning said, indicating the list.

"Have a heart, Rakes?" Blevitt practically pleaded. "There must be something here you'd like?"

Lightning shook his head and was about to leave when his gaze fell on a row of silver flasks on a shelf to the right of the counter. A row of wooden kegs sat on a bench below them. He did not need to be told what those kegs contained. It brought to mind the pleasant memories that had flooded through him the night Yellow Hair persuaded him to drink until his head hurt. For a moment he hesitated, debating. Then he made for the door.

Halfway there, the warrior paused. "Where can I find Courtney Walker?" he asked.

Blevitt had been fondling the coins. He glanced up and licked his thick lips. "Why do you want to know?"

"Yellow Hair wants me to say hello for him."

"Oh? Is that all?" The trader chuckled. "Well, you're out of luck. Walker went to the coast, to Fort Vancouver. He won't be back for another week or two yet, I'm afraid." Blevitt went back to fingering the coins, absently adding, "Will there be anything else?"

"Yes," Lightning said, and waited until the man raised his sweaty head. "I am not a chief. I am not a buck. I am not a heathen. Insult me again, and even though you have no hair, I will lift your scalp." He inwardly smiled at the terror that blossomed on the other's face, then walked on out.

It was distasteful for the warrior to make threats when he would much rather have slit the man's throat. But he had given Yellow Hair his word that he would not cause any trouble.

A glance back showed the trader and the one-eyed trapper huddled together. Dismissing them from his thoughts, Lightning strolled about the post. The only thing that had changed since his last visit was the addition of a small shack used to store grain for the company's horses.

Lightning listened to a Flathead and a white man haggle over how many Point blankets a bale of prime beaver hides were worth. He watched a game of bone dice being played by Shoshonis and a trapper. And he took special interest in a knife-throwing contest between a Flathead, a Shoshoni, and a scruffy company man. As the Kit Fox warrior watched the Shoshoni prepare to take a turn, a hand smeared with streaks of dirt fell roughly on his shoulder.

"Here you are, Rakes. I've been lookin' all over the compound for you."

It was the company man who wore the eye patch. Lightning did not know him well and felt uncomfortable being touched. Facing around, he stared at the hand until the trapper coughed, grinned, and removed it. "Why did you look for me? Did the trader send you?"

"No, Rakes. Your order ain't ready quite yet," the man said glibly. He had been holding his other hand behind his back and he now raised it with a flourish, exposing a silver flask. "I just figured the two of us should get better acquainted."

Lightning could not take his eyes off that flask. His throat became strangely dry and tight. Combined with the

memory of how happy he had felt for a while the last time
he drank, it was all he could do not to snatch the whiskey
from the white man's hand and guzzle the contents. Common sense stopped him. "Acquainted?" he repeated, since
he did not know the word.

"Friends, Rakes. The two of us should be friends. I
mean, it's only right, since your kinsman Bennett and I are
on such good terms, that the two of us should be the
same."

Lightning recalled seeing the one-eyed man talk to
Cleve a few times before. So far as he knew, they were
known to each other, nothing more.

The man went on without missing a breath. "I'm sure
Bennett must have mentioned me once or twice. Didn't he
ever tell you about old Patch? Or maybe he used my
Christian name, Dirksen?" The man shrugged while opening the flask. "Not that a name matters much between
friends, eh?" Taking a long swig, he smacked his lips and
beamed. "Ain't nothin' like tonsil varnish to get a man's
blood perked up, is there?"

Patch offered the flask to Lightning. Every instinct the
warrior had screamed at him to refuse. Every instinct
warned him that taking so much as a sip would be a grave
mistake. A lifetime of inbred caution filled him with a premonition that all was not quite right.

Then Lightning pictured Twisted Leg's lovely features as
he had envisioned them so vividly that night at the cabin,
and before he could help himself, he had reached for the
flask and pressed it to his lips.

The firewater burned, like the last time. It seared Lightning's throat, and for a moment he thought that he would
choke and gag. But the sensation was milder. The whiskey
seemed slightly different, somehow. He took several swallows and slowly lowered the flask.

Patch grinned and clapped the warrior on the shoulder.

"Well, look at you! It's nice to see a man who knows how to hold his liquor." He gestured. "Help yourself to more if you want. I have my own to drink." From his possibles bag he took a smaller flask. "I'm partial to rum, myself. It wouldn't do for me to have too much more whiskey. Mixing the two can make a fellow as sick as a dog."

Lightning took another swallow. And another. Warmth slowly spread down through his body and radiated to his limbs.

The Hudson's Bay man beckoned. "Come with me, friend. We shouldn't stand out here in the open like this or every lazy waste-about will be beggin' us for a sip." He made for the side of the trading post. "I know where we can do our drinkin' in peace."

Again Lightning's intuition blared. It waged an internal war with his desire to relive those wonderful days he had shared with his wife and to feel once again that delightful giddy sensation of untroubled bliss that had come over him at Cleve's. The contest was never in doubt. Tipping the flask to his mouth, he followed Patch Dirksen into the shadows.

Second Son never expected to see a Crow in the Chipewyan village. Yet the features, the style of hair, and the beaded necklace of the woman who now straightened by the entrance were definitely those of the tribe that lived in the mountains to the northwest of Tsistsista country.

The Crows and Cheyennes had had limited contact over the years, mostly in the form of mutual raids. There had been a brief period many winters past when the two tribes had enjoyed a brittle truce, which both sides later claimed the other broke.

The Crow who nervously stood there staring at Second Son with frank curiosity was ten to fifteen winters older than the warrior woman. Streaks of gray lightened the hair at her temples. She had a long, plain dress fashioned from the same animal skins the Chipewyans used to make all their clothes. Her moccasins were short and unadorned.

Second Son sat straighter as the woman came over and knelt. She responded in Tsistsista when she was addressed in what had to be the Crow language. "I do not speak your tongue."

Billy-Wolf had feared trouble when the flap opened, so he was glad to see only an unarmed woman. He observed that she was different from the other Chipewyans and took her for another captive. Her lack of hostility put him at ease. Leaning toward his mother, he remarked in English, "Maybe she knows sign. If we didn't have our hands tied, we could talk to her."

To the amazement of both of them, the Crow woman declared, "Me speak white man's tongue." Her pronunciation was atrocious but understandable.

"You do?" Billy-Wolf exclaimed. "Who are you? Where did you come from?"

"Me Rattles Track. Me Crow," the woman confirmed Second Son's deduction. "Mattonabee send. Him want me try talk you." She pointed at Second Son, who posed a question.

"Where did you learn the white man's tongue?"

Rattles Track's brow furrowed in concentration. "Many moons past white man live Crows. Him my man." Sorrow came over her. "Him killed by Utes."

"How did you come to be here?"

The woman struggled to find the right words. "Me take other man. Crow warrior. Have girl." Her sorrow deepened. "Blackfeet attack. Kill man. Kill girl. Take me be Blackfoot woman."

Neither Second Son nor Billy-Wolf broke the heavy silence that descended. Having lived through many trials of their own, they felt strong sympathy for this woman they hardly knew.

The Crow's tale was not unique. Indian warfare was constant. Seldom did any two or three tribes get along for any length of time. The Blackfoot Confederacy was a notable exception, cemented by the member tribes' shared hatred of all whites.

One of Second Son's uncles, the husband of Buffalo Hump, had firmly believed that it was a mistake for red men always to be at each other's throats. Standing Bear had been a fierce warrior of renown when he was younger, but as he got on in years, he forsook the warpath to become a strong voice at the councils for peace with all tribes.

Standing Bear had wanted the Tsistsistas and others to present a united front to the whites, who were just then making themselves known west of the Muddy River. Without unity, the whites would one day overrun them, a lesson he had learned from a Delaware he had befriended.

There was a story in itself. The Delaware, whose own name was so hard for the Tsistsistas to learn that he adopted the new one of Gray Raven, had migrated westward with others of his people after their land was seized by the very whites they had befriended.

From Gray Raven, Standing Bear had learned how the British and French set the tribes against one another and then displaced the weakened winners. He had warned that the whites would do the same to the tribes who called the rolling prairie and majestic mountains their home, but few had heeded his prediction.

Warfare had been an ingrained part of Tsistsista life for too long, as it had been for the Lakotas, the Comanches, the Kiowa, and others.

Now, watching the Crow woman compose herself, Second Son counted herself fortunate that she still had her man and her son. She had a lot to give thanks for. Her life could have been worse. Much worse.

Rattles Track continued. "Later Blackfeet, Chipewyans trade. Blackfeet want copper. Chipewyan warrior take me. Me his this many winters." She held up nine fingers.

Billy-Wolf thought that an awful long time to remain a captive. "Why have you stayed so long? Why didn't you escape from these Chipewyans or the Blackfeet before them?"

"Blackfeet catch, Blackfeet kill," Rattles Track explained, running a finger across her throat.

"But what about since the Chipewyans took you? You must have had a chance."

"Many chances."

"Then why have you stayed?" the boy persisted, and was puzzled when his mother glanced at him in reproach. It had seemed to be a logical question.

"Have girl. Have small boy," the Crow woman said as if that explained everything.

To Second Son, it did. Rattles Track was a devoted mother who would not risk the lives of her two children on a trek so perilous that there was very little likelihood of their reaching Crow territory alive. The woman was trapped there until her children were old enough to make the journey, and by then they would probably not want to go. Why should they? Being Chipewyan was all they knew.

Rattles Track glanced at the closed flap, then bent at the waist to say quietly, "You listen, Tsistsistas. You escape quick. These bad people. Much bad medicine. Not go, you maybe die soon."

"Does Mattonabee plan to kill us?" Second Son inquired. If that was the case, they'd make their bid to regain their freedom as soon as the sun set.

"Maybe once, old days. Not now. Chipewyans need women. Chipewyans need boys," Rattles Track said. "This big band once. Few left now. Much bad times. Many men, women, children killed." Her voice trembled and her lips quivered as she concluded, "Bad place for all not men."

"I do not understand," Second Son said, and would have quizzed the Crow at length had the flap not been shoved wide a second time, and into the lodge came Mattonabee, Takwugan, and two other warriors.

The Chipewyans formed a half circle around the captives with the chief facing Second Son. In the dim light his face had the aspect of chiseled stone. He spoke testily to Rattles Track, who bowed her head and responded in a submissive tone.

Billy-Wolf was disturbed to see that Takwugan had taken a special interest in him. The warrior studied him as he might a horse he contemplated buying.

Primly folding her hands in her lap, the Crow woman turned a face as impassive as the chief's on the warrior woman. "So sorry. Not think ask name."

"Second Son."

"Chief want me say his words. Want me say yours." Rattles Track paused to listen to Mattonabee. "Him say you strange. You woman, but fight like warrior. You kill Chetwynd. You hurt Takwugan. You hurt Wabamun. Him should kill you."

No reply was necessary. Second Son matched the leader's haughty stare.

Mattonabee went on for some time, then nudged the Crow. She immediately translated. "Chief want you savvy. Want me tell why band here." She paused and was nudged again, harder. "Long time, Chipewyans, Cree make war. Many die. Cree very strong. Cree have plenty warriors. Cree drive Chipewyans from land." She motioned. "Cree attack this band. Kill many warriors, steal many women, many young ones. Drive us south. Four moons we walk. Some die on way."

Second Son immediately decided that this was why the men who had taken her prisoner had acted so apprehensive on the trail. They were indeed in hostile country.

"Mattonabee say band need more women. Women do much work. Women cook, women sew. Women chop wood. Women haul. These things not for men." Rattles Track's shoulders slumped. "Not like Crows here. Not like Tsistsistas. To Chipewyans, women be like slaves. Men tell what do. Women listen, or women beaten."

Understanding prompted Second Son to review their arrival at the village. Only the women had been doing hard labor. Not one had been smiling. Not one had been laughing. None had been singing, as would have been the case in a Cheyenne village.

"Me tell this so you know," Rattles Track said, her sad, dark eyes on Second Son. "Chief say you Chipewyan now. Chief say you do as told."

Second Son glared at the leader. She was a warrior and the wife of Yellow Hair, not someone to be treated worse than the Tsistsistas treated their dogs.

Rattles Track spoke louder, announcing formally, "Second Son, Mattonabee take you be his woman. From this day on, you do what he want. Or you suffer."

chapter
—— 14 ——

Rakes the Sky with Lightning did not remember passing out. He must have, though, because the sun had been replaced by stars. A breeze cooled his perspiring brow as he pushed himself up off the ground and leaned against the trading-post wall.

Where had Patch gone? he wondered. The two of them had been drinking, the last he recalled. He'd had to nearly finish the flask before that wonderful feeling returned, the sensation that he was floating on air, part of him detached from his body.

A sequence of vivid memories of Twisted Leg had passed through his brain. For the longest while he had sat and stared at the empty air. The white man had talked to him from time to time, but Lightning had not listened. He was savoring those memories as a starving man savors every morsel of a meal. At some point he had drifted asleep.

Lightning was pleased that his head did not hurt so ferociously as it had before. He put his hands on the ground to rise when footsteps heralded the return of the Hudson's Bay man. Dirksen carried another flask.

"Here you go, Rakes. Just like you wanted."

"I asked for this?" Lightning responded, taking it.

"Sure did, friend. It was the last thing you said to me before you passed out." Patch smirked. "I had that cheat Blevitt deduct the cost from the change you have comin'. Don't fret, though. It's not all that much."

Sinking down beside the warrior, Patch took his small flask from his pocket, opened it, and held it up. "Let's drink to your health, Rakes. For an Injun you're all right."

Lightning did not care to have any more. He lowered the flask instead of raising it to his mouth.

"What's the matter with you?" Patch asked. "What did I do that you're insultin' me?"

"I do no such thing."

Patch made a clucking noise. "Yes you do, friend. I just offered a toast to your health and you turned me down. Why, that's the same as slappin' me in the face or stealin' my horse. Believe you me, no white man would be so rude."

Reluctantly, Lightning did as the trapper wanted. The initial sip tasted so good that he swallowed more, and before he knew it, he had downed a third of the whiskey. His head felt as if it were going to float away on the next strong wind and there appeared to be two of everything. Not realizing that he was doing so, he muttered aloud.

"What was that?" Patch asked, and belched loudly.

"You whites and your customs!" Lightning declared,

slurring every syllable. Once again his tongue was as thick as his wrist.

"Ours are no stranger than yours," Patch shot back. "Why, I hear tell that some of you like to smear your hair with bear fat and piss."

"A Tsistsista never would!"

"Maybe so, but warriors in other tribes do. And how about the custom of stickin' pieces of bone through the skin on your chests and hangin' from ropes until the bone rips out? If that ain't almighty peculiar, I don't know what is." He took a swallow. "I don't reckon either of us can call the kettle black."

Lightning did not see what kettles had to do with their discussion. Kettles were for cooking and no one had mentioned anything about food. Giggling at the white man's silliness, he let more firewater trickle into his mouth.

"I'll be back in a minute, Rakes," Patch declared. Setting down his small flask, he rose and hitched at his pants. "Nature calls, if you get my drift."

Lightning did not, but he smiled and nodded as the man weaved off toward the rear of the building. He leaned his head back and was going to close his eyes to rest when he caught sight of Dirksen's flask. Rum, the man had called it. Curious as to how rum compared with whiskey, he checked to make sure the trapper was gone, then brought the flask to his lips.

The warrior expected a taste similar to firewater. He thought it would burn, or at the very least tingle. Yet nothing happened. Rum was the most tasteless drink he had ever swallowed. It was like drinking water. Surprised that a white man would drink something so bland, he put the flask back down.

Shortly, Patch returned. Lightning paid him no mind until the Hudson's Bay man snickered.

"I tell you, Rakes, I wish a few more of the boys had

been in there to see the look on Blevitt's puss when you flashed those gold coins in front of him. Did you see how his eyes practically bugged out?"

"Over stupid yellow metal."

"Stupid to you, maybe, but not to whites," Patch admitted. "Yellow metal is to us what buffalo are to you Injuns."

Lightning had never thought of it that way before. To the Tsistsistas, the buffalo were everything: food, clothing, shelter, spirit helpers, and more. "Can yellow metal feed you? Can yellow metal keep you warm on a cold day?"

"As a matter of fact, yes."

"You joke, white man."

"Like hell." Patch sidled closer. "With yellow metal I can buy all the food I can cram into my belly, or enough blankets to keep me cozy in the middle of a blizzard." His good eye narrowed. "That's why I'd sure take it as a personal favor if you'd tell me where that Yank Bennett got those coins. The way I figure, he must have a stash somewhere. Tell me where and I'll split it with you."

The suggestion that he betray Yellow Hair's trust stirred Lightning's temper. "Never," he spat. "My aunt asked me not to tell and I never will."

The white man's single eye gleamed with greed. "So Bennett does have a cache! I was right!" Patch pointed at the warrior's flask. "Tell you what I'll do. Tell me where to find it and I'll keep you in that stuff for as long as you live. Think of it! All the whiskey you can drink! Every night of your life you can feel like you do right this moment. What do you say?"

Marshaling his energy, Lightning shoved awkwardly to his feet. He did not mean to be awkward, but his arms and legs had minds of their own and would not do as he wanted. Swaying, he jabbed a finger at Dirksen and forced his tongue to move. "I say that you try to trick me. I say

I want nothing to do with you." Proud that he had been able to get all that out without slurring every word, Lightning went to leave.

Suddenly Patch sprang to his feet, showing none of the unsteadiness he had exhibited when he went around the corner earlier. He barred the warrior's path and said in a threatening tone, "Maybe it hasn't sunk in yet, Injun. I mean to learn where that cache is, one way or the other. I've tried doin' it easy like, but you're too damn hard-headed for your own good."

"Out of my way."

"Or what? You'll shoot me? I unloaded that fusil of yours while you were asleep."

Lightning dropped his hand to his knife. Only it wasn't there. He groped the empty sheath, amazed at his own foolishness. "I should not have trusted you."

Patch laughed. "You caught on a bit too late, friend. Take him, boys."

Brawny hands closed on Lightning from behind. In his stupor he had not heard any footsteps. His finely honed senses had failed him. Or rather, he had failed them. He fought back, but there were three of them, and in no time he had been overpowered and was held in grips of iron. Patch materialized in front of him.

"What now, white man? Do you kill me?"

The man with one eye patted the warrior on the cheek. "You haven't been listenin'. Why the hell would I kill you when you're the only one who can tell me where to find the Yank's gold?" He made that clucking noise again. "Besides, if I did, Bennett would raise such a stink that Walker might launch an investigation." The trapper gestured and the men holding Lightning swung him around and headed for the back of the trading post.

"No, Rakes," Lightning heard Patch say. "There's more

than one way to skin a cat. And I think I know just the thing to loosen your tongue."

All the white men found that humorous.

Billy-Wolf Bennett was so mad that tears of burning fury moistened his eyes. He glared at Takwugan, then over his shoulder at the warrior who had gripped his arms when the trouble started.

It had all happened so fast.

Rattles Track had been telling his mother what Mattonabee expected of her. The chief wanted Second Son to start off every day by gathering wood for his fire and cooking his breakfast, after which she would cure hides or sew clothes or do whatever else struck his fancy. She was to prepare a hot broth for him every day when the sun was straight overhead, and during the afternoon she would be kept busy cleaning and patching or whatever else needed doing. In the evening she would cook his supper and later lay out his bedding for him. And she was expected to do all this with her ankles hobbled.

Billy-Wolf had overflowed with pride when his mother looked the chief in the face and told him that she was no man's slave, and that she would never be anyone's woman other than the man she had already taken as her mate.

Then it began.

Mattonabee rose and ordered her to follow him to his lodge. Second Son refused to go. She wanted to know what the Chipewyans planned to do with Billy-Wolf. The chief told her that it was none of her concern. From that moment on, Billy-Wolf was no longer her offspring. Again Mattonabee commanded her to stand, but she stayed where she was.

At a word from the leader, one of the other warriors had stepped to Second Son's side and bent to lift her up. She exploded off the floor, ramming her head into his stomach and knocking him against the side of the lodge. Before she could brace herself, Takwugan and the fourth warrior had jumped her and held her fast.

Billy-Wolf had sprung to help Second Son, but he could do little with his hands tied. He had been grabbed and pulled to one side as his mother was dragged from the lodge.

Seldom had Billy-Wolf felt so helpless. He wanted to rend the Chipewyans limb from limb, but there was nothing he could do other than stand there and glower.

Rattles Track, surprisingly, had not gone with Mattonabee. She had backed up during the struggle and now stepped forward to listen to Takwugan. When the warrior finished, she translated.

"Mighty warrior Takwugan say you lucky. Him take you as son. Him be your father. Rest of days live his lodge."

Billy-Wolf Bennett could not help himself. "Never!" he cried. "I already have a pa and I don't need another! Tell this toad that unless the Chipewyans let my mother and me go, they will regret it."

Rattles Track had been shocked by the outburst. "You must stay calm," she cautioned kindly. "If not, they hurt you."

"I don't care. Let them try."

"They maybe hurt mother, too."

That gave Billy-Wolf pause. He didn't want his mother harmed on his account. It was smarter to play along with the Chipewyans for the time being, he mused, and await an opportunity to free them both. Although he would rather have eaten raw polecat than give in, he nodded and declared, "All right. Let him know that I'll go along quietly."

Takwugan took the news with a smug smile. He ushered Billy-Wolf outside and headed for a larger lodge at the east end of the encampment.

The youth sought a glimpse of his mother, but she had already disappeared. He looked back and was surprised to see Rattles Track tagging along. "Why are you coming?" he asked. "Don't you have your own lodge?"

"We go my lodge." The Crow woman bobbed her chin at Takwugan. "Me his woman."

"Oh," was all Billy-Wolf could think to say. It helped matters that she would be there since she was the only friend Second Son and he had in the entire village, but he would rather have her be with his mother. He had a hunch Second Son was in far worse danger.

At a large lodge, Takwugan stood aside so that Rattles Track could open the flap for them. He motioned for Billy-Wolf to go in first.

The interior was warm and cozy. Well lit by a small fire at the very center, it reminded the youngest Bennett of a typical Tsistsista tipi. Bedding, robes, blankets, cooking utensils, and other belongings were neatly arranged around the perimeter. Leaning against the far wall were a bow and quiver. So were Billy-Wolf's Hawken, ammo pouch, and powder horn.

Billy-Wolf was taken aback to find the lodge occupied by another woman and a boy half his age. They were evidently expecting him and were on their knees on the other side of the fire, the woman a few paces in back of the boy.

Two dogs were also present. Mongrels, they lounged along the left-hand wall, both gnawing bones. As the lord and master of the lodge entered, they dashed up to him with tongues lolling and tails wagging. Takwugan smiled and gave each a rub and an affectionate pat.

The warrior turned to the Chipewyan boy and addressed him with a few terse words. For some reason the other woman was completely ignored.

Billy-Wolf stepped to the side and waited to be told

what to do. His mother's people adhered to a formal code of tipi etiquette, and he imagined the Chipewyans did the same.

Takwugan stepped around the fire. He sat facing the entrance, with his son to his right. Rattles Track moved around behind the warrior and knelt next to the other woman.

A smack of Takwugan's hand on the hides to his left showed Billy-Wolf where he should sit. Holding his head high, he did so. Not until that moment did he note the cooking skin balanced on a wooden frame and filled to the brim with bubbling stew. His stomach rumbled so loud that the others heard.

Takwugan laughed, produced his copper knife, and in a single swipe cut Billy-Wolf's bonds. The warrior then leaned over the skin, inhaled loudly, and smacked his lips. He rubbed his stomach and said something.

"My husband want you eat," Rattles Trap said. "Plenty food. Him say fill belly."

Billy-Wolf needed no prompting. Birchbark bowls lay near at hand, so he helped himself to one and to a big copper spoon. Ladling the bowl full to the brim, he commenced shoving the food into his mouth just as fast as he could move his arm. It was scorching hot but he didn't care. He was too hungry.

Takwugan took delight in Billy-Wolf's antics. Clapping him on the shoulder, the warrior went on at some length, pausing often so Rattles Track could relay what had been said.

"My husband say you boy, but eat like man. Him say you be strong. Need good hunter now. Have one more must feed. Take much food to keep all bellies full."

The warrior and the small boy spooned stew into bowls of their own. The boy wolfed his food, casting sideways glances at Billy-Wolf between gulps. Takwugan took his time.

Finishing the first portion, Billy-Wolf eagerly began to help himself to seconds when he noticed that neither of the women had moved. "How about you, ma'am?" he asked the Crow. "Aren't you and the other lady hungry?"

"As hungry as you."

"Here then," Billy-Wolf said, picking up another bowl to hand to her. "Don't let us hog all the food. Help yourself before it's all gone."

"You very kind," Rattles Track said softly. "But no. We cannot touch food yet."

"Why not?"

"It Chipewyan custom. Women not eat until men done."

"What? That's crazy. What happens if the men are so hungry they eat it all?"

"Women go hungry."

Billy-Wolf abruptly lost his appetite. Hunkering on his haunches, he watched the dogs chewing on their thick bones crammed with marrow.

Takwugan had been paying close attention to the exchange and now quizzed the Crow. He did not like what he heard. Lancing a finger at her, he spoke loudly, sharply.

Rattles Track cleared her throat. "My husband say me mistake. My husband say explain more Chipewyan ways."

"There's no need," Billy-Wolf told her.

"Please. Me must. Or him beat me."

The plaintive appeal in the woman's voice struck a resounding chord deep within Billy-Wolf. He thought it outrageous that the women were so mistreated and was going to give Takwugan a piece of his mind when a bundle of hides over by the right wall moved and from under them issued a high-pitched squeal.

Rattles Track was beside the hides in a twinkling. Carefully lifting the top one, she revealed a small circular bed on which rested an infant. Tenderly taking the baby into her arms, she moved back to her place behind the warrior and casually adjusted her dress so the infant could nurse. "This my girl," she said proudly.

With a start Billy-Wolf realized the boy must be hers also. A troubling image occurred to him and he could barely conceal his contempt as he faced the warrior, who was speaking.

"Husband say not be upset. Husband say eat all you want. Not worry for women." She stopped when the Chipewyan did. "Husband say men, women not same. Men hunt. Men fish. Women make fires. Women haul water. Women cook."

"Then ask him why the women don't get to eat when they want," Billy-Wolf interrupted. "It's only fair if they have to fix all the meals."

Rattles Track did not appear happy about doing so but she relayed the question. "Takwugan say fair not part of it. Men must eat so be strong. Men protectors. Men defend village from enemies, from bears, from wolves, from wolverines, from Windigos." She listened to the warrior a moment. "Many times food scarce. If men not eat, if women, children fill bellies, who protect Chipewyans?"

In a warped way the warrior's logic made sense, although Billy-Wolf still branded the practice as downright selfish. He stated as much. "Maybe he has a point, but that doesn't make it right." He jerked a thumb at the cooking skin. "Tell him that I won't eat another bite unless the two of you are allowed to eat with us."

"No," Rattles Track said.

"You've got to."

"Him be upset."

"What do you care after the way he treats you?"

"Him my man. Him good provider. Me love him."

Billy-Wolf was stupefied. How could a woman care for someone who treated her worse than he did the family dogs? A man who would beat her if she acted contrary to his wishes? It was too ridiculous for words, a mystery beyond his understanding. Since he was not about to delve into their personal affairs any further, he changed the subject to take the warrior's mind off the matter of how many portions he would down. "You just mentioned a bunch of animals. Wolves, bears, and wolverines I've run into or heard about. But what in the world is a Windigo? I don't know that critter."

Every last person there except the baby visibly tensed. Takwugan and Rattles Track talked briefly and she turned to Billy-Wolf.

"Bad medicine talk of Windigos. Very, very bad medicine," she stressed. "Husband say never want meet one. Be last thing ever see."

"What makes them so dangerous? Are they a kind of bear or a big cat or something else?"

"Windigos not animals. Windigos more than animals." Rattles Track paused, her forehead furrowed in deep concentration. "Windigos hard explain. Only found this north land." She hunched her shoulders upward. "They big." She drew back her lips and mimicked the growl of a beast. "They fierce." She tilted her head as if listening to the wind and gave a tiny shudder. "They eat people."

"But what *are* they? Where do they come from?"

"Windigos live in deep woods. They strong like ten men. But they more than men. Walk on two legs. Have sharp claws. And much hair."

Unbidden, into Billy-Wolf's head popped the horrifying image of a clawed hand trying to choke the life from his mother. "Well, I'll be!" he blurted. "I do know what you're talking about, after all. My ma and I fought one off the night before your man and his friends caught us."

Sheer terror etched the Crow's face. "You what?" she asked as if she did not believe her ears.

"We were holed up in some boulders," Billy-Wolf detailed, and elaborated. For some reason Rattles Track hung on every word. When he was done she urgently passed on the information to her husband. His reaction was even more extreme than hers had been. No sooner was she done than he put down his bowl and hustled from the lodge.

"What is going on?" Billy-Wolf wanted to know.

"Takwugan go tell Mattonabee," Rattles Track said. "Important chief know Windigo still after us."

"You mean this thing has been stalking your band?"

Another shudder racked the matron. "For two moons now Windigo hunt us. Men try kill it, but no luck. That what men out doing when find you."

"They were trying to track this Windigo thing down?"

"They try, and try hard. Because if evil creature not killed, it eat us all. One by one by one."

chapter

— 15 —

Rakes the Sky with Lightning wished he were dead. His whole body hurt, from the roots of his hairs to the tips of his toes.

It wasn't the kind of hurt a man felt as the result of being beaten or shot. Rather, it was the gut-wrenching hurt of being so utterly sick that all he wanted to do was bend over and retch until nothing was left to bring up.

Only Lightning couldn't, because he already had. His stomach was as empty as a punctured water skin. There had come a point where his body had been unable to take any more firewater.

The warrior did not know how long he had been wherever he was. He had no idea whether it was day or night.

All he knew for certain was that he had been tied to a chair, and the gag and blindfold the whites had applied were so tight that his head beat to the pounding of a buffalo stampede.

And he so wanted to die.

An awful stink assailed Lightning's nose. He tried not to breathe it in, but not doing so was impossible since *he* was the source. His unwashed, sweaty body, combined with the foul odor arising from the floor in front of him, were enough to provoke dry heaves and had been doing so off and on for a long time.

The warrior guessed that he had been thrown into one of the many small shacks that dotted Fort Hall. Some, like the grain shack for the horses, were in daily use. Others, like this one, hardly ever saw a soul.

With the thought came a rasping click in the middle distance. Lightning sat up in case it proved to be friendly trappers who would help him. He tried to speak, but the best he could utter was a strangled cry no louder than a squeak.

Boots clumped. The door clicked shut and a haughty voice chortled.

"Never give up, do you, Injun? Usually I admire that trait, but all you're doin' is making things harder on yourself. You are going to spill the beans sooner or later. Get that through your thick red skull and the better off you'll be."

The gag was yanked from Lightning's mouth so hard that he swore some of his teeth had been torn out with it. "You!" he croaked. "Only a coward treats another man like this! Give me a knife and let us end this man to man."

Patch Dirksen's sly laugh was echoed by a pair of men who were with him. "No can do, Rakes. That would be plumb dumb, and my ma didn't raise any yacks."

Fingers pried at the knot to the blindfold. Moments later

it was snatched off, and Lightning blinked even though the only source of light was a small candle. There were no windows, just the narrow door. In front of him stood Patch, hands on hips. To the left loomed a burly mountain man, to the right a trapper whose cheek bore a jagged scar. They were the same pair who had helped haul him to the shack and bind him. How long ago now? he mused. Three days? Two, at least.

"Guess what, friend?" Patch said. "It's that time again. You've sobered up enough to be ready for the next go-around." Stepping to the wall, he picked up a jug. "More of the straight stuff. Maybe this time will be the one that loosens your stubborn lips."

Lightning stared at the door. All he had to do to be set free was to reveal where Yellow Hair had his cache. It was so easy! Just open his mouth and let the words spill out and he would be cut loose and could walk through that door.

No! Lightning's mind screamed at him. That was not what would happen. Dirksen could not afford to let him live once he told. The moment he did, his throat would be slit or his neck would be snapped and his body would be whisked from the post and dumped in the forest somewhere for the scavengers to feast on. No one would ever know what became of him. And his aunt and her family would suffer because he was not man enough to hold his tongue.

"One more chance before we begin," Patch coaxed. "Where's the damn gold at?"

Lightning bowed his head as if thinking when really he needed to moisten his mouth and lips without being noticed. A loud yell might bring others on the run. Not all the Hudson's Bay men were as vile as Dirksen. If the others knew what was happening, they might put a stop to it.

The Kit Fox warrior threw his head back and opened

his mouth wide to shout. But his enemies were not caught napping. The burly one clamped a big hand over his mouth while the trapper with the scar stepped in close and cuffed Lightning on the jaw. Pinpoints of light pinwheeled before the warrior's eyes and his chin slumped.

"You just never learn," Patch said. "Even if you did give a holler, no one would hear. This shack is way at the back of the post, almost to the rear wall."

Fingers wound in Lightning's hair and his head was viciously snapped higher. The burly man's other hand wrapped around his throat but did not squeeze.

"That's in case you get any more bright notions," Patch said amiably as he uncorked the jug. Lifting it to his nose, he sniffed, then scrunched up his face. "Whew! One whiff of this would drop a horse in its tracks. I reckon it would make dandy varnish."

His defiance rekindled, Lightning hissed, "You waste your time, white dog. I will die before I talk."

Patch stepped forward and held the jug near the warrior's mouth. "Maybe you will, Injun. Alcohol can kill a man if he gets too much of it. In which case me and my pards will chop up your body and scatter the parts to the four winds." Leaning down, his face lit by a sadistic grin, he asked, "What happens to your silly dream of gettin' to the Other Place, then?"

It was hard to say which was the greater shock, that Dirksen knew of the Tsistsista belief in the Other Place or that Lightning would languish in eternal torment if his body were in bits and pieces.

The Cheyennes held that those who passed on to the other side arrived there in the same state as they left this life. Which meant that if a warrior died of a lance wound, that wound would plague him in the Other Place. The tradition was not unique to the Cheyennes and explained why many tribes condoned mutilating the bodies of slain enemies.

For Rakes the Sky with Lightning, the threat of being chopped to bits was profoundly upsetting. It almost made him waver. Almost, but not quite.

Lightning was a warrior. He had come to terms with the prospect of his death long ago. The imminent likelihood did not inspire fear in him. He would much rather have been shot or stabbed or had his neck broken, but that was out of his hands. A man had to accept his lot and make the best of it.

Patch Dirksen frowned. "I can see that you aim to play this out to the end, Rakes. Pity. You're young yet. You have your whole life ahead of you."

"Again you lie. We both know what you will do if I talk." Gathering what little spittle was in his mouth onto the tip of his tongue, Lightning spat at the one-eyed man's face but missed and hit his shirt.

Unaffected, Patch wiped a sleeve across his chest, then gripped the warrior's lower jaw. "I don't know what it is about the Cheyenne. None of you know enough to quit when you're licked." He swished the contents of the jug. "So here we go again. Fight all you want to. It'll make the time go that much faster."

And so it began. Again.

It had been days and still Billy-Wolf had not seen any sign of his mother. To all his many and persistent questions, Rattles Track would only say that Second Son was alive and well and in the leader's lodge. Or *wigwam*, as the Chipewyans called their tipi-type structures.

Whenever Billy-Wolf ventured outdoors, he could not take his eyes off Mattonabee's dwelling. All he wanted was a glimpse of Second Son, enough to see for himself that she had not been harmed in any way.

On this particular cloudy morning, as the boy sat watching the Crow's son, Cepizan, fashion special blunt points for several old arrows they could use in hunting birds, he kept staring off across the camp.

Rattles Track had gone over to the chief's wigwam over an hour ago. Several times each day she was summoned to translate, and she always reported the gist of what went on.

The strain of waiting was next to unbearable. Billy-Wolf could not sit still for more than a few seconds. He fidgeted. He picked at the whangs on his buckskin shirt. He jumped at any loud noises.

At last the flap parted and Rattles Track emerged. An enigmatic smile creased her weathered features as she crossed to where they worked.

Springing upright, Billy-Wolf grasped her arm and asked, "How is she? Has he hurt her? Did she give you a message for me?"

"Your mother fine. She say be patient. She say not do anything make Chipewyans mad."

Hearing that Second Son was all right was one thing; Billy-Wolf would much rather see for himself. Not that he doubted the Crow. During the short time they had been together she had proven to be a gentle, honest soul who would never tell a lie. He liked her considerably. "But what is Mattonabee up to? Why does he keep her cooped up in there? I thought she was supposed to fetch wood for him and do all sorts of things."

"Me think, too," Rattles Track said, and gave the leader's wigwam a perplexed look. Shaking her head, she put her hand on the boy's arm and added, "Not be worried. Me not understand, but Mattonabee not harm Second Son. He tell her do things. She tell him no. Yet he not hit her. Not beat her. Him never do this before."

Billy-Wolf digested the information. "I don't get it. Why is he treating my mother so special?"

"Me not know," Rattles Track answered as she stepped to the flap of her own lodge. "Me wish me did." She went in.

Cepizan nudged Billy-Wolf's elbow and pointed toward the forest to the south. The three arrows were done and he was set to go hunting.

"I reckon we should," Billy-Wolf said, although he had no hankering to go any great distance from the village and his mother. Refusal would get him into hot water with Takwugan, who needed feathers to make two dozen new shafts. Unwillingly, he fell into step behind the seven-year-old.

The village of the Whitefish Clan was quiet, as always. Billy-Wolf had learned a lot about his captors over the previous few nights, thanks mainly to Takwugan. The warrior was intent on teaching him all there was to know about Chipewyan history and traditions in order that he might fit in better.

The lessons had proven interesting and helped Billy-Wolf take his mind off Second Son. That very morning he had heard how the Chipewyans believed they were created.

Long ago there had been but one person in the whole world, a woman who lived in a cave. Mother, as the Chipewyans called her, lived on berries and green plants.

One day a creature that resembled a dog came into her cave. It slept beside Mother that night, and she dreamed that it turned into an attractive man with whom she made love.

The next day a giant of a man appeared. He was the Creator of all things. He dug rivers and gouged out lakes with a stick he held. He caused trees to grow and mountains to rear up out of the ground.

The Creator seized the dog creature and tore it to pieces. Its inner organs were thrown into the water to become fish. Its flesh was scattered in the forest to become the many types of wild animals that lived there. Its skin was ripped and thrown high into the air, where the pieces became birds.

Having done this, the Creator turned to go. He told Mother that he had seen to the needs of all her children soon to be born. They would never go hungry since the Creator gave them the power to kill all the creatures he had created for food, shelter, and clothing. Then the Creator vanished, never to be seen again.

Those children were the Chipewyans. And the fondly cherished tale of their origin explained their special reverence for dogs.

The animals were treated royally. They were always fed amply and never made to work. When camps were moved, it was the women, not the dogs, who hauled heavy litters heaped high with possessions. In the winter, the women had to trudge through deep snow pulling heavy toboggans while the dogs were permitted to run free.

It struck Billy-Wolf as being just as unfair as making the women wait to eat. He could not comprehend why they had to do all the work when it had been a woman who gave birth to the tribe, not the dog creature.

Ahead grew a thick tangle of vegetation. Billy-Wolf admired his young companion's speed and agility as they dashed into the trees and paused to look and listen.

Cepizan was a wiry but thin boy whose hair was as black as pitch. Like every other Chipewyan, his shirt and pants had been fashioned from caribou hides.

Billy-Wolf had listened in stunned amazement to accounts of elklike animals that traveled in herds so vast they rivaled the endless streams of buffalo he had seen on the plains to the south. He had learned that just as the buffalo were all things to the prairie tribes, so were the caribou unending sources of food and hides to the Chipewyans and other tribes of the far north.

Chipewyans were also fond of fish. Every man owned a net to which had been attached a special charm believed to lure fish. When a group of men went fishing, no two nets were ever allowed to touch one another out of fear the nets would become jealous of the other's charm and so spoil the fishing for everyone.

Warriors used arrows to fish, too, just as they did to down caribou and other game. This made obtaining feathers a never-ending chore.

Billy-Wolf did not have a bow, or any other weapon except for the folding knife hidden under his belt. He had been sent to observe and learn. Takwugan had made it clear that weapons were off limits until he had demonstrated he could be fully trusted.

At night it was a test of willpower for Billy-Wolf not to jump up, grab the Hawken, and attempt to rescue his mother. He was fairly confident he could hold the warriors at bay long enough to reach the woods, but a smidgen of doubt stopped him. Outnumbered as they were, he could wind up getting the both of them slain.

His rifle, he had discovered, was the only one in the village. The Chipewyans owned few guns, but not due to lack of interest. Until recently the tribe had not had much contact with white men and so had obtained few trade rifles.

Their bitter enemies the Crees, on the other hand, owned many guns. Because the Crees lived farther to the south and east than the Chipewyans, the Crees had established trade with the Hudson's Bay trappers first. And now the Crees enjoyed a distinct advantage in the ages-long warfare between the two peoples.

Thanks to the superior range and accuracy of their firearms, the Crees were slowly but surely driving the Chipe-wyans from their homeland. Band after band had been wiped out or forced to flee.

Mattonabee's had been one of the largest and strongest until an early-morning sneak attack under cover of heavy fog had enabled the Crees to kill half the men and make off with dozens of women and children before Mattona-bee's warriors could rally.

Unless something was done soon, unless the Chipewyans learned to fight fire with fire and got their hands on as many guns as the Crees had, their tribe was doomed.

That was why Takwugan had shown such an interest in the Hawken. For the past two mornings he had made Billy-Wolf take him out for target practice. Other warriors had accompanied them, although whether out of curiosity or to guarantee that the boy did not put a ball into Takwugan's back, Billy-Wolf could not say.

Suddenly Cepizan uttered a fluttering whistle and pointed. Off through the brush were four grouse, three perched on a log, the fourth pecking at the ground. The boy slowly eased onto his hands and knees so as not to draw their attention and crawled toward them.

Billy-Wolf did likewise. He made no noise. The meat on those birds was as important as their feathers, since the Whitefish Clan was always short of food.

Since being driven south, Mattonabee's people had been compelled to subsist on game other than caribou. Even in the middle of summer, when wildlife was most abundant, the hunters were hard-pressed to keep food in every pot.

During the preceding winter it had been much worse. Smaller animals had stayed in their burrows most of the time while many of the larger animals had migrated the previous fall, leaving the Chipewyans with precious little to eat.

The tribe feared the colder months. Even in their own

land, winter was known as the time of empty bellies, the time when Chipewyans succumbed to starvation and the elements in high numbers. Rattles Track had told Billy-Wolf that it was not uncommon for the family to get by on moss and what edible plants could be dug out of the snow.

When the winters were really bad, the Chipewyans would resort to eating their precious dogs. Once the supply was gone, they would eat anything: tree bark, grass, even the clothes on their backs. If that did not suffice until warmer weather came, they did the unbelievable. Rattles Track claimed the Chipewyans would eat their own dead, and if there were no bodies available, the weakest members would be slain and devoured.

Billy-Wolf had felt half-sick on hearing that story. He could never imagine one person consuming another. As for eating dead bodies, that was too repulsive to give a second thought.

Cepizan brought an end to the youngest Bennett's reverie by stopping and motioning for him to be still. The Chipewyan boy slowly rose on his knees and elevated his bow to sight down the arrow. As he did, he glanced at the bare earth ringing the bush he was behind and his whole lean frame shuddered and shook as if he were having a fit.

Billy-Wolf leaned to one side to see why. His own breath caught in his throat at the sight of a track identical to the one he had examined at the deadfall. It had been made shortly before dawn, judging by the dew marks. The toes were pointed northward, telling him that the Windigo had been spying on the village.

Cepizan forgot about the grouse. Whirling, he fled like a frightened deer.

Billy-Wolf turned to follow. As he did, the grouse suddenly took wing. He figured that he had spooked them until he heard a rustling noise deeper in the undergrowth.

Takwugan had warned them not to go very far. The

Windigo, it was believed, would lie in hiding near the encampment, waiting to pounce on the unwary.

Mattonabee, since learning of the encounter in the gully, had directed that everyone take extra precautions. Children were not allowed to stray. Women went for water and wood in groups. The men had to hunt in pairs.

On hearing the noise, Billy-Wolf lit out as if his backside was aflame. He streaked through the brush, skirting trees and boulders. Behind him a twig cracked. Then another. Feet slapped the ground in regular cadence.

Billy-Wolf was too terror-stricken to look behind him. He knew the creature was overtaking him. He braced himself, anticipating he would be ripped apart by steely claws at any second. The shaded forest, which had been so tranquil a minute ago, now seemed no more than a gloomy refuge for a hideous monster.

The tree line appeared. Cepizan was already in the open and racing for his father's wigwam.

Mere yards were all Billy-Wolf had to cover when he felt something scrape his right shoulder blade. He poured on the speed. The drum of the creature's feet was so loud in his ears that he thought the beast would run him down.

In another few seconds Billy-Wolf burst from the pines. Cepizan had raised an outcry and Chipewyans were converging from all directions. Since he couldn't defend himself with his back to the monstrosity, Billy-Wolf took several more strides and whirled. His hands were balled tight. He was set to sell his life dearly if need be.

But there was no Windigo.

No hairy two-legged creature of any kind.

There was nothing at all.

Billy-Wolf Bennett blinked in surprise, then scanned the woods. The beast was nowhere to be seen, yet it had been right behind him mere moments ago. There had been no time for it to hide. So where had it gone?

Dumbfounded, Billy-Wolf stayed where he was until a quartet of warriors arrived. Among them was Takwugan, who had the Hawken in hand and warily edged toward the pines. Billy-Wolf dogged his captor's footsteps. He knew he was asking for trouble, but he had to learn what had happened to the Windigo.

More warriors showed up. Mattonabee was at their head and he immediately issued orders. The men fanned out into a skirmish line to protect the south flank of the village.

Billy-Wolf halted shy of the first trees. He could see the footprints he had made fleeing into the village. He could see those Cepizan had made. But there were no others. No huge tracks of great hairy feet with long hooked claws. Not so much as a partial print to prove the Windigo had been there.

Confused, Billy-Wolf stood there until Takwugan and others had searched the immediate area and come up empty-handed. They did not find any evidence the Windigo had been there other than the lone print discovered by Cepizan. To them, that wasn't extraordinary. The Chipewyans believed Windigos had superhuman powers that enabled them to perform incredible feats, such as only leaving tracks when the creatures wanted to.

Billy-Wolf had been skeptical of that claim until now. Either he had imagined the monster was after him—or the Chipewyans were right.

chapter

— 16 —

Mattonabee was deeply troubled. Mattonabee, highly respected and widely feared leader of the Whitefish Clan of Chipewyans, whose word among his people was iron law. Mattonabee, who as a young man had been jumped by four Crees and slain them all in personal combat. Mattonabee, who had stood up to a charging grizzly and killed it with a single arrow from his stout bow when it was so close that it dropped dead at his very feet. Mattonabee was troubled by a woman.

Thinking about it had put the chief in a distressing mood. He sat cross-legged in front of the fire in his wigwam, his dark, brooding eyes centered on the dancing flames.

His two wives and three children, recognizing his mood, hugged the wigwam walls and made little noise.

Mattonabee did not even know they were there. He was deep within himself, pondering. He had closed out the world around him, everything except for the woman who sat behind him against the back of the lodge, her wrists and ankles bound. For some reason Mattonabee could not fathom he was unable to shut her from his mind as he had all else.

It was unthinkable, Mattonabee reflected. By this time he should have broken her spirit. He should have beaten her into submission. She should be doing whatever he told her whenever he told her.

Instead, the Tsistsista still sat proudly, her defiant gaze boring into his back. Mattonabee did not need to turn to see for himself that it was so. He could *feel* her eyes on him, feel the potent force of her personality as if it were as physical as her body, or his.

Never had Mattonabee met such a woman. It had been a mistake for him to bring her into his wigwam. It had been a worse mistake for him to boast that she would be as tame as a puppy in no time.

The word had been spread. His people were expecting him to bend the strange warrior woman to his will. But he couldn't! As the Mother was his witness, he had tried. Again and again he had tried. And each time the result had been the same.

It was her eyes, Mattonabee decided. Whenever he looked into them, it was like gazing into the eyes of that grizzly on the bank of the Snow Bear River so many winters ago.

The chief had thought he would die that day. He had seen his death mirrored in the grizzly's eyes. No one had been more surprised than he himself when his arrow killed the brute.

Second Son's eyes had death in them. His death. Mattonabee knew as surely as he lived and breathed that if he ever struck her, she would slay him. Oh, not right away. She would bide her time and pretend to be as docile as the other women. But the day would come when she would slip a blade between his ribs or maybe take an ax to his neck or drop him from a distance with a bow.

On five occasions over the past few days Mattonabee had picked up the switch he used to keep his wives in line. He had walked up to Second Son intending to lash her until she pleaded for mercy. On each occasion Mattonabee had stood over her, raised the stick on high ... and froze. On each occasion she had calmly looked into his eyes and done what no other man, woman, or wild thing had ever done before. She had filled Mattonabee with fear.

It sickened him. It made him gnash his teeth in private moments. It made him want to tear at his hair or break something.

Now Mattonabee pondered what to do. Enough was enough. He had not risen to his position of prominence by being weak or indecisive. He must examine the problem with a clear head and decide the best course to take.

The Tsistsista was bad medicine. Of that there could be no doubt. Mattonabee wondered if perhaps she was a shaman among her people and had turned her power against him.

It would be in keeping with recent turns of events. So much bad medicine had befallen the Whitefish Clan that Mattonabee sometimes suspected they might be under a curse. Why else had everything gone so wrong?

There had been the raid by the Crees. Until then, Mattonabee had been hugely successful at avoiding marauding war parties and repulsing attacks when he could not avoid them.

There had been the long, cruel journey, which had worn the women and children down and left the band with little food on hand to tide them over in times of want.

Then the worst affliction of all: the Windigo. The evil creature had been shadowing their trail ever since, picking off those who grew careless. About ten sleeps ago people had stopped disappearing and the clan had breathed a collective sigh of relief, thinking the worst was over.

But now the Windigo was back. And as if that were not enough for Mattonabee to deal with, he had the captive to plague him. Between the two, his people and his leadership were both in jeopardy.

Suddenly the chief had an interesting thought. Was it coincidence that the Tsistsista and the Windigo had shown up at the same time? Takwugan had told him the woman's story about fighting the Windigo off. Naturally, he had not believed it, at first. No one ever fought off a Windigo. No ordinary person, anyway.

It gave added credence to Mattonabee's suspicion that the woman was a shaman or witch. How else could she have resisted the creature?

Useful information, maybe, but it did not help Mattonabee solve either of his pressing problems. Somehow he had to get rid of her and the Windigo both. It was regrettable that he could not set them at each other's throats and let them destroy one another.

Mattonabee stiffened. He could feel her eyes on him again. His skin prickled where her gaze touched it. He shifted and bent to add a limb to the fire, but the sensation persisted. What was she thinking? he wondered. About how she would kill him?

Mattonabee, proud leader of the powerful Whitefish

Clan of the Chipewyans, stared glumly into the fire, his mood worsening.

Unknown to the chief, Second Son was thinking of her son. It had been days since she saw him last. And although Rattles Track came frequently and secretly reported that Wolf Sings on the Mountain was fine, Second Son worried.

Given the gamble she was taking, she should be more worried about her own welfare. By defying Mattonabee, she risked incurring his wrath.

The wise thing to do was to pretend to submit, to do as he wanted until a chance presented itself for her to escape with Billy-Wolf. Yet every time he approached her with that stick of his, something inside of her would not let her give in.

The same independent streak that had inspired Second Son to emulate Badger and become a warrior, the same independence that had led her to be the first Burning Heart to take a white man as her mate and to roam with him far afield of Tsistsista country, now inspired her to resist the arrogant Chipewyan leader, heart and soul.

One of the children went out, leaving the flap partway open. Second Son glimpsed a patch of sunlight and felt a breeze caress her face. How she yearned to be able to spend some time out there, to enjoy the wide-open spaces again! Being penned up in the wigwam except for short intervals every morning and night was worse than any torture her captors might devise.

Second Son also spied the forest. It reminded her of the commotion earlier. No one had told her what caused it. Mattonabee had not spoken to her since he returned, and his wives and children were under strict orders to have nothing to do with her.

Even so, Second Son had deduced much. She had seen

Chipewyans running toward the woods. She had heard the name Windigo being yelled. And after things had calmed down, the chief's wives had chattered on for the longest while, often punctuating their talk with the same word.

Rattles Track had told Second Son about the evil hairy giants that stalked the northern woodland. With the Crow translating, Mattonabee had grilled Second Son about her encounter. She could tell by his tone and expression that he doubted her every word, perhaps because the creature she had seen, while tall, had not been a giant, and it had exhibited none of the supernatural powers attributed to Windigos by the Chipewyans.

Second Son gathered that the creature was lurking in the vicinity of the village, waiting to snatch another victim. She didn't want that victim to be Wolf Sings on the Mountain. It galled her to have to sit there helpless when her son was in dire danger.

This time, at least, the creature had not been successful. But what about the next? And the one after that?

She wanted to learn more about the beasts to add to the meager store of information already imparted by the Crow, but she had no one to quiz. She did know what she would do if she were in Mattonabee's moccasins; she would have every last warrior track the Windigo down and not allow them to rest until it was slain. To accomplish that, however, the warriors needed to know a lot more about their nemesis than they seemed to.

Any hunter worthy of the name knew that the key to success lay in knowing the habits of any game being hunted as well as the hunter knew his or her own.

Animals were predictable. They adopted patterns of behavior. They were a lot like people in that they tended to do the same things every day, month in and month out. They drank at certain watering holes. They ate certain kinds of plants. Meat eaters or otherwise, it didn't matter. They staked out a territory and routinely covered the same route again and again.

Most of what the Chipewyans claimed to know about Windigos was utter nonsense: they had the strength of a hundred men, they could turn invisible, they did not leave tracks if they did not want to, they could hear a leaf fall on the other side of a mountain, and they liked to rip the still-beating hearts out of their human victims, then eat the hearts raw.

Second Son discounted such information as exaggeration born of fear. She had seen a Windigo with her own eyes. She had touched it, had felt its hair and sinews. It was made of flesh and blood, just as she was. In which case it had to have habits of its own, habits a hunter could exploit.

Rattles Track had mentioned a few other things about Windigos that Second Son did not discount: they were rare, they appeared in the dead of winter more than any other time of the year, their howls made grown men quake, and they were so bloodthirsty that their victims were invariably found ripped to pieces.

It wasn't much to go on. So much was left unanswered. Where did the creatures go to hole up? In deadfalls, like the one she had encountered? Why did they suddenly appear in the middle of winter and just as suddenly disappear later? Did they migrate? And why were they so fond of human flesh?

Just then, from outside, came Rattles Track's voice.

Mattonabee stirred. It annoyed him to be interrupted when he was so deep in thought. Then he remembered that he had told the Crow to come to his wigwam when the sun was straight overhead so she could translate for him. Now he wished he hadn't. The outcome would be no different from all the other times.

Again Rattles Track asked politely if she should come in.

The chief adopted a stern visage and bid her enter. "I will not keep you long this time," he revealed. "I weary of the games this Tsistsista plays. I am at the limits of my patience." He beckoned her to take her place and slowly turned.

Second Son straightened and adopted her customary air of quiet defiance. She must not show any weakness or Mattonabee would be quick to take advantage. "Hello, Rattles Track," she greeted the woman. "Is my son all right?"

"He be fine," the gentle woman said. "Windigo chase him, chase other son. They get away."

It took all of Second Son's self-control not to show her anxiety. *The Windigo!* Her worst fear had nearly come true. For his sake she had to regain her freedom quickly. Yet there was only one way to do this and her pride would not let her.

Mattonabee glanced at the Crow woman. He had noticed that she often said more than seemed necessary to relay his questions, and he had begun to suspect she had grown to like the Tsistsista, although she tried hard not to show it. "What did you tell her?" he demanded.

Rattles Track responded truthfully.

"Did I say to let her know about the boy?" Mattonabee snapped. "He is not her son any longer, so what he does is not her concern. In the future say only what I instruct you to say and nothing else. Is that clear?"

"Yes," Rattles Track said.

Second Son saw the Crow blanch. Although she did not understand a word they were saying, she could see that the chief was in a foul mood. "What did he just say?" she inquired. "Why is he so mad at you?"

Rattles Track went to answer, but Mattonabee cut her

off. "And another thing. From now on you will not answer the captive when she speaks to you until you have told me what she has said. Then you will translate my words exactly as I say them."

"As you wish."

Second Son leaned forward. "What did he say?" she repeated. "Why won't you tell me?"

Mattonabee smirked and folded his arms. "She acts curious. Good. Say this." He paused. "The time of reckoning has come. I have tolerated your behavior long enough. You will agree to obey me or you will live to regret it."

The threat was no different from any other the chief had made. Second Son did not take it seriously. Smugly, she mocked him, saying, "Surely the great Mattonabee knows by now that I will never do as he wants. I am a warrior of the Tsistsista, not a timid Chipewyan woman who rushes to carry out his every whim. Only when he treats me with the respect I deserve will I do the same to him."

"Respect?" Mattonabee practically exploded. "You forget yourself, woman. You talk as if we were equals when we are not. I am the leader of the Whitefish Clan of my people. You are a captive. You are less than nothing in my eyes. You get no respect because you deserve none."

"And you do? Which one of us beats those weaker and smaller than he is? Which one of us makes threats he never carries out? Which one of us is afraid to hunt down the Windigo?"

Being called a coward was more than Mattonabee could abide. Springing to his feet, he advanced on the Tsistsista and wrapped his fingers around the hilt of his big copper knife. He had bloodlust in his heart. He wanted to be rid of this wicked woman who had never learned to bend her

knee to her betters. Yanking out the knife, he seized her by
the chin and pressed the tip to the side of her neck. In another instant he would bury it. Then he looked into her
eyes.

Second Son believed her time had come. She had finally
pushed him over the brink. The copper nicked her skin
but she did not flinch. Matching his glare with her own,
she waited for the death stroke. She might die, but she
would do so as a warrior should.

Mattonabee wavered, and wanted to scream in frustrated rage. It should be so easy. He had killed so many.
Yet he could not do what needed to be done. His strength
seemed to flow out of him through his eyes and pass into
her. His arm dropped. He was almost glad when a frantic
smacking sounded on the front flap and a thin voice urgently called his name.

Giving the captive a push, Mattonabee spun on a moccasin heel and tramped to the entrance. He bent and
stepped through the opening so quickly that he scared the
small boy who waited outside. It was Toktoyaktuk, son of
another warrior. "What do you want?" he rasped. "Do
you know no better than to disturb people who do not
wish to be disturbed?"

Toktoyaktuk was trembling all over. "It got him," he
squeaked.

"What got who?" Mattonabee asked, surveying the
peaceful camp.

"The Windigo took Aklavik."

"My son?" Mattonabee said, alarm flaring within him.
He vaguely recalled the boy going out earlier and leaving
the flap half-open as he always did, even though Mattonabee had told him countless times not to. The chief
took several steps, hoping against hope that Toktoyaktuk
was wrong.

"We were there," Toktoyaktuk said, pointing toward a

cluster of tall pines growing close to the footpath that con-
nected the south shore of the lake to the village. "A big,
hairy arm came out of the bushes and grabbed him."

"No," Mattonabee said softly, aghast. Aklavik was his
oldest, having seen ten winters, and his favorite. One day
he counted on the boy taking over the mantle of leadership.

"I am sorry," Toktoyaktuk was saying. "There was
nothing I could do. I was so afraid that I could not
speak."

"No!" Mattonabee said, louder than before. There was
no time to lose. Dashing into the wigwam, he told his
wives and directed them to go from dwelling to dwelling,
rousing all the warriors. He hurried to a corner and hastily
donned his quiver and strung his bow. As he started to
leave, he remembered the Tsistsista and the Crow.

Storming over to them, Mattonabee said, "Tell the
witch that she has gone too far this time."

Rattles Track recoiled. "Surely you do not blame her for
the taking of your son?"

"Why shouldn't I?" the chief angrily countered. "This
woman is bad medicine. From the moment Takwugan
caught her, she has brought nothing but misfortune on our
clan. I think she has cast a spell over us. I think that is why
I cannot kill her. And now she has dared to have the
Windigo steal my son."

"But—"

Mattonabee snapped. Lunging, he shoved Rattles Track
aside and slapped Second Son with all his might. The
blow stunned her, but still she stared at him without fear.
"I warn you, woman! If my son dies, so does yours! You
will see his eyes torn from their sockets and his fingers
chopped off one at a time. You will see his stomach
opened and his intestines pulled out." He bunched his fist

to strike her again, but a hail from outside stopped him. The warriors were arriving.

"I will deal with you later," Mattonabee announced, hastening from the wigwam. Five men were there. He did not wait for the rest. "Follow me!" he cried, and made for the spot Toktoyaktuk had indicated. He thought it unlikely that the Windigo had left any sign, so he was all the more elated when he pushed through the bushes and found fresh tracks in a patch of dirt. He saw where the creature had lain in wait, saw where it had taken a single long stride to reach out and grab his son. Scuff marks showed where the boy had briefly fought back. Then the Windigo had made off to the southwest at a swift lope.

Other warriors had joined them. Mattonabee faced around and pointed to four. "You will stay to protect the women and children. If we are not back by dark, build big fires at each end of the village. Stay awake all night in case the Windigo circles around us."

"We will be out all night?" said one of those who had not been picked to stay behind.

"It has my *son*," Mattonabee responded, and no man there dared object again.

The tracks were plain and easy to follow. Mattonabee wasn't the most skilled tracker in the band, but neither was he the poorest. He held to a steady jog. The men were strung out behind him in single file. Glancing back, he saw Takwugan right behind him. "I hope you are not attached to the Tsistsista's offspring," he warned.

"He has given me no trouble. He is a good boy," his friend answered.

"He is a dead boy if the Windigo harms Aklavik."

Takwugan was upset by the news, but Mattonabee was past caring. Second Son would suffer as no other woman ever had. He came to the bottom of a talus slope and scoured the heights above before climbing. Where the grass gave way to broken stone, the tracks ended.

Mattonabee gestured. The warriors knew what to do. Spreading out on either side, they began a methodical sweep of the slope. He went straight up, paying special attention to patches of bare earth. Nowhere did he find even a partial track.

By the time Mattonabee gained the top, he was deeply worried. It was just as he had feared. The Windigo had vanished, and Aklavik with it.

Until the sun rimmed the western sky the warriors carried on their search, covering every spot of ground. One of the men stopped and sat down on a boulder. Immediately Mattonabee berated him for being lazy and told him to keep on looking. The man jumped to obey.

Sighing, Takwugan approached their leader and commented, "It is no use. We have lost them. And soon it will be too dark to track."

"I am the one who will say when we quit," Mattonabee said bitterly. "And I will put an arrow into any man who thinks he knows better than me."

"None of us would be rash enough to challenge you," Takwugan said. "But think for a moment. We have gone over this entire slope and the ground on all sides. They are gone. The creature has taken your son to a place where we cannot follow. What hope have we against such powerful medicine?"

The truth was undeniable. Mattonabee halted and bowed his head, overcome by resentment. "If I had the Tsistsista's medicine, I could save Aklavik. She has more power than any person I ever—" Suddenly Mattonabee froze. An amazing idea had burst in his brain like a mental avalanche, sweeping all else before it. The plan was so simple yet so perfect that he was astounded he had not thought of it sooner. Overjoyed, he tossed back his head and laughed.

Takwugan and every last warrior there stopped what they were doing to regard their leader as if he had gone insane. They were bewildered when he waved an arm and shouted for them to return to the village. Nor did they comprehend why, on the way back, he frequently uttered the name of the Tsistsista woman, then cackled.

chapter

—— 17 ——

Rakes the Sky with Lightning did not understand why he was still alive. He should have died long ago.

The warrior had no sense of the passage of time. It might have been only two or three days since he'd ridden into Fort Hall, or many sleeps might have gone by. All he knew for certain was that he was in torment and the torment just kept getting worse.

Slowly Lightning raised his head and squinted, striving to make sense of the jumbled blur before him. This simple effort provoked spasms in his abdomen and between his ears. He would have cried out if not for the gag over his mouth.

How many times had Patch Dirksen and the trapper's

friends forced firewater down his throat to get him to tell them all he knew about Yellow Hair's cache? How many times had they beaten him when the whiskey did not loosen his tongue?

Lightning did not need to see to know that his body was covered with welts, bruises, and cuts. He did not need to touch himself to know that his cheeks were swollen, his nose twice its normal size, and several of his teeth were so loose that they might fall out if he sneezed.

In addition, one of his ears had been hit so hard that blood had trickled out and dribbled down his neck. His shirt had been torn off and his chest had been gashed by the tip of Dirksen's knife.

There was no feeling at all in his arms and legs. They had been bound so tightly to the chair for so long that he doubted if he would ever be able to use them again.

Yet with all he had endured, Rakes the Sky with Lightning was proud of himself. The Hudson's Bay men had done their worst, but he had not told them what they wanted to know. Yellow Hair's secret was safe.

An instant later the door was jerked open. A puff of fresh air cooled Lightning's brow and he caught a whiff of grass and pine trees and other fragrant scents he had always taken too much for granted. Three dark forms slid into the shack and lined themselves up in front of him. The door closed again.

"So you're still kickin', are you, Rakes?" Patch Dirksen said as he pulled the gag off. "You're one tough Injun. But tonight it all ends. I know when I'm floggin' a dead horse."

Lightning did not answer. The moment he had been longing for had arrived. At last the suffering would end. At last he would be reunited with his beloved Twisted Leg.

"Most of the boys are gone," Patch remarked. "The Shoshonis are holdin' a dance in our honor." He snorted.

"I reckon I should thank them. Now it'll be real easy to cart you from the fort and dispose of your mangy carcass."

"Let me have the honors," said his burly companion, reaching for his butcher knife.

"Great notion, Larsen," cracked Patch. "Slit his throat right here. That way maybe someone will walk in one day and see a big pool of dried blood and wonder where it came from."

"So what if they do? He'll be buzzard turds by then. No one will ever link us to his death."

Patch shook his head. "It's a loose end, friend. And if there's one thing a hunter learns early on, it's to never leave a trail of any kind." He lowered his face to within inches of the warrior's. "I wouldn't want it said that I'm not a generous man, so I'll give you this one last chance. Tell us, and I give you my word that you won't suffer. I'll do you myself. It'll be real short and sweet."

Lightning could barely speak. He had to swallow a half-dozen times and force his protesting lips to move. "I do not care how you kill me, white man. My time has come. I am ready."

Sighing, Patch straightened. "I never have made sense of the Injun outlook on death. It seems to me that the whole damn lot of you are ready to die at the drop of a hat. Pretty stupid, if you ask me."

The trapper with the scar gestured impatiently. "Quit the jawing, will you? Let's get this over with."

"Nervous, Timms?" Patch baited him.

"Damn right I am," the man replied, "and you would be, too, if you had the brains God gave a turnip. If we're caught, or if that Yank finds out, there'll be hell to pay. Everyone says he's not one to trifle with, him nor that heathen wildcat of his."

"Scared of the red bitch, are you?" Patch said, and chuckled.

"Don't poke fun at me," Timms groused. "You've heard the stories. They say she cut off a fellow's pecker once for messing with her. Now I ask you, what sort of woman would do such a thing?"

"A woman after my own heart. One with more grit than ten men combined," Patch admitted. "But the way I've worked things out, we've no need to fret. She'll never connect us to her nephew's disappearance."

"Let's hope not. For all our sakes."

Lightning had listened with half an ear. He wished the white men would quit talking and get it over with. Every moment they wasted was another moment he was kept from seeing his wife. It was like that time he tried to provoke the grizzly into charging him and the bear had run off. When he wanted most to end his life, life would not cooperate.

It made the Kit Fox warrior think of his skirmish with the Blackfoot war party. Any one of them would gladly have counted coup on him. But it was one thing for a warrior to seek his end in a manner of his choosing and another to let lifelong enemies do the job.

Suddenly rough hands were untying the ropes that bound him. Lightning smiled grimly. At last they were getting it over with! He realized that Patch had drawn a pistol and trained the barrel on his chest. His smile widened. Were they so blind that they could not see he was too weak to lift a finger against them? The ropes fell to the floor.

"On your feet, Rakes," Dirksen commanded. "And do it slow, if you please."

Lightning knew he could do it no other way. His arms had fallen at his sides and his legs tingled as if they were being pricked by a thousand buffalo-bone needles at once. The tingling hurt more than it tickled, so much so that waves of pain washed up him.

"Come on, damn your hide. We don't have all stinkin' night," the one-eyed man declared.

"I will try," Lightning said. Awkwardly sliding his legs in front of him, he planted his feet firmly and attempted to rise. Nothing happened. It was as if he had no muscles. He tried once more, gritting his teeth to ward off the pain. All he succeeded in doing was twitching his toes.

"He'll never make it on his own," Larsen said. "He's too weak."

Patch backed to the door and wagged the flintlock. "Then the two of you will have to tote him. I'll lead the way and keep watch. If I wave, hide."

Lightning sagged as the pair of trappers slipped their hands under his shoulders and roughly hoisted him off the chair. Both men grunted. They steadied him, then propelled him to the door, which Patch had opened.

A gust of wind struck the warrior as they emerged. It caressed his body from top to bottom, much like the fingers of his wife had done when they lay under their buffalo robe at night. A moan escaped his lips.

"Shut him up!" Patch hissed.

Larsen pivoted and slammed a rock-hard fist into the Kit Fox warrior's gut. Lightning doubled over as excruciating agony shot through him. Barely able to breathe, he gasped for air. He was left so weak that he could not stand. The two company men had to carry him, letting his feet drag.

Although Lightning was in torment and could not lift so much as a finger, his senses were extraordinarily sharp. He attributed it to being locked in the shack for so long. Every little noise was like a thunderclap in his ears. His nose registered every scent, no matter how faint. The dank earth, the smell of horses in the stable, the pungent scent of the white men, his own sweat, he smelled them all.

The trappers bore him toward the northwest corner of

the palisade, passing behind the trading post and the main building. Since the gate was on the south side of the post, Lightning was puzzled until he saw that a wagon had been backed up against the far corner and crates piled high on the bed, reaching almost to the top of the wall.

They were nearly there when the murmur of voices caused Patch, Larsen, and Timms to flatten. The latter two yanked Lightning down beside them and Timms placed a hand over the warrior's mouth to keep him from crying out.

"One peep and you die that much sooner!"

Lightning could not have cried out if he wanted to. He rested quietly, feeling a smidgen of strength return to his arms and legs.

The voices faded. Patch promptly motioned and they hastened on to the wagon. Timms and Larsen heaved Lightning onto the bed. The warrior winced as his right shoulder slammed onto the hard wood. He rolled onto his back and lay there sucking in air. The wagon squeaked when the two white men climbed up.

Timms stepped around behind Lightning and lifted the warrior as high as he could. Larsen moved in close, stooped, and draped him over his wide right shoulder.

The crates had been arranged like steps. Timms got onto the first one and helped Larsen hoist Lightning up. The burly trapper had such short legs that he had to be pulled up by Timms. And so it went until they were up to the highest one. Timms gripped the tapered tops of the cottonwood logs, swung himself up, carefully eased over the side, and dropped.

For a terrible moment Lightning thought that Larsen was simply going to fling him over. From that height, in his condition, the fall would probably break half the bones in his body. But Larsen hoisted him high enough to slide him through a notch, held him by his wrists with his body dangling, then let go.

The drop was short, yet it jarred him. His legs crumpled as if they were soft reeds. He felt Timms grab him and drag him toward the trees. A heavy thud told him Larsen had joined them. He lifted his head and saw Patch Dirksen come over. They hurried to help Timms, casting anxious glances at the bastion on the northwest corner.

No outcry was raised. The sentry had not noticed.

It was not long before the forest enveloped them. The three trappers stopped to catch their breath. They were grinning now, partly in triumph and partly in sadistic glee at what lay in store for their captive. At a nod from Patch they dragged Lightning deeper into the pines.

The warrior knew the end was near. He focused on a mental picture of Twisted Leg. Soon he would be by her side again, where he belonged.

The white men came to a small clearing. To one side lay a large log. Lightning was propped against it and Patch squatted in front of him.

"Well, Rakes, you've come to the end of your trail. It's too bad you didn't take my advice. You could have spared yourself a heap of pain." With that, the one-eyed trapper swung his right arm.

Lightning could not duck or dodge. His head exploded in a whirl of colors and dizzying sensations. His jaw felt as if it had been snapped in half. He was knocked onto his side, dazed.

"You can't say I didn't warn you," Patch said, pulling the warrior back up. "I told you flat out that I was going to make you suffer if you didn't open up. It's your fault that you didn't take me at my word."

Dimly, Lightning realized that Dirksen had drawn his knife. He braced for the killing stroke. "Do it," he croaked, overjoyed that at long, long last it was all over.

"Not so fast, friend," Patch responded. "Haven't you been listenin'? We aim to have some fun first. Sort of pay you back for all the grief you've caused us." He pressed the razor-sharp tip of the blade against Lightning's left biceps until he drew blood. "We're fixin' to carve you into bits and pieces. By the time we're done, your own aunt won't recognize you."

Lightning did not care to have them whittle him down as if he were a block of wood. He stared at the knife, a hand's width from his chest. Gathering what little energy he had left, he threw his body forward, seeking to impale himself. But Patch was too quick. The blade was snatched back out of reach and Lightning was slammed against the log.

"Oh, no you don't! You're not goin' to cheat us of our due. Take your lumps like a man, Rakes." Patch grinned and wagged the dully glittering knife. "Where should I start? The fingers? The toes? Or how about an ear?"

Lightning clamped his teeth together. He was not going to give them the pleasure of hearing him scream. No matter what they did, he would endure it.

The only regret the warrior had was that he would never have the chance to properly thank Second Son for all she had done for him. His aunt had always treated him with the utmost kindness and respect. When he had been small, she had taken him under her wing and instructed him in many warrior ways. And she had been the one who introduced him to Twisted Leg. He owed her more than he could ever repay.

Suddenly Lightning became aware that Patch was talking again. He caught the last few words.

"—all you went through for nothing."

"What do you mean?" Lightning asked.

"Your dyin' is a waste, Injun. That's what I mean. Sooner or later I'll get my hands on Bennett's gold. Since you won't tell me the big secret, I'll have to persuade one of the others to talk. Your aunt, maybe. Or that breed brat of theirs."

Outrage lent Lightning unexpected strength. He whipped his right hand to Patch's throat even as he grabbed the trapper's wrist to hold the knife at bay. His intention was to throttle Patch lifeless, but Larsen and Timms were on him in a twinkling. They seized his arms and held them fast so that he could not budge a muscle.

Patch was doubled over, coughing violently. When he raised his head, a feral gleam lit his sole eye. "You shouldn't ought to have done that, Injun. I've changed my mind. Instead of takin' off your ear or your tongue, I think I'll start lower down." He paused to let the full import sink in. "Boys, do me a favor and strip those britches off this buck."

Lightning tugged and heaved, but he was powerless to stop them. They slammed him down on his back in the middle of the clearing and tore off his buckskin pants, Timms snickering all the while. Larsen then stepped close to his feet and pinned his ankles in place.

Patch approached, slowly waving the butcher knife from side to side. "Know what I think I'll do?" he asked. "After we're done here, I'm going to take your pecker and pickle it in a jar. That way I can show it around when I get back home. Hell, folks might even pay to see a genuine Injun doodle."

Larsen laughed. "Damn, Patch, but you come up with some great notions. No one but you would have thought of that."

Halting, Patch looked down and sneered. "I've never done this before, Rakes, so you'll have to bear with me if I make a mess of it."

The other two laughed.

Lightning tried to tear his arms and legs free, but it was

hopeless. All he could do was lie there and watch in horror as Patch sank to a knee beside him and held the knife poised over his groin. His skin broke out in goose bumps and he shivered even though he burned with fever. The blade began to descend.

"Hold it right there!"

The three trappers jumped to their feet at the grating bellow and swung toward the trees. Figures charged out of the shadows.

"Son of a bitch!" Larsen roared.

Lightning gawked in confusion. He saw the newcomers close in from several directions. He saw Timms draw a pistol and extend it. A rifle cracked. Timms staggered, clutched his temple, and collapsed. Several buckskin-clad forms pounced on Larsen, who went down swinging.

Patch Dirksen whirled to run. Suddenly a towering figure with long yellow hair reared in front of him. "You!" Patch snarled, and stabbed, but the blow was deflected and a massive fist caught him flush on the ribs. He doubled over. Sputtering, Patch cursed, then thrust low, at his attacker's loins. His arm was seized. Frantic, he wrenched backward but could not tear loose. The big man with the blond hair whipped his knee up and there was a loud crack as the elbow shattered.

Patch screeched. The knife fell at his feet. He started to sink to the ground and raised his head just as a fist descended. There was a crunch and a thud and Patch Dirksen was prone on the ground, motionless.

Lightning wanted to sit up but could not will his body to obey. In a bound the big man was at his side and holding him, a warm hand at the nape of his neck. He stared at the familiar face above him, incredulous.

"Yellow Hair?"

Cleve spoke, but whatever he said was swallowed by the same black veil that claimed the Kit Fox warrior.

• • •

Second Son expected trouble when two Chipewyan warriors came to get her.

For some time there had been a great commotion in the village. People had been shouting and bustling about.

The chief's wives had departed long ago, leaving Second Son all alone for the first time in days. She immediately attempted to free her hands. It would take some doing. Mattonabee had made it a point to check the knots every morning and to tighten them if they seemed the least bit loose.

The warrior woman had been working at the task for quite some time when the two men showed up. Both were painted as if for war and had their weapons with them. One cut her ankles free. The other brusquely hauled her to her feet and shoved her toward the entrance.

Outside awaited a greater surprise. Every last member of the Whitefish Clan had gathered in front of the wigwam. Formed into two rows on either side with a wide path between them, they stood as silent as ranks of trees. At the other end of the path waited a tall figure wearing a bizarre wooden mask.

In the flickering light cast by the two large fires that lit the scene, it took Second Son a few seconds to recognize the figure as Mattonabee. She hesitated, unsure of what was expected of her, and was given a hard push by one of her escorts. The sight of Billy-Wolf sparked momentary happiness, which was quickly eclipsed by the anger she felt when she saw that husky warriors flanked him and held his arms so that he could not interfere with whatever had been planned for her.

Second Son caught his eye. His distress was evident. She smiled and he smiled back, but it was easy to see that his heart was not in it. He glanced at the chief and gnawed on his lower lip.

One of the men let out with a fluttering cry much like the piercing shriek of a hawk. It was the signal for the entire band to begin a singsong chant that rose in volume the closer the warrior woman drew to their leader.

Second Son had to keep moving or be prodded by the pair behind her. She had gone a third of the distance when she noticed a large war club propped against Mattonabee's left leg. Embedded in the top was a curved copper blade of sufficient size to shear off a head with a single swipe.

Mattonabee had his arms folded across his chest. He was the perfect picture of solemnity, but under his mask he was grinning. At long last he had the Tsistsista right where he wanted her! He came close to laughing aloud at her wariness. She didn't know it yet, but she was as good as dead. One way or another, he would pay her back for her effrontery.

The mask the chief wore represented the legendary dog creature that had mated with the Mother to produce the Chipewyans. Generations ago it had been crafted by a gifted shaman and been passed from leader to leader ever since. It was worn only on formal occasions.

When Second Son passed the last of the onlookers, Mattonabee commenced the special chant that would bring good fortune to his people. He broke into a shuffling dance, the club in his left hand. Moving in a circle, he bobbed his head with every step.

The Chipewyans took up the refrain, stomping their moccasins in rhythm.

Fifteen feet from the chief, Second Son drew up short. The significance of the ritual was incomprehensible to her, yet the chanting and dancing were remarkably similar in certain respects to rituals of her own people.

Second Son would have stayed where she was had one of her escorts not poked her with the tip of his bow. She advanced, taking small steps, alert for any abrupt moves on Mattonabee's part. The fact that he had a war club did not bode well.

Without warning the two escorts stepped in close and grabbed her arms. Second Son thought they were going to hold her there, just as the other two were doing with her son, but she was wrong. One of them stuck out his foot while simultaneously giving her a shove. She fell hard onto her knees. Hands on her shoulders prevented her from rising.

Second Son saw Mattonabee come toward her. He skipped lightly from right to left and back again, the war club in front of him. The big copper knife swayed from side to side like the russet head of some immense serpent. He stopped when he was close enough to touch her. Crying out in his own language, he swept the club overhead, then brought it sweeping down at her upturned face.

chapter

—— 18 ——

Billy-Wolf Bennett had been expecting treachery of some
kind. When the chief arced the war club on high, his blood
turned to ice. Before he could help himself, he screamed at
the top of his lungs in Tsistsista, *"Mother!"*

Second Son had also expected treachery. She went to
throw herself to the right but was held fast by the warrior
behind her. In the blink of an eye the war club flashed toward her face. She thought for sure that her head would
be split like an overripe melon, yet at the very last instant
Mattonabee checked his swing, stopping the blade within
a hairsbreadth of her nose.

Mattonabee relished that moment. For an instant in
time she had been totally at his mercy, just as he had

wanted her to be all along. The scream of her offspring was an added delight. He had demonstrated his superiority in front of all his people. No one could doubt his fitness to lead.

Shifting the ax to his side, Mattonabee stared at the clan through the thin slits in his dog mask. Shouting so all could hear, he declared, "You have seen with your own eyes! This woman was in my power, yet I spared her life." Puffing out his chest, he strutted from side to side, studying each and every clan member for any hint that they doubted him. Satisfied he had made the impression he wanted, he pointed at Rattles Track and bid her, "Come. You will translate."

The Crow woman obediently hurried forward.

"I have important words for our people," the chief informed her. "You will share them with the Tsistsista exactly as I say them. Do not add any. Do not subtract any. She must understand clearly what is required of her. Is that understood?"

"I will do my best," Rattles Track pledged.

"You had better." Mattonabee faced his people and raised his arms to get their attention. "It is no secret that we have fallen on hard times. We have been driven from our land. We are denied the caribou which mean life itself. A Windigo has plagued us for many sleeps." He paused. "Some of you, I know, think that we have angered the Creator without meaning to, so we are being punished. Others think that a powerful Cree shaman has put a curse on us."

Murmuring broke out as the opposing points of view were debated.

"I will be honest. I cannot say if either is the case. But I do know this." Mattonabee moved close to Second Son. "This woman might be the answer to at least one of our problems. As all of you are aware, Aklavik was taken by the Windigo. We tried to save him, but the Windigo's trail vanished into thin air as it always does."

The Chipewyans grew somber.

"My son is the seventh victim this Windigo has taken." Mattonabee rattled off the list of names, then went on. "How many more of us must be slain before the creature loses interest and goes elsewhere? Is there no way for us to put an end to the slaughter *now*?"

Second Son had been paying close attention. She resented being used to boost the chief's influence, but she was more concerned over where his speech was leading.

"I think there is," Mattonabee declared. He gestured at the Tsistsista. "This woman is no ordinary woman. You can see for yourselves that she dresses like a man. Ask my wives and they will tell you that she acts like a man. And Takwugan and those who were with him will verify that she also fights like a man. She killed Chetwynd, did she not? And wounded two others? What Chipewyan woman could do such a thing? None. It is a clue to her secret."

All eyes were on Second Son. Few were friendly.

"By now all of you have heard how she fought off the Windigo. How she was able to do that which no Chipewyan has been able to do in the history of our people. 'How did she do it?' you might ask yourselves. 'It is impossible.' "

Second Son did not move when Mattonabee rested a hand on her head. It would have done no good with the two warriors right there to hold her still.

"I have asked myself that same question. I have pondered day and night. And I have discovered the truth." The chief waited a moment for effect. "This woman has powerful medicine which keeps her from harm. A charm, perhaps. Or something else. How else did she hold her own against six of our bravest warriors? How else did she fend off a Windigo?"

Second Son nearly laughed. "I need no war charm to win in battle," she told Rattles Track.

"Why do I bring this up?" Mattonabee continued. "Because I propose to use this woman to save my son and slay the Windigo. I will bend her to my will to show you that my medicine is more powerful than hers." Turning toward the captive, he squatted. As always, her features were molded in defiance. But this time she was in for a surprise.

"I will not do it," Second Son stated bluntly. "You have wasted your breath for nothing. Soon your people will see that your claim to power is false and they will reject you."

Mattonabee spoke slowly so that the Crow would have no difficulty translating.

"Him say you be wrong, warrior woman," Rattles Track said. "Him say you do as he want. If not, your son be staked out in woods. Left for Windigo to find."

There wasn't a shred of doubt in Second Son's mind that Mattonabee would do exactly as he threatened. He had her, as Cleve would say, over a barrel. She would do anything to save Wolf Sings on the Mountain and he knew it.

"Well?" Rattles Track prompted at the chief's urging.

Second Son remembered the time her husband had cursed out a trapper who had been too forward with her. "Tell the son of a bitch that he has won. I will hunt the Windigo."

Rakes the Sky with Lightning had almost forgotten how it felt to be warm and comfortable. He felt half-afraid to open his eyes for fear he might be dreaming and would find that he was still strapped to the chair in the small shack. But when he did, there sat Yellow Hair and Courtney Walker, the man in charge of Fort Hall.

Cleve had been anxiously waiting for the warrior to come around. Smiling, he said, "Welcome back to the land of the living. You've been out most of the night. Sunup is not far off."

Lightning had to try three times before his vocal cords would work. "My heart is glad that you are here, Yellow Hair. Yet I do not savvy why."

"It's no big mystery," Cleve said, shifting to lean on the bed. "I felled and shaped all the trees we needed. Since there wasn't much else I could do without the nails and your help, I figured I'd light a shuck for the fort." He pursed his lips. "And, too, I was just plain lonely with no one to talk to."

Courtney Walker rose. He was a meticulous man who customarily wore neatly pressed clothes and a stiff hat. "I have to be off. Before I go, accept my assurance that I will mete out proper punishment to Patch and Larsen. Timms would share in their guilt, but he's dead." With a nod, he departed.

Cleve chuckled. "Decent man, that Walker. I ran into him on the way here. He was coming back early from the coast." He gestured at the room. "You're in his quarters, you know. He wouldn't hear of anything else."

Exhaustion and lack of food were taking their toll, and Lightning could barely keep his eyes open. "How did you know . . ."

"Where to find you?" Cleve finished the question. "I didn't, at first. Your bay was in the stable, so I asked around. Blevitt over at the trading post claimed he'd never seen you. But then I learned that he'd been flashing gold coins, so I went back and boxed his ears in until he fessed up. It seems he knew of Patch's little scheme but he'd wanted no part of it."

Lightning was drifting asleep again. His friend's words rapidly grew fainter.

"We didn't know where Patch was holding you, so we kept watch on him and those other two. We saw them cart you from the shack, but we held back as long as we dared for fear they'd shoot you before we could close in." Cleve rubbed the knuckles of his right hand. "I can't tell you how much I liked breaking Dirksen's nose."

Cleve heard a fluttering snore and fondly regarded the scarred warrior. "You rest, nephew. You take your time and mend. When you're fit enough we'll head for home. There's no rush. Knowing my wife, she won't be back for a week or two yet. I bet you anything Billy-Wolf and her are having the time of their lives."

Pink streaks tinged the eastern sky when Second Son stepped from the wigwam and adjusted the quiver slung over her back. In her right hand she clasped a Chipewyan bow. A long copper knife hung on her left hip. A small ax had been wedged under the belt on the other side. In addition, a leather bag had been slung across her chest. It contained pemmican and jerky, enough for several days.

At so early an hour none of the Whitefish Clan was yet abroad, with a single exception. Second Son was surprised to see Rattles Track bundled in a caribou robe decorated with colored quills. "Have you been waiting for me?" she asked.

"Yes, friend. Me make you this."

Second Son was handed a bracelet composed of large polished elk teeth. Her puzzlement was obvious.

"Yesterday you say have no charm," Rattles Track explained. "Me make you one. Bring you good medicine."

The warrior woman looked at her. Second Son felt a strong liking for this gentle person who had suffered so many tragedies in her life yet still had a heart brimming with goodness. Most people would have succumbed to bitterness and resentment. "I am honored," she declared, donning the gift.

"Also want you not worry," Rattles Track said. "If you

not come back, me take care of son. Him grow be strong man."

Second Son put a hand on the other's shoulder. "You are a fine friend, Rattles Track. I wish we had met another time, another place." She would have said more, but the flap rustled and she sensed who was standing there. "What does Mattonabee want, Rattles Track?"

The chief stepped into view. He didn't bother telling them that he had heard voices and investigated. It angered him to see Takwugan's woman on such close terms with the Tsistsista. He would have forbidden Rattles Track to see her, but he didn't deem it prudent to upset the Crow when she was the only means he had of communicating with Second Son. "Tell her that I came to see her off and wish her well," he commanded.

"What do you care if I live or die?" Second Son relayed through the Crow.

"True, I care nothing for you," Mattonabee said. "But I do care very much for my son. I want Aklavik back safe where he belongs. You are the only one who has any hope of saving him, so your well-being is of great importance to me."

"And once I save him what will you do?"

Mattonabee tried to keep all expression from his face and all emotion from the tone he used so she wouldn't guess that he was lying. "You'll have done what no other Chipewyan ever has, and for that you should be rewarded. I will give serious thought to freeing you and your son."

The man's mouth said one thing, his eyes another. Second Son did not believe him for a minute. She made up her mind then and there to outfox him. Before she was through, Mattonabee would learn the hard way that women were every bit as competent as men.

"There is one other reason I came out to see you off,"

Mattonabee said, and rose on his toes to survey the encampment. "I wonder where he can be?"

"Who?" Second Son asked through Rattles Track.

"The one who is going with you."

Second Son glanced at Rattles Track, who shook her head to indicate she had no idea what he was up to. "I hunt best when by myself," Second Son insisted. "I will go alone."

"I do not recall asking you to take him," Mattonabee responded indignantly. "I am *telling* you to take him." He saw a man appear over by the lake and smiled. "Ah, here comes your hunting partner now."

Second Son turned. It was rare for her to be dumbfounded, yet she was now. For shuffling toward them came the young warrior she had seen that first day she arrived, the warrior who was all skin and bones, the one whose only garment consisted of tattered pants. He hadn't changed. His hair still hung in filthy strands. His body was still covered with dirt and scratches. But this time he was armed. A knife hung at his waist and he carried a thick lance. "You cannot be serious," she declared.

Rattles Track translated.

Mattonabee laughed lightly. "I am very serious." He waited for the young warrior to reach them, then said, "Second Son, permit me to introduce Kelownan. Two moons ago his father, Qualicum, was taken by the Windigo. He has not been the same man since."

"He is in no shape to fight the creature."

"Never judge by appearances," Mattonabee replied. "He is uncommonly strong. And he has his clear moments." He patted the younger man's arm. "He heard that you were going after the creature and begged me to allow him to go along."

Which was not quite true. Kelownan had shown up at the chief's wigwam late the night before and informed

Mattonabee that he would be joining the Tsistsista. Mattonabee had been inclined to argue, but the gleam of madness that lurked just under the surface of the young warrior's eyes had stilled his tongue.

Anyone with intelligence knew not to antagonize those who had snapped. Some of the older members of the clan claimed that the Chipewyans were prone to madness, that in their many years they had seen it come over men and women alike time and time again. The hard lives they lived were largely to blame. That, and the merciless winters, which drove every clan member to the brink of death and often beyond.

"Remember the directions I gave you and you will have no problem finding the talus slope," the chief declared. "Remember, too, to watch your backs. Windigos like to attack their victims from the rear or from above."

Kelownan gave Second Son an uneasy smile and spoke rapidly, so fast that Rattles Track seemed to have difficulty catching every word.

"Him say thank you. Him long want kill Windigo. No other warriors would go. Now he avenge father. Him very happy."

Second Son sighed. Debating the point would be useless. "Tell my son that I will be back," she told Rattles Track. Then she swung to the southwest and hastened off. The young warrior fell into step beside her, running as silently as she did, his bony features pale in the dim light.

At the edge of the village Second Son slowed to look back. The chief had gone into the wigwam. Rattles Track had not moved; she waved. Second Son responded in kind.

Plunging into the forest at the point Mattonabee had told her about, Second Son traveled at a brisk rate until the sun had cleared the majestic mountains. On a narrow

shelf partway up a slope she stopped to survey the countryside.

Kelownan appeared to be upset. He nudged her,
pointed to the southwest, and rattled off a string of sen-
tences.

Second Son knew what was bothering him. He wanted
her to continue on to the talus slope, as Mattonabee had
advised them to do. But she wasn't going to waste most of
a day trying to pick up a cold trail. Based on the little she
had learned of Windigos, she had come up with a plan
that stood a much better chance of success.

Kelownan plucked at her sleeve and motioned again.

"No, we are not going on," Second Son stated.

Unexpectedly, the madman grabbed her shoulder and
shoved her in the direction they had been going. He gestured angrily with the lance, a fiery gleam making his face
as feral as the monster they hunted.

Second Son stayed calm. She reminded herself that the
young warrior had suffered an emotional blow that had
stripped him of his reason. He could not be held fully ac-
countable for his actions.

Slowly straightening, Second Son locked her gaze on his
and advanced. Kelownan halfheartedly jabbed at her, but
she stepped aside, placed a hand on the shaft, and spoke
firmly. "No!"

The young man frowned. He whined. He shifted from
one foot to the other. Finally he lowered his weapon.

Moving to the edge of the shelf, Second Son motioned
for Kelownan to do the same. Since she was stuck with
him, she had to make the best of a bad situation. Somehow she must explain her plan.

Haltingly, Kelownan inched nearer. He had the air of a
wolf about to bolt.

Second Son swept her arm to encompass the length and
breadth of the verdant tableland. From the steep moun-

tains in the east to the higher range in the west, from the ragged peaks to the north to the spot where they were standing, she included it all, then looked at him to see if he was paying attention. She pointed at the lake, then at the village. From that distance the wigwams resembled ant-hills.

Kelownan just stood there, staring in mute incomprehension. He voiced that plaintive whine of his to show his distress.

"Windigo," Second Son said to get his attention. That did the job. He glared at anything and everything with the lance poised to thrust. "Windigo," she repeated, pointing at the village again and making a circle in the air as if she were drawing a line around its perimeter.

Her plan was simplicity itself. She based it on the only habit the Windigo had that she could exploit. The beast apparently spent most of its time spying on the Chipewy-ans, waiting for an unwary victim to draw too close to its hiding place. It never hid in the same spot twice, but it was always close by. She had a much better chance of catching the creature in the act than if she spent days traipsing over the tableland.

The madman was perplexed. He scratched his head, his chin, his chest. He stared long and hard at the village, then at her. "Windigo?"

Second Son held her right hand upside down with the first two fingers pointing at the ground. She moved them as if they were tiny legs and "walked" her hand toward the village. "Windigo," she said hopefully. Then she stamped her feet to make clear tracks in the dirt.

Kelownan held up his own hand and mimicked her. "Windigo?" he said, wriggling his fingers.

Second Son hunkered down to tap the tracks she had made. He looked at them but evidently did not make the connection. Several times she went through the same motions, trying to get it through his head that they were going to look for the beast's footprints. Just when she had about convinced herself that it was hopeless, the young warrior's face lit up like a campfire and he excitedly bobbed his chin.

"Windigo! Windigo! Windigo!" he exclaimed, stomping his feet.

To verify that he had gotten the idea, Second Son leveled an arm at the village and drew the circle in the air. Some of his confidence evaporated, but he leveled his arm and said the creature's name.

Second Son descended, angling to the northeast, sticking to the thickest cover. Since the beast's senses were undeniably keener than hers, she had to compensate by exercising extra caution and making no noise. Her newfound ally demonstrated superior skills of his own, trailing her in total silence, a virtual ghost.

A wide band of firs gave way to spruce lower down. Second Son commenced a sweep from west to east, on the lookout for patches of bare earth where the Windigo might have left tracks.

Kelownan had indeed caught on, for he was just as diligent in scouring the ground they covered.

Over an hour went by. When Second Son felt they had gone well east of the eastern limit of the village, she veered to the northwest. In this zigzag fashion she planned to make a sweep of the forest right up to the edge of the trees that bordered the encampment.

They were constantly climbing slopes, crossing gullies, and circumventing obstacles such as boulders and downed trees. Second Son was on the watch for deadfall areas, but there were none.

Meanwhile the sun climbed steadily. By the middle of the morning they were tired and dusty, but neither of them gave any thought to resting. Kelownan, in particular, behaved like a man obsessed. Ceaselessly in motion, he checked every possible spot where tracks would show, even venturing into thickets bisected by game trails.

Second Son changed her mind about having the young warrior along. They were able to cover twice as much territory as she would have done on her own, which hiked the odds of success. But as the morning wore on and they came across no sign at all, she began to question whether her plan was sound.

Then they came to a knoll and made for the crest, Second Son taking the right, the Chipewyan slanting to the left. They were halfway up when a loud rustling broke out on the other side. Something growled softly.

Second Son drew up and signaled for Kelownan to do likewise. She quickly notched a shaft to the bowstring and sidled toward him. If it was the Windigo, they were better off confronting it together. Alone, they would be overwhelmed.

The warrior woman saw high weeds move at the top. Loud sniffing ensued as the animal sought to catch their scent. She sighted on the spot and pulled the string clear back to her cheek. None too soon.

The weeds parted to reveal the savage thing stalking them.

chapter

— 19 —

Kelownan flung his spear arm back and bounded higher to get close enough to use it. In his unstoppable thirst for vengeance he did not take the time to confirm that the animal was the Windigo.

For a precious instant Second Son doubted her own eyes, then she threw herself at the Chipewyan. "No!" she cried, swinging her bow so that it clipped the lance just as the warrior snapped the weapon forward. She barely brushed it, but that was enough to cause the lance to bite into the earth well shy of its mark.

Startled, the madman glanced at her as if she were the one touched in the head.

Second Son had eyes only for the yellow bundle of

grime and energy that bounded down the slope and launched itself at her. She let go of the bow and braced her legs, but still the dog bowled her over. Grinning and giggling as if she were ten years old again, Second Son hugged the animal close and said breathlessly, "Snip! You are alive!"

The mongrel yipped and licked her face, her neck, her hands. He could not get enough of her, nor she of him. They tumbled playfully about in the grass until they were both spent.

Second Son rose to her knees to examine him. Snip had a knot on the side of his head as well as dried blood plastered to his fur. His coat was thick with burs and mud and his paws were filthy.

Either the dog had been mistakenly left for dead, Second Son mused, or he had crawled off into the brush during the fight and been overlooked when Takwugan's party led Billy-Wolf and her off. Either way, the animal must have started in search of them as soon as it was strong enough, but had lost the trail at some point and been scouring the region for them ever since.

Second Son could imagine how glad her son would be that Snip had survived. It had been just one year ago that Wolf Sings on the Mountain had lost his other prized pet, Jase.

Kelownan leaned on his lance, impatiently tapping his foot. He wanted to be off.

"I am coming," Second Son said out of habit, even though he would not understand. She gave Snip a last rub, then reclaimed her bow and went up and over the knoll. The dog glued itself to her side. She was doubly pleased that fate had smiled on them since Snip's powerful sense of smell would be of definite help if they ever struck the creature's trail.

But it seemed as if they never would.

Noon came and went. They rested briefly, munching on pemmican and drinking at a narrow stream. Snip wolfed three thick pieces of jerky. Judging by the tightness of the skin over his ribs, he had not eaten regularly since their separation.

On they went. At a flat tract bordering huge trees that had stood for many hundreds of years, Second Son stopped. From a shaded cluster of trees to the north issued an odd buzzing. She pivoted, and nearly gagged. A revolting stench made her put a hand over her mouth and nose. She breathed shallowly. The young warrior did the same. Snip was unaffected.

The foul odor was familiar to anyone who spent any length of time in the wilderness.

Every so often in her travels Second Son came across the bodies of deer and other animals slain by predators or disease. She figured that this was another instance until she stepped between two of the trees and saw the headless body swarming thick with flies.

It was the boy, Aklavik. Or what was left of him. His chest and abdomen had been torn open and his organs ripped out. Coils of intestines lay strewn across his hips. A partially eaten liver was beside him. His flesh bore dozens of bite marks.

Kelownan groaned, stepped close, and sank to his knees.

Second Son moved upwind so the smell would not be as bad. She looked about for the boy's head but didn't see it. So much blood had spewed from the corpse that a large puddle had formed and hardened. Bloody footprints led off to the northeast.

Oversized footprints with long curved claws on each toe.

The young warrior set down the lance and scooped dirt and leaves onto the boy's legs. Whining pitiably, he covered the entire body, then mumbled in the Chipewyan tongue for the longest while.

Snip, meanwhile, had been sniffing the ground, his hackles raised. He had followed the tracks a score of feet, then sat on his haunches and looked back.

How had the boy gotten there? Second Son wondered as she hurried to catch up with the mongrel. As near as she could work it out, the Windigo had doubled back on Mattonabee and the search party after losing them at the talus slope. It was unlikely that the poor child had still been alive at that point. The creature had probably carried the body until it grew hungry. But what had it done with the head?

Snip stood and broke into a steady lope.

Second Son ran faster in order not to let the dog out of her sight. Behind her, his wasted features lit from within by the rekindled mad glow of his fanatical thirst for revenge, jogged Kelownan.

Based on the prints, Second Son pegged the trail as at least twelve hours old, possibly longer. The creature could be anywhere, but she was counting on its insatiable appetite for human flesh to be its undoing.

Time crawled by. Second Son's left leg cramped. She ignored the pain and it went away. Snip glided through the deep woods with his nose to the ground, rarely raising his head. The warrior never spoke to her, although his lips often moved soundlessly.

The bloody prints ended at the point where the blood had worn off the Windigo's feet. From there on they had to track it as they would any other animal. For a while that posed no problem, as the tracks were quite distinct, thanks to the Windigo, which had been running in long bounding leaps.

The tall timber gave way to shorter spruce mixed with saplings. Here the beast had slowed and moved cautiously.

Its tread had been light; consequently the tracks were few and far between.

Snip, though, did not need to rely on the prints. His nose guided them due north. Toward the village.

Suddenly the dog stopped. Second Son gazed past it and felt her stomach churn. She had seen so many grisly sights over the years that they had become a matter of course. But not this one.

It was the boy's head. It sat perched on a log, facing them. The eyes had been gouged out and the nose consumed. Both cheeks had been gnawed through. Both lips had been bitten off.

Before Second Son could stop him, Kelownan dashed past her, fell to his knees, and scooped the head into his arms. Tears gushed as he stroked the matted hair and blubbered incoherently. Gore and rotted flesh clung to him, but he appeared not to notice.

Second Son went over. She touched Kelownan's shoulder, pointed at the head, and motioned for him to set it down. He refused. She attempted to pull his arms loose, but he violently jerked away and turned his back to her. Thinking that he might like to cover it as he had the body, she hunkered and scooped out a large enough hole. When she tapped him, he glanced at the hole and made an emphatic gesture.

Recognizing a hopeless cause when she saw one, Second Son continued on with Snip. By her estimation they were almost within earshot of the village. She had been right. The creature was spying on the Chipewyans again.

Second Son slowed. A dense stand of berry bushes blocked their way and Snip had veered to go around them. Following, she saw the mongrel leap over a broken limb that had fallen from a tree that flanked the berry patch. She glanced down and noticed that the thick end of the limb was twisted, as if it had been wrenched from the trunk.

Idly lifting her head, she glimpsed a bulky hairy figure just as it launched itself from a thick lower branch. Too late, Second Son remembered the chief's warning: *Windigos like to attack their victims from the rear or from above.*

She already had an arrow notched. All she had to do was sweep the bow up and pull the string back. But hardly had she started to level it when the thing was on her.

Uttering a piercing howl, the Windigo slammed into the warrior woman with all the force of a stampeding bull buffalo. She was flung rearward like a leaf in a Chinook and smashed onto her back. The impact knocked the wind from her, leaving her stunned and vulnerable. Shaking her head to clear it, she grabbed the antler hilt of the copper knife and went to push to her feet, then froze.

The Windigo was there. It reared above her, a snarling, bestial apparition that reeked of sweat and urine and more abominable odors. For a moment it paused, studying her just as she studied it, its nostrils flared, its dark eyes dilated, its lips pulled back to expose its gleaming teeth.

It was a man. A tall, powerfully built man with a barrel chest and corded sinews on his legs and arms. His filthy hair had not been cut in so long that it hung well down past his waist. Plastered to his body, it gave the illusion of being a coat of fur.

The impression was enhanced by a heavy growth of hair on his arms and legs and eyebrows, which were as bushy as woolly caterpillars. Where no hair grew, the skin was caked thick with dirt. From a distance, or in the dark, he looked every bit the monster the Chipewyans took him to be.

The nails on his fingers and his toes had been allowed to grow unhindered, with the result that both were inches long and curved like the claws of a great cat or the talons of a hawk. He held his fingers bent to slash and rend.

All of this Second Son observed in a span of seconds. She noted that the man-beast's features were Chipewyan and entertained the thought that before her stood a former warrior who had fought the wilderness on its own terms and lost. Perhaps, years past, during a particularly severe winter, he had been on the verge of starvation and turned to the only ready source of nourishment available: human flesh. Ever since, he had been wandering the north woods, a demented shell of his former self.

Venting a strident yowl, the Windigo lunged and slashed at Second Son's throat. She rolled to the side, drawing the knife as she turned so that when she came to a stop she could push into a crouch with the blade extended. But the man-beast was on her before she could rise.

Arms endowed with the strength of a grizzly looped around the warrior woman's arms and pinned them to her body. Fetid breath assailed her nose as she thrashed and kicked in a vain bid to break free.

Teeth sheared into Second Son's shoulder, just missing her neck. She bucked but could not break his grip. Whipping her head to the side, she drove her forehead into his face.

The man-beast jerked back and roared. He let go and rose, blood streaming from his mashed lower lip. Touching his mouth, he stared at his scarlet fingertips, then shrieked and waded into her with his arms flailing just as she straightened.

It was Second Son's long curved knife against ten over-sized fingernails, yet she was the one who had to give way. Those nails had been worn to sharp points, and wielded as they were by someone with his inhuman strength, they could rip her open as easily as any blade. She parried swing after swing, pricking his hands and forearms repeatedly. Her own arms were nicked again and again, drawing blood.

The man-beast fought with insane fury. He constantly pressed her, trying to break through her guard. Quick as a striking rattler, he darted to the right and left, never still for a moment.

It had all happened so fast that Second Son had momentarily forgotten about Snip. Now the mongrel streaked past her with a growl as fierce as those of her adversary. The dog leaped at the Windigo's throat but was brutally batted aside. Snip landed close to the man-beast's feet, unconscious. Immediately the man-beast turned toward him and reached for the dog's neck.

Second Son glided in close and speared the knife into the Windigo's side. The copper severed hair and flesh, biting deep.

Arching its back, the creature howled in agony, then whirled on her and struck with blinding speed. Second Son received a ringing blow to the head that exploded bright points of light before her. She felt herself falling but could do nothing to stop. As she hit, her arm was viciously bent and the knife was ripped from her grasp.

Steely fingers encircled the warrior woman's neck. She thought that her end had come. In another instant the man-beast would gouge his fingers into her knuckle-deep or give her neck a savage twist that would snap her spine like a dry twig.

A flurry of footsteps sounded, and an inarticulate cry of utter rage shattered the air.

Second Son's vision cleared just as the Windigo stiffened and vented a bloodcurdling outcry. The tip of a lance had burst from the center of his chest. The man-beast glared at the gore-encrusted tip, then reached around behind his back. With a mighty yank, the monster tore the lance from his body and started to turn.

Kelownan had drawn his knife. Voicing a roar every bit as fierce as the man-beast's, the madman sprang. The Windigo dropped the lance to meet him halfway. They grappled. Locked together, they turned this way and that, neither able to gain any advantage.

Second Son, meanwhile, pushed erect. She wanted to help Kelownan. Drawing the ax from under her belt, she raised it aloft but could not strike for fear of hitting her companion.

Suddenly the Windigo twisted and heaved. Kelownan sailed over eight feet and crashed into the tree headfirst. He landed prone, his arms outflung.

The warrior woman leaped. She brought the ax flashing down at the crown of the man-beast's head. The Windigo dodged aside, then evaded a sideways slash. He snarled, scarlet spittle flecking his lips. Badly wounded as he was, the Windigo still had the agility of a bobcat and the ferocity of a wolverine.

Over and over the berserk cannibal sought to get his hands on her, but Second Son held him at bay by constantly swinging the ax. She creased his shoulder. She sliced into his wrist. She took a chunk of flesh out of his side. Yet still the Windigo pressed her.

In the swirl of combat, Second Son lost track of where she was in relation to Snip and Kelownan. It took all her concentration to ward off her inhuman foe. So it was that she did not realize she had moved in a circle and was close to the yellow dog until the heel of her left foot bumped against him.

Second Son tripped. Her balance started to go. She threw herself to the side, and as she did, Snip stirred, his legs extending and closing in pure reflex. One of his rear legs snagged on Second Son's ankle. The next thing she knew, she was on her back.

The man-beast was quick to close in.

A quick swipe kept the Windigo from seizing her. Before Second Son could reverse her swing, the man-beast pounced. He grabbed hold of the ax by the blade and wrestled it from her, leaving her unarmed.

The Windigo rose to his full height. A sneer curled his lips as he tossed the ax into the weeds.

Second Son dared not attempt to scramble to her feet with the cannibal standing so close. She looked to the right, thinking she would roll in that direction, and saw her only hope of survival lying a few feet away.

A wavering cry erupted from the man-beast's throat, just such a cry as Second Son had heard a seeming lifetime ago, on that night she and Billy-Wolf had sat by their fire, mending fences.

Spurred on by desperation, Second Son dove sideways. Her fingers wrapped around the stout shaft. She twisted as the Windigo swooped down at her, ramming the lance into his belly. The point cut into the skin above his navel, spiked through his internal organs, and ruptured out the small of his back.

Impaled, the man-beast vented his most piercing wail yet. In a rabid frenzy he clawed at her face and chest but could not quite reach her.

Second Son held on to the lance with all the strength she had left. His hands fanned her cheeks, his nails nearly raked her eyes. Gradually his movements grew weaker, but there was still enough life left in him to rip her to shreds when his body began to slip lower on the lance. His nails passed within an inch of her face. Then only half an inch. She bunched her shoulders to try to shove him off, knowing full well he was too heavy, that she was too worn-out.

The man-beast hissed. He snarled. He slipped lower than ever and drew back his right hand for one more swing. A heartbeat later his body went rigid. His arms fell, as limp as wet hides. Those fiery eyes of his dimmed.

Second Son angled the lance to the side and heaved. The Windigo thudded beside her. She rose onto her side, prepared to defend herself if need be, but the cannibal was dead. His face was so close to hers that she could smell the foul odor that came from his open mouth.

Tapping into the meager reserve of stamina she had left, Second Son rose onto her hands and knees and moved to Snip. The dog was unharmed, as best she could tell, and coming around. She went on to Kelownan. The madman's head was tilted at an impossible angle; his neck had been broken. Oddly, in death his features were more composed, more sane, than she had ever seen them.

Slowly the warrior woman sat up. Her whole body hurt and she was short of breath. She needed some time to rest, to recuperate. But she could not afford much. Well before nightfall she had to be on her way. There was one task she still had to do.

Second Son stared at the Windigo.

No. There were two.

A sliver of moon hung high in the firmament when a shadow slipped from the forest encircling the village of the Whitefish Clan of the Chipewyan tribe. The shadow was Second Son. She crept to where her mare, Billy-Wolf's horse, Blaze, and the packhorse were tied, quickly freed all three, and quietly led them into the woods to where Snip waited.

Second Son next made for Takwugan's lodge. She paused at the flap. From within issued the sound of snoring. Slowly lifting the bottom of the hide, she scanned the wigwam for her son. Her heart leaped when she saw Wolf Sings on the Mountain lying on the other side of the low fire.

A pair of dogs were to the left of the entrance. Both were awake and staring at her. They should have barked to alert the master of the lodge, but they did not. They did not because seated between them, stroking their necks and whispering to soothe them and keep them quiet, was Rattles Track. The Crow smiled, then motioned for Second Son to stay where she was.

A louder whisper brought Billy-Wolf to his feet. He held the Hawken. Across his chest hung his powder horn, ammo pouch, and possibles bag. On cat's feet he crept to the opening and slipped out into the cool of night. So ecstatic was he to see his mother safe that he threw his arms around her and hugged her close.

Second Son was nearly overwhelmed by emotion. She had to remind herself that it was not the proper time and place. Embracing her son briefly, she stood back just as the flap opened.

Rattles Track held a bulging parfleche. "Take this," she whispered. "Me prepare food for journey."

"You knew I was coming for him?" Second Son asked.

"Me knew. If not this night, then the next. Or the one after." The kindly Crow chuckled. "Me mix herb in Takwugan's food so him not wake up."

There were no words to describe Second Son's feelings. "Come with us," she urged. "Bring your children. I will see you safely back to your people."

Rattles Track bit her lower lip. She glanced at the wigwam, then at the inky mountains to the south. "Too far for children. Too many enemies. Too many animals. You not be able protect us all."

"I will do my best," Second Son pledged. *"Please."*

The Crow took a breath. She placed a hand on the warrior woman's shoulder. Moisture glistened in her eyes as she responded, "So sorry. Go. Now. Other dogs maybe hear. Maybe bark." Spinning around, she darted inside.

Second Son took a half step, then stopped, racked by turmoil. She could not force the Crow against her will. And every moment they dawdled increased the risk of discovery. Reluctantly, she guided her son into the trees. "Stay here," she directed. "I have one more thing to do."

On a nearby log, wrapped in Kelownan's pants, was the object she had carried tucked under her arm for hours on end. Picking up the bundle, she hastened back into the village a final time. Straight to Mattonabee's lodge she went. In front of it she arranged her surprise so that it faced the flap. It would be the first thing the chief saw when he stepped outside in the morning.

Billy-Wolf waited impatiently. After all that had happened, he couldn't wait to get out of there. When his mother returned, he hugged her again, and this time she did not push him away. Fighting back tears, he choked out, "Thank you for saving me. You're the best ma in the whole world."

Second Son thought of Buffalo Hump and knew that never again would she doubt herself. Her aunt had been wrong. It *was* possible for a woman to be a warrior and a mother both, if it was what she wanted more than anything else.

They mounted. Second Son took the lead and swung in a loop to the west to go around the lake. Once beyond it, they would ride all night, ensuring that the Chipewyans would never catch up.

Billy-Wolf could not stop grinning. Already he was thinking of their secluded valley, of their cozy cabin, and of his father and uncle. "Say, Ma," he said, remembering. "I've got a question."

"I am not surprised."

"What was that thing you left in front of the chief's lodge? I never got a good look at it."

"It was a gift from me to him."

"But what kind of gift?" Billy-Wolf pressed her.

Second Son, superb warrior of the Tsistsistas, devoted mate of Yellow Hair, and as proud a mother as ever lived, shifted to look back and smiled. "One that will give him nightmares for many winters to come. It was the Windigo's head."

AUTHOR'S NOTE

For those who might wonder, the Chipewyans did exist in the area described and they were driven from their homeland by the more powerful Crees. And yes, their attitude toward women was recorded by several reliable sources.

No race, it seems, was exempt from treating its women as inferior at one time or another. Second Son's modern sisters should be proud of the great strides they have taken since the days when they were treated as little better than dogs.

As for the warrior woman's reaction to her son's deceit, it must be remembered that her people abhorred those who lied. The Cheyenne were among the most moral of the Plains tribes. Their women were noted for their chastity, their men for their honesty. Parents went to great lengths to instill these values in the children. So for Second Son to be upset by one little lie is not at all out of character.

As for the north land, I wish to express my high regard for the many friendly people I met on my visit to Harrison Hot Springs and beyond.

Canada is a land of boundless splendors. The towering

mountains, the lush valleys, and crystal-clear lakes combine to evoke an abiding sense of awe at both the majesty of creation and its Creator.

For the skeptical, allow me to point out that the Windigos were feared by *all* the Algonquian peoples of the subarctic. Psychiatrists have even identified a "Windigo psychosis," of which some seventy cases have been documented. In forty-four of those, the afflicted performed acts of cannibalism. Thirty-six ate members of their own families. Most had to be executed. It was the only way to put an end to their rampant craving for human flesh.

The exciting frontier series continues!

 RIVERS WEST

Native Americans, hunters and trappers, pioneer families—all who braved the emerging American Frontier drew their very lives and fortunes from the great rivers. From the earliest days of the settlement movement to the dawn of the twentieth century, here, in all their awesome splendor, are the RIVERS WEST.

____27401-5	THE YELLOWSTONE	WIN BLEVINS
____28012-0	THE SMOKY HILL	DON COLDSMITH
____28451-7	THE COLORADO	GARY McCARTHY
____28583-1	THE POWDER RIVER	WIN BLEVINS
____29180-7	THE ARKANSAS RIVER	JORY SHERMAN
____29770-8	THE SNAKE RIVER	WIN BLEVINS
____29769-4	THE GILA RIVER	GARY McCARTHY
____56511-7	THE HIGH MISSOURI	WIN BLEVINS
____29925-5	THE RIO GRANDE	JORY SHERMAN
____56794-2	THE PECOS RIVER	FREDERIC BEAN

each available for $4.99/$5.99 Canada

Ask for these books at your local bookstore or use this page to order.

Please send me the books I have checked above. I am enclosing $____(add $2.50 to cover postage and handling). Send check or money order, no cash or C.O.D.'s, please.

Name _____

Address_____

City/State/Zip_____

Send order to: Bantam Books, Dept. RW, 2451 S. Wolf Rd., Des Plaines, IL 60018
Allow four to six weeks for delivery.
Prices and availability subject to change without notice.   RW 9/95